UNSPOKEN *Words*

"Beautifully written, emotional, and so realistic. I loved it!"

~ *Katy Evans, New York Times and USA Today bestselling author*

"H.P. Davenport delivers a beautiful, heart-warming, friends to lovers story in her debut novel, Unspoken Words, with a touch of suspense that causes you to tear through the pages."

~ *Michelle Lynn, USA Today bestselling author*

"Camryn and Jamieson's story will take up a part of my heart forever. H.P. Davenport weaves her words into gallant emotion that literally pours off every page and straight into your soul. I laughed out loud, winced and cried and grew to love not only these two characters, but the whole cast, within moments of opening this book. This love story will raise the bar for every one you read after it. Stunning."

~ *Michelle Kemper Brownlow, Author*

"This is the debut book of H.P. Davenport. And I have to say she really knows how to pull out the emotional roller coaster for her first book! This book has it all. Swoon worthy moments, hot mess moments, and moments where you can not put the book down because you need to know what is going to happen next."

~ *Karrie, Panty Dropping Book Blog*

"H.P. Davenport has taken my heart on a rollercoaster ride of emotions."

~ *Tami, The Book Enthusiast*

UNSPOKEN *Words*

H. P. Davenport

Editor: Elaine York,
Allusion Graphics, LLC / Publishing & Book Formatting

Cover Design: Elaine York,
Allusion Graphics, LLC / Publishing & Book Formatting

Cover photo: © Bigstockphoto.com

Interior Design & Formatting: Christine Borgford,
Perfectly Publishable

Two lives . . . as close to perfect as they can be.

Camryn Townsend has everything she's always dreamed of . . . an amazing family, supportive friends, and the perfect job. Everything a girl could want. Or is it? A trip back to her childhood home threatens to unravel her web of perfection.

Her problem . . . she's in love with her best friend and she's too scared to sacrifice their friendship for a love she's always wanted.

Jamie Banks' life is the epitome of perfection. His company is thriving, his band is on the cusp of stardom, and the girl he loves is returning home.

His problem . . . the girl he loves has been his best friend for as long as he can remember and he's not sure he's ready to sacrifice his best friend for a lover. Pursuing a relationship with the possibility of losing her has him second-guessing everything he knows.

Unspoken words are the only thing standing in their way.

To *Jason* . . .

You are my world, you are my *everything*

Prologue

"SOMEONE HELP ME! HELP ME!" I scream. Hoping someone will hear me. The reality is, no one can. The music in the club is so loud, the bass is bouncing off of the walls. My chest tightens in the pitch black room as I plead with God to make him stop. Please no. Don't let this happen.

"You bitch, this is going to be rough now," he growls.

I struggle to get free. His body presses against my back, forcing me against the wall. All I feel is his breath against my neck before his tongue swipes up the left side of my face. "Why are you fighting me? You were begging me with your eyes to come dance with you out there, to touch you."

What the hell is he talking about?

Gentle hands lightly shake my body side to side. "Wake up, Camryn. You're safe now. He can't hurt you." Gripping the sheets wrapped around my body, I tremble.

My mom pulls me into her arms. "You're safe, sweetheart. Wake up. Look at me. You're home, no one can hurt you. You're having an-other nightmare, baby." My mom repeatedly whispers in my ear, as her hand rubs up and down my back. She wraps me in the comfort of her arms and my rapid breathing slows down.

"Mom, when will this stop? When will the nightmares stop?" I plead.

"I don't know, sweetie. I wish I knew, I just don't," she whispers.

CHAPTER

One

Beginning of October

Camryn

AFTER MAKING MY WAY THROUGH security, I grab a Caramel Macchiato from Starbucks. As I take my first sip, I savor the intense espresso flavor that hits my taste buds. The creamy vanilla-flavor with a topping of velvety-rich foam, finished with a buttery caramel drizzle, these are my guilty pleasures. This is one of the many reasons why I run every day.

I approach the gate, and notice my flight is going to be packed from the lack of unoccupied chairs. I plop down my laptop bag and carry-on and lean against the window to wait for the attendant to announce my flight. I'm praying the seat next to me is vacant so I can catch up on sleep after my late night checking out a local band for a piece I'm working on.

My internship while attending Stanford was at one of the most prestigious music magazines, *Key Notes*. It paid off and I was offered a permanent position with the magazine after graduation.

I love living in LA, but my favorite perk of the job is the fact my company flies me to New York often. *Key Notes* has an office in New York City, so when there are bands on the East Coast that my boss wants me to see, they send me out there. Although *Key Notes* provides me with an expense account, I'd rather not stay at a hotel. Especially when my family lives there. So, I usually crash at my parents' house, with my twin brother, Christian, or with the only other man in my life—my best friend, Jamieson.

Just thinking of Jamieson—or as everyone calls him, Jaime—puts a smile on my face. Being home for a few months means I will get to spend a lot of time with him, just like old times. Knowing we are both single, the possibility of us hooking up has crossed my mind a few times but the timing has never been right and I always fear he doesn't feel the same.

I've wanted to say something to him for quite some time. But I don't know if I could handle the rejection if he didn't feel the same way as I do. Once I cross that line, there is no going back to what we used to be. I never wanted to risk our friendship. With me living in Los Angeles now, I savor the time I get with my family and friends when I am on the East Coast. I love having quality time with my girls, whether it's a day at the spa or even taking a run in Central Park.

The sudden movement of the crowd of people at the gate shakes me out of my daze. People start to line up and wait for their rows to be called. One of the perks of traveling for business is first-class. *Key Notes* treats me well. Once they announce first-class is boarding, I grab my laptop bag, carry-on and head toward the attendant.

After my ticket is scanned, I proceed down the jet bridge. Making my way to my seat, I notice that the seat next to me is vacant. Saying a silent prayer, I hope it remains that way for the entire flight. The last thing I need is a chatterbox sitting next to me. On my last trip an older woman talked to me the entire flight. I don't think she came up for air. I swear, she was sucking the oxygen out of the cabin and my ears were bleeding by the time we landed.

I shove my overly-stuffed carry-on in the overhead compartment and grab my iPod to prepare for the possibility of a chatty seatmate. Sliding into my seat by the window, I instantly begin to feel my body relax. With my busy schedule these past months, I didn't realize how much I missed my family and friends.

When I received my itinerary for this trip, I was shocked to see how many events were on my schedule. My boss, Shelby, made sure she packed my schedule with events that I need to attend. My *Key Notes'* column, "Pulsations" focuses on emerging artists and bands. Shelby loves for me to find the hidden gems and make them shine in the spotlight.

She's not only booked me in New York for the next few months, but Boston, Connecticut, Philadelphia, Baltimore, and Washington, DC, are on the list as well.

I pop my earbuds in, hoping to drown out the conversation coming from the two people sitting behind me. I am just about to close my eyes, when a guy takes the empty seat next to me and another in the seat across the row. Trying not to be too obvious, I glance over and find two total hotties. One has a baseball hat pulled down low to his face, and the other has brown hair that is cut short around the ears, yet longer on top, which seems to stick out as if he just ran his fingers through it. I can't really see the one across the aisle, but the one next to me has eyes that are a piercing deep blue, and from what I can see, he definitely looks like he spends some time at the gym. His black shirt hugs him in all the right places as it stretches across his shoulders and biceps. I take a deep breath to appreciate the alluring cologne he is wearing. It's not too strong, a clean smell that has me deeply inhaling without being too obvious. It smells familiar though, and I know I've smelled it before, which makes me do a double take. I don't remember his name, but I've seen him before. Where though?

I turn my head away as he catches me gawking. He clears his throat, so I look out of the corner of my eye, and notice he is staring at me. I drop my chin, my cheeks flushing red. Just as I am about to turn my music on, I feel a tap on my left forearm. Glancing over, a huge grin is splashed across his face. His smile is beautiful and by the smug look on his face, he knows it, too. The guy next to him sits quietly looking at something on his phone.

"Excuse me, you look very familiar. My name is Chad Murphy. Have we met before?"

I've been told my face tells the whole story, I can only imagine what it looks like right now. I simply say, "Nope," slightly popping the 'p' as I speak, "I don't think we've met."

"Are you sure we've never met because you look really familiar?"

While trying to figure out where I recognize him from, I say, "Maybe we've seen each other out or something. I spend a lot of time in nightclubs, bars, and music venues. Not that I'm a bar rat or a huge partier, but it comes with my job."

At that very moment, his eyes widen as if a light bulb turned on in his head. "I know where I know you from. You interviewed my band last fall and wrote an article about us for *Key Notes*. It just took a little time for the rolodex of beautiful faces catalogued in my brain to find you."

Chad has this smile that lights up the room, but at the same time, it's a little devilish. He knows he is good looking and I am sure he uses it to his advantage. I remember how he flirted with me. I brushed it off. I never mix business with pleasure. That is a line that I will never cross.

My cheeks get hotter from embarrassment. Quickly trying to remember what band he's part of, I come up empty. Not surprisingly, I meet a new band each week when I work in the field. After a while it's hard to remember them all.

"Thank you for the compliment, you seem to be quite the charmer. Yes, I do work for *Key Notes*. My name is Camryn, but most people call me Cami. What's the name of your band?"

"Troubled Pasts," he says in that deep voice of his. "This here," he points to the guy who hasn't spoken a word since they sat down, "is Buffer. He's the guitarist in the band." There's something sexy about this man. I don't usually get frazzled easily, but something about him unnerves me.

Buffer leans forward so I can see him. His boldly handsome face smiles warmly at me. He lifts his chin, "Hey. Nice to meet you."

His profile was rugged and somber. It didn't do him justice until he gave me a full view of his face. Damn, he is good looking. He is attractive and unscrupulous enough to take any woman. Women must find him deliciously appealing. Those eyes. They are serenely compelling.

After boldly staring at Buffer, I direct my attention back to Chad. "Ah . . . I remember your band. You guys rocked the house that night at The Hollywood Bowl. The ambience and sound there is amazing. It's my favorite venue."

"So do all of the rockers hit on you while you're checking their band out?" Chad asks.

I laugh. "Not hardly. I keep everything professional while I work. Every once in a while I *get hit on,* as you say," making quote marks with my fingers, "But, rockers are usually on their best behavior not knowing what I'll put in my review of their performance."

"So I guess I'm in the minority then. Good thing you already wrote your piece on my band. I can flirt all I want with you now." He raises his eyebrows at me, while he takes in my appearance. His eyes roam my body. They fixate on my chest. Feeling a little self-conscious at his blatant appraisal, I quickly pull the zipper up on my work-out jacket.

"Dude, are you going to bother that poor girl the entire flight?" Buffer asks.

"What? I'm not bothering her. I'm simply being friendly," Chad says.

Buffer leans forward, giving me another look at him. His eyes are an emerald green. The shadow of his beard gives him an even more manly aura. He smiles wide, his teeth strikingly white against his tanned face. "If his friendliness begins to irritate you, I suggest you put your earbuds in now. Maybe he'll get the hint."

I laugh at his comment. "Thanks, I'll keep that in mind."

"Just ignore him, I usually do," Chad says jokingly.

We make small talk while we taxi to the runway for takeoff. He tells me about some of the other venues his band has played, and I tell him some of the other bands that I've interviewed and promoted.

Once the plane is in the air, I search my iPod until I find the playlist labeled 'Travel'. I created the playlist of relaxing ballads sprinkled with a little funk between every couple songs. Music is my passion, there isn't a time in my life that music didn't play a huge role.

With my head resting on the pillow and the blanket pulled up around me, my eyes focus out the window, as the plane climbs higher into the sky. This is going to be a long flight, six hours with no layover, which is great; but with Chad sitting next to me, I can only hope that exhaustion takes over my body. I am not in the mood to talk the entire flight. I want to catch up on some much needed sleep.

The music floods my ears and eventually Boyce Avenue, one of my favorite bands, soothes me to sleep.

"Jamie push me higher." I yelled as he pushed me on the swing in our back-yard. Morgan was on the swing next to me and Christian was pushing her. "Higher, Jamie, they can't beat us. You can't let Christian push Morgan higher than me."

Laughter filled the air, as Morgan and I were shouting at the boys to push us higher. Christian was telling Morgan to use her legs to help get better momentum, I hollered at Jamie to underdog me. Jamie was pushing me and pushing me and then he pushed me so hard that he ran underneath me as I went above his head. I looked over at Morgan and Christian and screamed like every seven year old would. "WE WIN. I WENT HIGHER!"

Morgan shouted. "No fair, you cheated. You didn't say Christian could do underdogs. That's not fair."

Jamie and I were laughing as my swing slowed down. Jamie said, "There were no rules, Morgan, you just said you wanted to see who could go higher." We high fived each other, claiming another win.

Jamie and I were always partners when we played games, especially when we played games with the boys versus the girls. I hated being partners with my brother. Yuck.

Morgan jumped off her swing when it stopped. "You and Jamie always cheat. Why can't you ever let anyone else win? It's always you two against everyone else. Why do I always have to have Christian as my partner? Why do you always get Jamie, Camryn?"

With my hands on my hips, I looked back at her. "Because he's my best friend, that's why." I think I hurt Morgan's feelings by saying that because she shouted in our back door and asked my mom to help her cross the street so she could go home. I wasn't being mean by saying that Jamie was my best friend. Morgan knew she was my best friend too. The four of us always played together. We were inseparable. But I always loved being Jamie's partner. I couldn't explain it, it just felt right.

Jamie lived next door to us, so he was always over. Morgan had moved in across the street when we started kindergarten.

My mom stood at the back door, "Is everything okay?"

Morgan put her hands on her hips. "Mrs. Townsend, Jamie and Camryn don't play fair. Can you please help me across the street, so I can go home?"

My mom came over and squatted down and looked me in the eyes. She took her finger and placed it under my chin, "Camryn, why is Morgan saying you and Jamie don't play fair?"

I shrugged my shoulders. "I don't know."

"I told you before, the four of you need to get along. You need to play nice with each other. It's not always about being the winner, Camryn. Sometimes you need to just play and have fun."

My mom went over to Morgan. "Are you sure you want to go home?"

Morgan looked over at me with unshed tears in her eyes.

I went over to where she was standing with my mom and I threw my arms around her neck. "I'm sorry. Please don't go home. We can go play Barbie's."

Morgan smiled and hugged me back and we ran off toward the tree house together, holding each other's hands.

I feel my body being pushed, and I slowly open my eyes. Chad is smiling at me. "Rise and shine, Sleeping Beauty."

I wipe the sleepiness from my eyes and look around. I try to gather my unfamiliar surroundings. My brain finally decides to work and I remember that I'm flying to New York. *Please, Lord, don't let there be drool on my face after sleeping for six hours.*

The flight attendant's voice crackles from the speakers. "We are approaching the landing, please make sure your seatbelts are buckled, all electronic devices are powered off, and your bags are placed under the seats in front of you or in the overhead compartments." Butterflies take flight in my stomach. Not because we are landing, rather from knowing that I will get to see Jamie on a regular basis for the next few months.

We land and begin to taxi toward the terminal. I look at Chad and Buffer. "It was nice meeting the two of you again. I hope your stay is great."

"I'm hoping it is, we're meeting up with the rest of our band. We have a few meetings set up and we're keeping our fingers crossed everything works out." Chad says in his deep, sexy voice. The more I listen to him speak, the more I remember how he excited the crowd at Hollywood Bowl. His tone is so sensual and inviting, it gives me goosebumps just being near him.

"Are you going to be in New York for a while?" Chad asks while Buffer stands there quietly, his eyes studying me with a curious intensity.

"According to my schedule I have events up and down the East Coast, so to answer your question, yes, I will be in New York for a while."

That smile I saw earlier makes another appearance as Chad pulls out a business card from his wallet and hands it to me. "Here's my card, my cell number is on it. Give me a call if you have a free night to meet up for drinks."

Reaching out to take his card, my fingers touch his and a sudden tingle shoots up my arm. I quickly pull my hand back and look at him. That alluring grin spreads across his face again. "Thank you. I'll give you a call when I get settled in. Maybe we can do drinks. I can bring a few of my friends, and you can bring a few of yours." I suggest.

"I was hoping maybe the two of us could have drinks . . . without friends there to chaperone us. I don't bite." A sly grin crosses his face. "Unless I'm asked to," he says with a mischievous smile.

My eyes go wide at his remark. Talk about being forward. "I'll let you know about the drink. You never know, maybe I will take you up on it."

A loud laugh pulls my attention away from Chad. "Nice line, dude, real nice. Camryn, please don't think our entire band acts like this one." He nods his head in Chad's direction.

Chad shoots his bandmate a look then gets up and grabs his bag from the overhead

compartment, placing it at his feet. "Which bag is yours?"

"It's the hot pink, leopard print one."

He hands me my carry-on, and when I bend over to grab my laptop bag I hear a whistle. I turn around and give Chad a dirty look. If looks could kill, he would have dropped dead right there in the aisle. He holds his hands up, as if surrendering. "I'm only joking, no need to shoot daggers at me." He chuckles and Buffer and I walk ahead of him down the jet bridge.

When we exit the bridge, Chad extends his hand to me. "Well, it was nice seeing you again. Call me."

"Or don't," Buffer interjects.

We go our separate ways at the terminal, since they both only had a carry-on. Following the signs toward baggage claim, I pray Christian and Jamie are here to pick me up. It has been three months since I've seen my friends and family and what a welcome home it will be to see them both in a few minutes.

CHAPTER

Two

Camryn

MY BROTHER, CHRISTIAN, LEANS AGAINST the wall in baggage claim looking up at the screens. Starting to walk in his direction, I'm swept up into a set of strong arms. I don't need to see the face to know who they belong to. I'd recognize the vibrant tattoos that cover his arms from his wrists all the way up to his shoulders and wrap around to his chest. These arms belong to Jamieson Banks . . . my Jamie.

Jamie squeezes me and snuggles his face into my neck. A loud squeal leaves my mouth, turning heads in our direction. Jamie places my feet back on the ground, just in time for me to turn around and throw my arms around his neck squeezing him tightly. After inhaling his scent, a smile spreads across my face. *Home.*

Jamie is beautiful. His features are perfect, so symmetrical, that any more delicacy would make him too beautiful to be a man. His skin pulled taut over the elegant ridge of his cheekbones. His brows and chocolate eyes are startling against his tan skin and dark hair.

In my eyes, he is literally a walking sex god. Granted, we've never had sex or anything, but with me being home for a while, I'm hoping to build up enough courage to tell Jamie how I feel about him.

Jamie whispers in my ear, "It's been way too long, Tink. I've missed the hell out of you." Just as I pull back to look at his face, Jamie leans in and plants a huge kiss on my cheek. Swatting Jamie in the chest, I mutter "Don't call me that in public. You know how much I hate that name."

Jamie raises his eyebrows and laughs, "Cami, I've been calling you Tink since you were little and dressed up as Tinkerbell five Halloweens in a row. You were obsessed with Tinkerbell, you even wore your costume in the yard to play. I can't help it."

"Oh, really, I also dressed up as a baseball player for Halloween a few times, and wore a uniform for years on the field, you could have at least called me 'Slugger' or 'Power Pitcher'. Something a little catchier."

Jamie lets out a hearty laugh, "Cami, you have no idea how much I missed our bantering back and forth."

When Jamie and I break away from our hug, my brother comes over in our direction. "Hey, what am I? Chopped liver? Get over here and give your big brother a hug. I've missed you more than Jamie."

"Big brother, really? You are not my big brother."

"I beg to differ and my birth certificate will vouch for that. I am, indeed, your big brother."

"Christian, you were born one minute before me. That does not constitute seniority. If you are playing the birth certificate card, I believe I am the big sister since I weighed more than you."

"You weighed in more than me because you wouldn't share the food that Mom was consuming while she was pregnant. You were greedy then, and you're still greedy now when it comes to food."

"Whatever, Christian, shut up and just hug me. It's been three months since I've seen any of you."

Christian pulls me into a bear hug and squeezes the air out of me.

"Alright, let me go. I said give me a hug, not break my ribs."

Jamie clears his throat, "Hello, I'm over here. Did the two of you forget about me? You're beginning to make me feel like a third wheel."

Laughing at Jamie, I move away from Christian and wrap my arms around his waist and lean my head against his chest. Jamie has been my best friend for as long as I can remember. Yes, he is my brother's best friend, too, but Jamie and I have a special bond. For years, Morgan and I tagged along with Christian and Jamie. The boys taught me how to play baseball, climb a tree, throw a football, drive a stick shift. The list of things is endless.

It was our eighth birthday, Christian and I had a baseball-themed party. Our parents offered to have a separate party for each of us, but Christian and I agreed on one theme. Our parents decorated the backyard like a baseball field. Our dad made stands out of wood and placed signs on the front labeled snacks, souvenirs, hot dogs, etc. As you looked around the yard, concession stands appeared in the corners. Our mom had every goodie you could think of on the counter of the snack stand along with an array of chips. My mom had set up a hot dog stand and a pretend souvenir stand with party bags filled with a baseball and a New York Yankees t-shirt.

When we were able to open our presents, Jamie ran inside. When he returned, he walked over to me with his hands behind his back. He reached out his hands and I scrunched my nose at his gift wrapped in Christmas paper.

Jamie quickly says, "I wrapped it myself. I know your birthday is July 3 but the paper had cute puppies on it and I know how much you love puppies."

I threw my arms around his neck. "I love it."

Jamie smiled. "Wait until you open it, you're gonna love my present more than you love the paper."

After tearing the paper off, I quickly tossed the lid to the side. My eyes immediately met Jamie's because inside the box was the best gift ever. Jamie got me my very own baseball glove.

A huge smile spread across my face. Glancing around the yard, my eyes finally found my dad. When our eyes met, I held the glove up in the air.

"You finally got that glove you've been asking for," my dad hollered over the other kids as they watched Christian open up his gifts.

Turning, my eyes met Jamie's as he stood there staring at me. "I knew you wanted your own glove. Anytime you want to practice throwing, come get me," he says with a huge smile on his face.

My eighth birthday was one of my favorite birthdays. That glove meant the world to me. When the boys would let me play with them, they would loan me one of theirs. My love for baseball was born that day.

Christian played baseball all through high school, his dreams of going pro were shattered when he tore his ACL . . . resulting in surgery and then a shitload of physical therapy. Rather than going to college on an athletic scholarship, Christian went to NYU and focused on his academics. He double majored in business and music engineering production.

I, on the other hand, attended Stanford on a full athletic scholarship for softball. Obviously, I had the grades as well. My decision to attend Stanford wasn't based solely upon my scholarship, Stanford has an incredible Journalism program.

Growing up with Christian and Jamie, sports was something I was always around. That is how my love for the game developed. The countless hours of training, whether I was at the gym, on the field, or at the batting cages, all paid off, playing softball at the collegiate level was a dream come true.

I never imagined I would have played the sport I fell in love with until I was twenty-two years old. But it was bittersweet, knowing that my brother's dreams were taken from him on the same field that brought me such inner joy. The guilt bothered me at times, but Christian being the loving supportive brother he is, supported me the entire time I was in college. He and Jamie would try to attend my games if they were able to or they watched them online when they wanted to keep up with my stats. I couldn't have had a better support system than I did with my family and best friends.

Jamie squeezes my shoulders, reminding me where I am. "What are you thinking about, Tink? You seem like you're a million miles away."

Shrugging my shoulders, I lean into him. "Just remembering my eighth birthday."

Jamie tilts his head to the side and looks at me. "When I gave you your glove?" He smirks, quite proud of himself.

"You remember? I still have that glove even though I outgrew it a long time ago. It's tucked away in a safe place in my closet at my parents' house. I hope one day to pass it on to my little girl."

Jamie's face softens when I mention my glove. Of course, I still have it.

"What's THAT look for, Jamie Banks? Have I shocked you?"

"How could I forget that day, your yard was set up like a baseball field. Your parents went all out for that party. I think they just loved the fact that Christian and you didn't make them throw separate parties." Jamie puts his arm around my shoulder, pulling me closer to him.

"Yeah, you may be right. With me not being high maintenance, my parents had it easy when it came to parties." Christian pulls my bags off of the carousel and looks in my direction, "Camryn, do you only have two bags with you?"

"Yeah, I packed light. *Key Notes* allowed me to ship some boxes home with more of my stuff since my stay will be longer than usual."

Both Christian and Jamie's eyebrows raise at that statement. Christian asks, "What do you mean longer than usual? You're not here for two weeks?"

Looking a little devious, I shrug my shoulders. "Oh, did I forget to tell you two that little bit of information?" Laughing, I say, "Boys, I am home till after the New Year."

Christian and Jamie both look at me with pure excitement written across their faces. Jamie grabs one of my bags from my brother and places his arms around my shoulders as we leave the airport. "This is going to be fun. Welcome home, Cami."

CHAPTER
Three

Camryn

THE THREE OF US WALK to the parking garage and my eyes wander around to see which car Christian used to pick me up. Christian leads us in the direction of our father's black Land Rover. Neither of us own vehicles with him living in New York City and me being in Los Angeles. When I'm home, I use one of my parents' cars. It makes more sense than renting one. Christian does the same if he needs to.

Christian pops the hatchback and loads my two bags in the back, while Jamie opens the passenger door for me to get inside.

Turning toward Jamie I smirk, "Well, aren't you quite the gentleman."

"I've always been a gentleman when it comes to you, Camryn. My mother raised me well."

I can't bring myself to look away from Jamie's face. He looks better than I remembered. Christian slams the hatchback down, startling me, causing me to hurry up and get in the car. "Alright, Casanova, get in or we're leaving you at the airport." I playfully flirt with Jamie. Nothing sexual has ever happened between the two of us, but we have shared a few kisses over the years.

Christian gets in the driver's side and buckles his seatbelt. Jamie jumps in the back of the truck and squeezes my shoulders lightly from the back seat. Glancing in my direction, Christian asks, "Where am I taking you? Are you staying with me, one of the girls, or am I taking you to mom's?"

Turning to look at Christian, I notice Jamie staring at me from the backseat. "Take me to mom's. I told her that I would have dinner with her and dad. Are you staying for dinner, or are you just dropping me off?"

Christian looks in the rearview mirror to address Jamie. "Dude, do you mind spending some time at my parents' house today or do you want me to drop you off first before taking Cami home?"

"Nah, it's cool. No need in going out of your way. I'll go with you guys and then I'll stop by to see my folks while we're there. This way my mom can't say that I haven't seen her. If she knew I was next door and didn't visit, she'd give me shit for not stopping by."

"So, what are your plans for this weekend, do you have any work events that you need to attend?" Jamie asks from the back seat.

"No. My boss left this week open for me to get settled in. I have a few events set up in the City over the next month, and after that I have to do a bit of traveling. You guys are more than welcome to join me if you don't have any plans. The rooms are paid for, I can always call and switch the reservations to two queen beds."

Christian speaks first, "I'll have to check my schedule and see what I have going on at the studio. Things have been a little busy lately. I'm finishing up an album and I have a few meetings set up with a couple new bands."

"Well, check your schedule and let me know. It would be fun. We could take a few road trips. Shelby set it up that I am in each city for two days so I'll have some time to go sightseeing or whatever."

If I know Jamie, he's mentally trying to figure out what Parker, the guitarist in the band, has lined up for their band, Side Effects. It doesn't surprise me when Jamie says, "I'll check with the guys and see what our schedule looks like. I know we have a few gigs lined up at Aces, but I'm not sure what else Parker has booked. If we don't have any shows, count me in. I'm in desperate need of a vacation for sure."

Smiling, I turn to Christian, "You better make this happen. I haven't seen either of you since you came to visit me in July for our birthday. We need some quality time together. I miss you guys."

He groans, "I already told you, I'll see what I have on the schedule. You know if I can make it happen, I will. Relax, you've only been off the plane for what, an hour?"

Reaching across the center console, I give Christian's shoulder a shove. "Hey, I'm only home for three months, and I want to make the most of it. You know how I am. I love spending time and making memories with the two of you. I may even ask Morgan and the girls if they want to tag along with me."

"Well, if Christian and I go, and the girls tag along, too, you might as well ask Lincoln if he wants to come."

We met Lincoln in middle school. The boys hit it off immediately with him. He balanced out Christian and Jamie's bold personalities. Both Christian and Jamie are hot heads where Lincoln is the more level-headed of the three.

I lean my head against the headrest, "Whatever. The more the merrier. Just let me know. I'll ask the girls. If the girls are up for it, then ask Lincoln."

The car ride to our parents' house takes a half hour tops. Living in Berkeley Heights, New Jersey, was convenient for commuting to the City. Our parents still live in the house that we grew up in. Jamie's parents, along with Morgan's parents, still live on the same street. Christian pulls the car into the driveway and I immediately see the front door open before Christian even has a chance to hit the garage door opener.

My mom stands on the front step waving at us. You would think that she hasn't seen me in years. I was home for Easter, six months ago. I love my job, I love being able to travel for it, and I love living in LA, but I do get homesick a lot. There's nothing better than being home with my family and friends . . . and Jamie.

I open my door, and my mom immediately throws her arms around my neck and squeezes me close. I love my mom. She is one of my best friends. Growing up she always treated Christian and me as if we were the prince and princess of the home. We never wanted for anything, but we were never spoiled brats. Even though our parents are well-off financially, they still made us work for the things we wanted. My father is a partner at one of the largest law firms in New York City, Townsend and Wilcox, PC. My mom was a guidance counselor at the local middle school until she had Christian and me. She made the decision to be a stay-at-home mom when she found out she was having twins. Juggling twins and working full time would've been too difficult for my mom to do with my father's hours at the firm.

From the moment we were outside of our mother's womb people referred to us as the "Townsend Twins." We both have brown hair and brown eyes, mine a little lighter than his, more hazel. Looking at us, you immediately know we are related, but you can't tell that we're twins. Christian is six-two, whereas I am only five-four. *Thank the Lord for heels.* Christian jokes around and calls me "Tink" just like Jamie. He says I'm a real life Tinkerbell fairy. That I am both sweet and sassy and loyal to all my friends. *Whatever.*

When I hear the hatchback of the Land Rover shut, I realize my mom still has her arms around my neck, my arms go around her waist and I place my head on her shoulder. She whispers in my ear, "Welcome home, sweetie. I've missed my baby girl." My insides warm as her words make me teary-eyed. I never stopped and thought about how me living in LA affects my family. I'm looking forward to spending time with my mom over the next three months. As much as I need my Jamie and Christian time, I also need to spend quality time with my mom because I miss her every day. I make a mental note to keep an eye out for an opening in the New York office. I miss being home.

CHAPTER

Four

Jamie

WATCHING CAMI'S MOM, GWEN, EMBRACE her makes me smile. They're my family, too. Looking around at the Townsend's house and my childhood next door, this is home. Living in the City is convenient because of the studio and Aces, the bar that one of my best friends, Lincoln owns, but I always feel more at peace when I am here in Berkeley Heights.

Growing up with Christian and Camryn, this house is a second home to me. To be honest, more of my childhood was spent in their backyard than my own. Our parents are friends, they grew up together, so it was only natural that we would do the same. Being an only child, one would think I would be lonely, but that is the furthest thing from the truth. Christian is like a brother to me. We've been through everything together, whether it was a fight at the playground, relationship break-ups, or career moves. The biggest event we've been through is that brutal day I carried my best friend off the field when he tore his ACL. The look in Christian's eyes when he knew his dream was crushed broke me.

I was there for him every step of the way after his surgery. I took him to and from the months of therapy sessions. Christian didn't want to see the pity or sadness in his mom's eyes when he would endure the long therapy sessions. So I volunteered to take him after school. I would sit in a chair in the corner with my elbows on my knees, my hands dangling between my legs, as I watched Christian struggle with the exercises. Those days were torture for him and me both, but it was another fight that we battled together that bonded us closer.

Gwen steps back from Camryn, takes her hand and leads her toward the house. Leaving Christian and me to grab Camryn's bags from the car and bring them inside. We place them by the front door, not knowing if Camryn is staying the night here or just staying for dinner and heading back to the City with us.

I love when Camryn stays with me or Christian. It feels like old times . . . when we were inseparable. When she is here, I feel complete. Christian and I live in the same apartment building in SoHo. We were lucky to find our places, the rent was affordable and it's close to the studio. Christ knows, rent in the City will bleed you dry.

I'm a partner in the studio with Christian. He and I attended college together, and studied the same majors. We recently opened the studio and called it Townsend and Banks, LLC. Our parents are investors, which worked out well, so we didn't have to use all of our savings.

The sound of laughter echoes into the foyer, drawing my attention to the kitchen. Walking down the hallway, the French doors to the kitchen are open, allowing me to see Camryn and her mom sitting at the island. Gwen is on the telephone, and I hear her say, "Come on over. Have dinner with us."

Having no clue who she is speaking to, I look at Camryn as she shrugs her shoulders and sips on her cup of coffee. "Don't be silly, your son is here." Ah . . . she's on the phone with my mom. She laughs, "You know how it is, Michelle, wherever Camryn is, Jamie is close by."

My eyebrows shoot up in the air. *Hello, I am right here. Do you mind not talking about me while I'm standing less than ten feet away?* Turning my attention to Camryn, she tries to hold back her laughter. Her hand covers her mouth and her eyes shine as if to think, *what?*

I walk over and stand behind her, gently moving her hair away from her neck, whispering in her ear, "What's so funny. You never seem to mind when I'm around, now do you?" The locket around her neck catches my attention. I exhale a long sigh of contentment, my girl still wears it after all these years.

A gasp slips from her mouth. She turns around to look at me, trying to seem as if I've offended her, but I'm the wiser. This is what Camryn and I do. These are the games that we play with each other. My relationship with Camryn is different than any relationship I have with my other friends. There's nothing hidden between the two of us. She knows all of my dirty little secrets; she accepts me and loves me with all of my flaws.

Standing here in the middle of the Townsend's kitchen with their mom, I am flooded with tons of memories from our childhood as I glance over at a picture that was taken the night of the Homecoming dance, a silly photo that my mom took of the three of us, arms wrapped around each other's waist before we left for the dance. The bestest of friends sharing and making high school memories that we'd cherish forever. Some of the strongest bonds we formed happened here in this kitchen.

Camryn had softball practice, so she wouldn't be home for a while. I stood on the Townsend's front step, repeatedly pressing the doorbell. Mrs. Townsend answered the door, while she dried her hands off on the towel.

"Come in, sweetie, I'm just getting dinner ready." I followed her into the kitchen and she pulled the stool out next to me to sit down. "Mrs. Townsend, I need to ask you something."

"What have I told you? There is no need to call me Mrs. Townsend. We have been over this before. You are like a son to me. I see that handsome face of yours every day. Call me Gwen, please."

Looking away from her, I remember that she told me this all the time, but I felt funny. My parents had always told me to call my elders by Mr. or Mrs. Why should Mrs. Townsend be any different?

Shaking my head, I said, "Yes, ma'am. I'll call you Gwen, but I have to ask my mom if that's okay."

Clearly happy with my response she replied, "So, what's on your mind?"

Nervously, I tried to find the words that I wanted to say. My fingers tapped frantically on the countertop of the island. "Um . . . would it be okay, um . . ."

Gwen continued to look at me, which only made me more nervous. Clearing my throat, "Um . . . would it be okay with you and Mr. Townsend if I ask Camryn to Homecoming?" I asked Christian earlier in school if he cared if I asked Camryn to go with me. He gave me the go ahead saying he wouldn't want her to miss out on a good time.

A smile appeared on her face and she drew me into a hug. She squeezed me, before pulling me back to look at my face. "It's Mark, sweetheart. You can call us both by our first names. And, of course, Jamie, you have our permission to ask Camryn to Homecoming. I'm sure she would be thrilled to have you as her date. You know, she wasn't going to go with everything that happened with Todd. Morgan and Lindsey told her to go by herself. But you know Camryn, she refused. I'm not sure if she didn't want to go because she may see Todd there with someone or she just felt uncomfortable going by herself."

"I'm gonna ask her tomorrow at her game. It has to be something big though. I want it to be special for her. Do you think you can run me to the store to grab a few things that I need?"

"Okay. Let me finish getting dinner ready, then we'll head out."

When Gwen finished, she walked toward the garage door and grabbed her car keys. "Come on. We need to get going if we're going to make it to the store and back before she gets home from practice."

I jumped off of the stool and quickly followed after her. After we got what I needed at the store, Mrs. Townsend helped me with my project.

I didn't sleep a wink that night after we had everything ready for the game. I played it over and over in my head, how I was going to pop the big question. It had to be perfect, Camryn deserved nothing less than perfection.

After the National Anthem, Camryn took her place on the pitcher's mound, looking relaxed as she always did. Christian helped me out by having the announcers let me have the mic for a few seconds. Standing by the announcer's booth, mic in hand, I said a silent prayer that I didn't make an ass out of myself in front of all these people. "Excuse me, ladies and gentlemen. I have something special I would like to ask Camryn Townsend."

Camryn's eyes lit up as she looked around the ball field. She frantically searched the bleachers for me until her eyes met mine by the announcer's booth.

I was standing there holding my sign over my head. On the poster board it read, You STRIKE me as the girl I want to take to Homecoming. What do you say? Did I STRIKE out, or did I hit a HOMERUN?

Her eyes widened and a smile appeared instantly. The look on her face was priceless. She immediately nodded her head up and down. I saw her mouth moving, but everyone in the bleachers was cheering, so I couldn't hear what she was saying.

That night, my Cami pitched her first no-hitter . . . I'd like to think that I had a little something to do with that.

After the game, Camryn came out of the locker room freshly showered and threw her arms around me. "I can't believe you did that." With her eyebrows cocked, "You know, if you wanted me to go to Homecoming with you, all you had to do was ask."

"I did ask." I smirked.

"I mean you didn't have to go to all that trouble just for me." She peeked up at me through her long lashes.

Laughing, I pulled her away so I could see her whole face, leave it to Camryn to feel unworthy of that attention. "Well, I wasn't going to allow you to miss out on a Jamie Banks Special. I couldn't think of any other girl to go to all that trouble for."

Christian nudges me, bringing me out of my daydream. "You got plans tonight?"

"Nah, I figured once we finished up with dinner, maybe we could all head to Aces. I can text Lincoln to see if he'll be around tonight. Cami can text the girls and have them meet us there if she's coming back to the City with us."

Christian nods his head in agreement. "Sounds like a plan. I'll see if Cami wants to pack a bag and stay with one of us in the City tonight. This way, we can just hang out tomorrow rather than coming back here to grab her."

I pull the stool out that's next to Camryn and sit down. Her mom finally hangs up with mine after laughing at God knows what. She announces that my parents are going to join us for dinner and that we'll be eating at six o'clock when our fathers get home from the office.

Bringing my attention back to Camryn, I nudge her with my elbow, "Hey, I was thinking maybe you could give the girls a call and see if they want to meet up at Aces for a few drinks. Sort of like a welcome home party."

She raises her eyebrows. "It's Friday night! Mr. Banks doesn't have a hot date?"

A laugh escapes my throat, holding my hands over my heart, I pretend I'm offended by her comment. "I do have a hot date tonight. I intend to spend the evening with a beautiful brunette, who has the most amazing hazel eyes. When she walks into the room, every man stops and stares at her. So I'll have to keep her close to me tonight. You know, to keep the vultures away." I wiggle my eyebrows up and down at her.

Her eyes widen and she tilts her head to hold my gaze. Without giving her time to respond, I swing my arm around her shoulder and pull her in to me, whispering in her ear, "You're my HOT DATE tonight, Camryn Townsend. I plan on spending my Friday night right where I want to be . . . by your side."

My lips touch her ear lightly. We are so close I can feel the heat from her body.

Her body trembles and she bites her lip, "Jamieson Banks, if I didn't know better, I would say you're flirting with me?" She laughs and pushes away from me.

Holding my hands up to surrender, "Hey, I can't help but flirt with a beautiful woman when I have the chance."

"Wow! That's the second time I've heard that line today."

"Who else told you that you were beautiful today?" I ask. She was on a freaking plane for the past six hours. Was someone trying to put the moves on her while she was in the air? Did the guy think he was going to become a member of the mile high club by flirting it up with my girl?

"It's not important who told me I was pretty." Camryn waves her hand in front of her, dismissing my question.

Christian clears his throat from across the kitchen island. "Are the two of you done with this little back and forth bullshit? The way the two of you act, it's no wonder everyone who sees you thinks you're a couple."

Before I have a chance to respond, Camryn turns her attention to her brother, "I don't care what anyone thinks about our relationship, you ought to know that by now. People have been talking for years, I don't pay any attention to it."

Christian knows I'm in love with Camryn. I think he has known for years. I got drunk a while back and professed my love for her to him. Of course, the next day I didn't recall a damn thing about that night, but he felt the need to enlighten me. He's given me his approval to go after her. He said that he would rather her be with me than some other douche. Christian knows that I can make her happy. I'm sure he isn't thrilled about the idea of me sleeping with his sister, but he knows I would never hurt her.

Christian told me to tell Camryn how I felt. But I don't think he understands, if I tell her how I feel, and she doesn't feel the same way, it could potentially ruin our friendship. Christian has never told Camryn about our conversation. He said it wasn't his story to share and that it was up to me to come clean to her.

"I know you don't pay any attention to it. Trust me, I know," he says with a glance in my direction. "Anyway, let's talk about our plans for tonight. Do you want to head to Aces when we're done here and stay in the City with one of us, or do you plan on spending the night catching up with Mom and Dad?"

"Let me see if Mom has anything planned. I feel bad just getting home, then heading to the City."

"You know Mom. She won't care," Christian says.

"Mom, do you mind if I head to the City with the boys tonight? They want to head to Aces to hang out with everyone." She bats her eyes in her mom's direction.

"Don't be silly, sweetheart. Go spend time with the girls. You haven't seen them in months. How about I pick you up on Monday morning? We can go to the spa and get a mani and pedi before you have to start work next week."

Camryn nods her head. "Okay, that sounds good. After dinner, I'll grab some things and throw them in an overnight bag. What is on the agenda for tomorrow? I need to know what kind of clothes to pack."

Jamie replies, "Whenever we get up, we can head to the gym, or for a run in Central Park. Whatever you want to do. I figured, we'd spend the day together, grab a show and dinner or something,"

"I'd like that. I've been dying to see *Lion King,* and who better to take me than you."

"Anything for you, Tink. After all, I've never been able to deny you anything before so no sense starting now." I grin as I say this, hoping she reads into my unspoken innuendo.

"Awe, Jamie, you're such a sweet talker," Camryn says as she pats my cheeks with her warm hands.

I'm looking forward to spending as much time as possible with Camryn while she's home. I may never get this opportunity again to tell her how I feel and I'm really hoping that we stop *denying* ourselves of what we both know is happening between us.

CHAPTER
Five

Jamie

ONCE WE FINISH DINNER, WE say our goodbyes and Cami's father, Mark, drops us off in the City. We had plenty of time to get ready before the girls were meeting us at Aces at ten o'clock. I texted Lincoln to see what club he would be at tonight. Aces is located in Chelsea, not too far from where Lincoln's apartment is. It's a laid-back bar with old rock and roll nostalgia on the walls, a stage, and a few pool tables. Aces isn't anything elaborate, just a great place to hang out, see some bands play, and eat some surprisingly tasty bar food. Christian and I spend almost every weekend here. He is always scoping for possible new clients, and my band, Side Effects, plays there every other Friday night.

Having Lincoln own Aces benefited Side Effects tremendously when we first started out. It gave us a steady venue to play. Now we bring in a large following, but Linc keeps us on the schedule. He gave us a chance when no one else would. Aces is and will always be like home to us.

Lincoln's other club, Redemption, has a totally different feel from Aces. Whereas Aces is more laid back and is a great place to hang out, Redemption is a full-blown club. Lincoln's girlfriend, and Camryn's best friend, Morgan, is in charge of this club. She handles everything from entertainment, private parties for high profile clients, hiring and firing of staff along with promotional work for both Aces and Redemption. Morgan is great with pulling in crowds, she spotlights up-and-coming bands and also scores some big names to play at both clubs. Morgan was also able to bring on DJ Magnum, one of the hottest DJs in the New York City scene. His name, alone, on the sign out front packs the house.

When I get a text from Christian, I grab my jacket and head down a few floors to his apartment.

When I walk in, he's in the kitchen grabbing shot glasses from the cabinet above the stove. "What poison are we starting the night off with?"

I shrug my shoulders, "Whatever you have is good with me. Just nothing sweet. That shit doesn't sit well in my stomach."

"Decision made, Absolut, it is." He pulls the freezer door open and grabs the bottle of vodka. He pours three shot glasses and grabs the lemon from the fridge, I assume in case Camryn wants to do her favorite shot, a Lemon Drop.

"Hey, Cami, how much longer are you gonna be? I told Lincoln that we'd meet him there around ten," Christian shouts down the hall. We do our shots, and he pours us another. We down our second shot, when the door finally opens. I hear the click of Camryn's heels on the hardwood before I see her.

When my eyes meet her standing before me, I damn near fall off the stool. My heart pounds against my chest and I feel like there is a lump in my throat. I attempt to discreetly clear my throat, as her eyes narrow in on me. "Are you okay?"

Standing before me is the most beautiful girl I've ever seen. Her hair is down tonight with wavy curls. It rests just above her breasts. Her make-up isn't painted on, she still looks natural but my attention is drawn to those damn hazel eyes. Camryn makes her way over to the counter to stand by Christian.

I can't pull my eyes away from the way her ass looks in her skinny black leather pants. The pants fit her like a second layer of skin. Her black shirt shows off her chest as it hangs loosely off of her left shoulder revealing the red bra strap she has on underneath. Camryn is a petite girl, not tipping the charts at more than five-four. But tonight with those damn 'fuck me' heels she has on, she is pushing close to five-eight. She's one of those girls who doesn't know she's gorgeous. She is the most down-to-earth girl I've ever met. And that's what makes her so beautiful.

Fuck . . . I can only hope that Aces isn't packed tonight, because my eyes will be locked on her all night. This girl is going to be the death of me.

I pray that I get a minute alone with her tonight to feel her out about us. I know she loves me as a friend, but I want to see if she picks up the feelers that I plan on putting out about possibly seeing if something could spark between the two of us.

Clearing my throat. "Um . . . yeah . . . I'm fine." I give her a once over. My eyes roaming the entire length of her body. Cami catches my appraisal of her attire.

"Don't EVEN start your critique of my outfit, Jamie!"

She thinks I'm tripping over my words and going to break her balls about her outfit. Is she kidding? Trying to make light of the situation and not make myself look like a fool, I mumble, "Um . . . yeah, you look gorgeous. I'm sure I'm gonna have my hands full tonight keeping the vultures away."

Christian comes up and slaps his hand on my shoulder and laughs, "Don't worry, buddy, she won't get too far out of our sight. We won't let her get into too much trouble."

Looking at Camryn dressed the way she is brings my feelings for her to the forefront of my mind. She is the reason why all of my relationships have failed. She has held my heart in her hand ever since she was a little girl. When she moved to California to go to college she took my heart with her. When she's around me, it's the only time I feel whole again. Knowing this is a struggle every day. Somehow over the years, my feelings toward her have changed from friendship to so much more. I no longer look at her as a sister or even as my best friend, I look at her as a want-to-be-lover.

I never had the courage to tell her how I feel. Risking our friendship was always my main concern. It was never something I had on my agenda, but things have changed. I can't suffer in silence anymore, I have to figure out a way to let Camryn know how I feel. I have been holding my emotions in for years. I can't keep this façade up. I have no choice. I have to risk everything in order to gain the woman I want. No pain, no gain, right? I can only pray that she feels the same, and if she doesn't that our friendship isn't ruined. With Camryn being home, I think it's a sign. Neither of us are in a relationship, so I'm going to have to go out on a limb and lay it all out.

Turning my attention toward Christian, I motion for him to pour me another shot. I need something to settle my stomach or simply to numb the tingling sensation I feel creeping up my spine.

Holding up his shot glass, he motions, "Here ya go, buddy. Cheers."

Knocking back my third shot, I feel my nerves begin to settle. I'm not much of a drinker, but the shots are definitely making me feel good. "How many of these have the two of you done already?" Hands on her hips, Camryn raises her eyebrows at us as if we are little school boys being scolded by the teacher.

"Just a few," Christian answers. Pointing to the bottle where a quarter of the vodka is now gone, he points to Camryn, "This is your fault. If you would have been ready a half-hour ago, then we would have already been on our way to Aces, not standing around here in my kitchen knocking back shots."

Camryn walks over to Christian and takes the bottle of Absolut and pours two shots. Taking the glass, she swallows it with one gulp, then grabs a piece of lemon that Christian has on the counter. She takes the second shot and downs that one and places the piece of lemon in her mouth and begins to suck on it. She makes eye contact with me, raising her brow silently asking if I am enjoying the show. I can't tear my eyes away from her lips wrapped around the wedge of lemon. Immediately my dick is hard. *I wish those lips were wrapped around something else.* What the hell is wrong with me? This is not good . . . so not good. I am hard in the middle of Christian's kitchen.

After Camryn is done putting on her show with the lemon wedge, she throws it in the trashcan. "Whatever, boys, you don't need to use me as an excuse to drink. You could have at least waited for me to join you in the festivities."

Christian's phone rings. He looks at the screen and nods toward the door, letting us know the cab is here. We grab our things and head out.

ABOUT FIFTEEN MINUTES LATER, WE pull up outside of Aces. There's a line to get in the place, but we go around to the side entrance where the bouncer is standing by the door waiting for us. Lincoln must have told him to keep an eye out for us.

When we walk in, Lincoln immediately waves us over to the bar located along the entire back wall. There are several bartenders shuffling around one another to fill requests. Patrons are lined up in rows around the small area. The waitresses are hollering orders to the bartenders, as they weave through the masses with trays held high in the air. Lincoln is finishing up talking to someone by the bar when we approach.

"Yo, whatz up?" Lincoln says, shaking my hand.

"Same shit, different day. You know how it is."

He motions us toward the table over by the stage where Morgan, Lindsey, Karsen, and my bandmate, Parker, are already sitting. "Everyone is already here."

When we approach the table, Morgan jumps up and throws her arms around Camryn's neck, making her fall back into me. I grab her so she doesn't lose her balance and end up on her ass.

"Oh my God . . . I missed you so much. Please tell me you are in town for a while. What are your plans for the rest of the weekend?" Morgan shoots out question after question, never giving Camryn enough time to answer the first question before she hits her with another one. When Morgan is finally satisfied with all of Camryn's responses, she is able to hug Lindsey and Karsen.

The girls make themselves comfortable around the table and fall into their own conversations. Filling Camryn in on what she has missed since her last visit home. It's nice to have Camryn back in the folds of the group.

We are a close-knit group, more like family than friends.

A tall brunette with legs that go on for miles approaches the table. Christian nods his head to the waitress who asks what we would like to drink. After she makes her way around the table, getting everyone's order, she heads back toward the bar.

Lincoln approaches our table and grabs a stool. "So, what brings you here tonight? I figured with Cami in town, you would have wanted to go to Redemption rather than here. Thought you'd want a night of drinks and dancing with the girls."

Christian speaks before I have a chance, "Nah, we figured we'd keep it low-key tonight, probably hit up Redemption tomorrow night. Cami had an early flight this morning, so we didn't want to be out 'til the sun comes up."

Lincoln nods, "Gotcha." He turns his attention to Camryn, "So, baby girl, what's a guy have to do to get a hug tonight?" Knowing that Lincoln adores Camryn but wouldn't miss a chance to break her balls at the same time, she crumbles up her napkin and throws it at him, hitting me in the process.

"Tink, are you off your game? You never miss a shot. Your arm must be rusty," I tease with raised brows.

A devilish smile appears on her face. "I've never had any complaints on my game, and I assure you . . . I'm anything but rusty," she says in a silky voice.

Lincoln lets out a huge laugh, smacking me on the shoulder, "Shit, man, I've missed seeing the two of you go back and forth."

Pushing him away from me, I grumble, "Fuck you, dude."

Staring across the table, my eyes meet Camryn's. She has this look in her eye, like 'Game on, Mr. Banks.' *Well, game on, Miss Townsend.* Both of our competitive sides show, and neither one of us ever backs down. With Camryn being in town for a while, I'm going to have to up my game. This is my time to make a move. I have been accused by many of my exes that I was in love with Camryn. Of course, I denied it, but in reality . . . I was in love with Cami.

The waitress arrives at the table with her tray balanced perfectly with all of our drinks. She hands me my bottle of Miller Lite, and continues to pass the rest of the drinks out around the table.

Music blares through the speakers and the girls squeal. *Hanging On*, which I immediately recognize from the movie *Divergent*, begins to play. Morgan grabs Camryn's arm and drags her to the dance floor. Karsen and Lindsey follow them out and they all begin to dance to the beat. Camryn has always been a great dancer. Her hips move so naturally. I have to admit that I'm visualizing her moving that way in bed and it's not helping out my current predicament in the least.

Morgan and Camryn are putting on quite the little show, while Karsen and Lindsey dance next to them. The girls are getting some attention from a group of guys who are playing at the nearby pool table. As the beat of the song slows down, the girls slow down, then when the beat picks up, their bodies match the tempo. You can tell that the girls are having a great time, with the huge grins on their faces. They know the attention that they are getting and they love it.

The song changes to *Toyfriend* by David Guetta and the girls grind up against each other. Morgan runs her hands up and down Camryn's sides, while Camryn sings the song to Morgan. They are definitely putting on a show for their audience. Camryn moves her hips quickly, never missing a beat. She turns around and dances with Karsen. The girls have formed their own little circle on the dance floor, each taking their turn in the middle.

"Yo, you like what you're seeing? The girls sure have formed a fan club out there," Christian yells across the table. He is being such a ball breaker today. Do I have 'I'm in love with your sister' written on my damn forehead?

"You gonna let those guys try and make a move on the girls, or are you going to show them what you got?" he continues with a raised eyebrow challenging me.

Sitting here at the table watching the girls dance is killing me. My fists are clenching under the table as I notice guys approaching the girls. The girls aren't paying them any mind until one dude walks up behind Camryn. He stands there, eyeing her up like she's a freaking piece of candy. He hasn't touched her yet, but the idea of him being that close to her has my blood boiling. My jaw begins to clench, and my body tenses. I look over at Christian, and he has this shit eating grin on his face.

Not being able to stand it anymore, I grab my beer and take a long swig. It's nearly empty, so I motion to Lincoln to order me another one then I head to the dance floor. Camryn's back is toward me so she doesn't see me approaching, but Morgan does and she has a huge smile on her face. If I were to bet, I would think Morgan knows more than she lets on about Camryn's feelings for me. But, of course, Morgan being her best friend, her lips are sealed yet she never misses an opportunity to make comments about the two of us.

Morgan continues to dance in front of Camryn, never letting her know that I nudged the guy out of the way. *Desnudate* by Christina Aguilera comes on and Morgan moves in between Camryn's legs so she can grind up against her. Morgan wiggles her eyebrows at me and yells over the music and motions to me behind her, "Cami, keep dancing. You're good." Camryn doesn't turn around to see who is behind her. I'm guessing she figures if Morgan said to keep dancing, she's going with the flow. It could also be that she had a huge grin plastered on her face when I approached, so Camryn knew it was okay to continue to dance.

My body is now against Camryn's back and my hands are on her waist moving her to the beat. Camryn hasn't attempted to turn around, and I want to keep it that way. I don't want her to know it's me . . . not yet. Camryn continues to dance, her hips moving to the beat and her ass is grinding against my straining dick. *Heel, boy . . . Down.* I move back a little, trying to adjust myself, but it's not working. Screw it, moving closer to Camryn I pull her ass into me and move my hips. I know she can feel how hard I am for her, but she doesn't pull away, so I move my hands so they are around her waist and rub her stomach. I can feel her muscles tense up under my touch, but she is enjoying this as much as I am.

Morgan laughs while she dances. She moves away from Camryn to Karsen and Lindsey, leaving Camryn with me. I lean down and gently move Camryn's hair away from her neck. The smell of her lavender vanilla body spray makes my mouth water.

Whispering, "Are you enjoying yourself?" I can feel her laugh as my hands glide across her stomach. She simply nods her head and continues to push against me. Camryn's body relaxes, so my hands continue to roam up and down her lean body. She knew it was me the entire time. Camryn would have never allowed a stranger to dance with her the way I am. When Morgan gave her the okay, she knew it was me. Camryn knows my body, this isn't the first time we've danced like this. Leaning into her ear again, I ask "Do you feel what you're doing to me, Camryn?"

I know I am being bold. Putting myself out there, but I am tired of fighting my feelings for her.

She quickly spins around and throws her arms around my neck. Now we're facing each other and she has a wicked smile on her face. That grin tells me she knows exactly what she's doing to me. She tippy toes so she's next to my ear and says with a seductive voice, "Were you jealous that those boys were close to me? Did you think I didn't know the minute you walked up behind me? I felt you, Jamie. I know when you're near me, I can sense it deep inside my body."

My words catch in my throat. This is not what I was expecting tonight when I came out. I know we flirt all the time, but I have never rubbed my hard-on up against Camryn's back. She gives me an evil grin, telling me she knows exactly what she is doing to me. I don't pull away, but continue to dance. I'm all in now. I'm crossing that line. There's no going back for me. She'll have to be the one to pull away.

The song ends and Camryn grabs my hand, leading us off of the dance floor toward the bathroom. "Wait here, I need to pee and wet my face."

All I can do is laugh at her. I lean against the wall and wait for her to come out of the bathroom. I can't believe she just pulled me off the dance floor. For a moment, I thought she was going to kiss me after she asked me if I was jealous.

Dancing with her was definitely a work out. Any little bit of buzz I may have had from the few shots I did is gone. The only buzz I have is the one that Camryn induced. When she walks out, she's glowing, I put my arms around her tiny waist, pulling her close to me. With me being six-two, and Cami being the size of a 'Polly Pocket', even with her heels, she's just shy of my chin.

My heart pounds against my chest. This isn't just from dancing. When she is close, she makes my pulse race. I can still smell her scent on my clothes. Having her body pressed against me felt so natural.

Looking at me with her wide, hazel eyes, she asks, "Are you attracted to me, Jamie?" She looks away nervously before continuing. "I mean . . . not just that you think I'm pretty. Like . . . you want to kiss me . . . maybe you'd want to be with me?"

Her questions catch me off guard. I never expected her to be so straightforward. I figured I would be the one who would have to ask her those questions. When I don't answer immediately, she pulls away from me, leaving me feeling empty, as she rushes past me to find our group.

I immediately reach for her, grabbing her arm. "Cami, stop," I plead.

She pulls her arm free, then turns and walks away before I can even try to explain myself.

Screaming "FUCK!" in the hallway draws a few curious eyes. *What the hell did I just do?*

I walk up to the bar and grab another beer then head back to the table, since the one Lincoln got me before I went to the dance floor is probably piss warm by now. When I grab a stool, Morgan glares at me from across the table. Camryn must have told her what just happened in the hallway by the bathroom. Not being able to keep eye contact with Morgan, I look at Lincoln and he has the same sour look on his face. *What the fuck?* Does everyone at the table know what just happened?

Taking a long swig of my beer, Parker nudges me. "Don't sweat it, dude. Camryn told Morgan and Lincoln but no one else was paying attention. They were all wrapped up in their own conversation talking about heading to Redemption tomorrow night. There's a band playing that Morgan said was pretty good."

I stand from the table, walk over to stand behind Camryn and place my hands on her shoulders. Immediately, her body stiffens from my touch. Leaning down, I speak in her ear, so only she can hear me. "Can I talk to you? Away from all these prying eyes."

She pushes my hands from her shoulders. When she turns to look at me, her eyes speak a thousand different emotions. Hurt, anger, rejection, embarrassment. I hate that I made her feel that way.

"No." She sneers at me through gritted teeth. "There is nothing that needs to be said."

I lean in closer, placing my finger under her chin, so she looks at me. Knowing that I have her full attention, I plead, "Don't do this. Please. Hear me out."

Her eyes are sad and it's all because of me. I feel like shit that I put it there.

"There is nothing to explain. I got the message. Just . . . go away. Please . . ."

I turn away, knowing that my absolute shock and lack of response to Camryn is the cause of this. I thought I was finally crossing the line with her and now I feel like I've jumped backwards twenty feet. I've got to figure out how to fix this and fix it fast before some asshole has the chance to steal her away from me while she's in New York.

After a few more beers I'm ready to head out. Christian said he and Camryn were heading to the diner down the street to get something to eat. Rather than sit through an awkward meal, I opt to catch my own cab home. I'll text Camryn in the morning and tell her we need to talk. I can only pray that she will listen to me and not brush me off again. She can be a little stubborn—hell, a lot stubborn—when she wants to be.

CHAPTER

Six

Camryn

I WAKE UP TO THE sunlight shining in through the blinds. You would think after living here for three years, my brother would have curtains up in his room rather than just blinds. My head is throbbing with pain. It feels like someone is beating drumsticks against my temples. I attempt to open my eyes, squinting to look at the clock. It only reads a little after nine and I let out a groan. The lack of sleep, the effects of the alcohol and the light are only making my headache worse.

Christian and I got back to his place sometime after three a.m. My brother, being the gentlemen that he is, told me to take his room, he would sleep on the couch. Even after me arguing that I'd take the couch, Christian wouldn't allow it. When Jamie was single, I used to stay there sometimes. We even slept in the same bed, but nothing happened besides a little cuddling. We usually spend hours talking, catching up on things. Jamie makes me feel safe, and at home when I am with him. Especially when I am wrapped in his strong arms.

Something has changed between us over the last year. Our flirting has surely picked up a notch. The two of us are a little more open with touching each other. There are things that Jamie knows about me that my brother or even Morgan don't know. I have always felt comfortable telling Jamie anything.

Jamie was dating a girl named Tabitha for the past year. She was a really nice girl, they met their senior year at NYU. We all hung out a few times when I was home, but Jamie never brought her with him when he came to visit me in California. They broke up sometime in the winter, and from what Jamie says, it was mutual. He really never went into details about the break-up, he just said things weren't working out between the two of them. They wanted different things in life, and when the relationship ended, they remained friendly.

I liked Tabitha. I really did. She was funny, energetic, and easy going. She was perfect for Jamie, if only I didn't have feelings for him. I've always wanted Jamie to be happy, but seeing them together made my heart ache. Being in their presence sometimes made me feel uncomfortable, especially when she showed him affection in front of me. My stomach would clench when I would see her kiss him and that's when I realized I wanted *him* to be kissing *me*.

I keep replaying last night over and over, trying to see if I misread the signals that Jamie was giving me. After the way we were dancing and the way I felt with his body molded into mine, I don't know how I could have misconstrued what was happening. In all the times we've danced together, I've never felt him aroused before. To know that I had that effect on him brings a smile to my lips. This is why I'm still shocked by his reaction when I asked if he was attracted to me.

I know he thinks I'm beautiful. He tells me all the time, but I wanted to know if he saw me differently. If he was attracted to me enough that he would want to pursue something more physical. If he was attracted to me where he may want to see if we could have a relationship together. When Jamie didn't respond, my heart stopped beating right then. I felt as if he took a sledgehammer and shattered my heart into pieces. I couldn't breathe. I couldn't speak. I'm not sure if I was upset with him for not answering my questions or mad at myself for being foolish enough to think that he wanted me.

The previous evening, when I left Jamie standing there in the hallway, I made my way back to the table where everyone was sitting.

Morgan and Lincoln seemingly picked up on the change in my demeanor. My body language must have clearly shown it. My gaze bounced around from place to place as I prayed that the tears would not come. I pulled deep breaths in to help calm myself down. I couldn't even look at Morgan when I got back to the table.

I grabbed the shot glass in front of me and tossed it back. I wasn't even sure whose it was, but it didn't ease the pain that I felt. There was another shot in front of Lincoln, so I grabbed that one as well. That shot burned like hell as it went down my throat. I took a deep breath trying to ease the burn, but that only made it worse. Wincing from the shot, Morgan handed me her drink. I took a large mouthful of it before sliding it back to her.

Lincoln pulled me close to him by putting his arm around my shoulder, where he gently squeezed it. I ignored him. I tried to look anywhere but at him. I couldn't look at him. I knew I was going to lose it if I did. He didn't give up though. He pulled my stool closer and turned it so I faced him. I had no option but to look at him.

"What's up, baby girl? Spill it." Morgan got up from her stool and moved it next to mine, so we both faced Lincoln. After filling Morgan and Lincoln in, they both just shook their heads back and forth. I sat there and watched Lincoln's jaw clench with his frustration. He just told me, "Don't dwell on this, Cami, everything will work itself out. Trust me."

Could I trust Lincoln? Would everything work itself out? Was coming home a mistake? When Shelby offered me the opportunity to head home for a few months, I jumped at the chance to be closer to my favorite people on the planet, now I was beginning to think I made a huge mistake.

When I walked down the hall last night and met Christian and Jamie in the kitchen before we left for Aces, there was something different in Jamie's eyes when he looked at me. It was as if we had a conversation with our eyes as we stared at each other. So many unspoken words were being conveyed. I could have sworn that he wanted me the way I wanted him. *Rejection sucks.*

Ugh, I am exhausted. It's only nine o'clock, I should still be sleeping.

My mind refused to shut off last night when I laid in bed. Now here I am, with only a few hours of sleep and a raging hangover.

Stretching, I reach over and grab my phone off of the nightstand. There are several texts from Morgan, Lindsey, and Karsen checking to see how I feel this morning. When Christian and I left them at the diner last night, they knew I was going to have one hell of a hangover this morning. They watched me consume a decent amount of alcohol last night. More than I normally do. I figured if I drank enough, it could numb the pain that I felt in my chest. Maybe the alcohol would have masked the embarrassment that I felt every time I looked at Jamie as he sat across from me at the table.

Morgan: Hey, drunk bitch, we're heading to Redemption tonight. I have a private room set up for us. Bar bill is on Lincoln and me. Be ready at 10, we'll swing by and grab you guys.

Me: After the amount of alcohol I consumed last night, I really DO NOT want to go out tonight. Was I that bad last night?

Morgan: WHATEVER, you're going out. Wear that tight strapless black dress you have and your red Manolo Blahnik heels. NO ARGUING. Yes, you were drunk, but not too much to handle ☺

Me: Ugh . . . Can't we just have a movie night?

Morgan: NOOOOOOOOOO!!!!!!! Don't make me have to come there and dress you myself. You had a shitty night last night. That is not the welcome home party I wanted for you. We will dance and drink all night. Tonight will be awesome!!

Me: Okay . . . Okay . . . I'm gonna jump in the shower and head out for a run. I slept like shit last night, so I need to try and burn some energy off.

Morgan: I can think of a few ways you can burn some energy off. It begins with a J and ends with an E, with AMI in between (lol) That boy has it hard for you. No pun intended.

Me: WHATEVER . . . His silence spoke volumes last night.

Morgan: Maybe you just caught him off guard. Cut him some slack, Cam.

Me: I gotta run. I'll talk to you later.

Morgan: Don't ignore my text about you catching him off guard. This conversation is NO WHERE NEAR OVER!!

Me: Love ya too . . . talk to you later. Putting phone on charger. MUAH

I finally get up, grab my toiletry bag and head down the hall to the bathroom. The apartment is quiet, so Christian must still be sleeping. I turn on the shower and wait for the water to get hot. Looking at myself in the mirror, I'm a little scared at the reflection staring back at me. My eyeliner is smeared and my hair looks like rats ran through it while I slept. Oh God, last night was rough. I step into the shower and when the hot water hits my body, my muscles immediately begin to relax.

By the time I am done with my shower and wrapped in a comfy towel, I decide to scratch the idea of going for a run.

I need to get this nasty taste out of my mouth. Quickly I brush my teeth and gargle some mouthwash, hoping it will help.

When I open the bathroom door, I hear *his* voice. *Shit . . .* Jamie is here, what the hell? It's only ten o'clock, why is he here already? This day cannot get any worse. I grip the towel tighter and try to sneak out of the bathroom without being noticed. I fail miserably, because Jamie spots me immediately.

"Don't think I don't see you. You and I need to talk. Like now," Jamie says, his eyes scowling and pleading at the same time.

"There isn't anything to talk about, Jamie." He and I stare at each other and I pull my towel tighter around my chest, suddenly feeling self-conscious and exposed.

I can tell he is pissed. "Like hell there isn't." He looks back at my brother sitting on the couch, "Give me a few minutes, I need to talk to your sister."

I ignore him and continue to walk into Christian's bedroom and slam the door.

I hear my brother say, "Go for it, Bro. I think you are going to need more than a few minutes. I'll get the coffee brewing and start breakfast. Breakfast should be done by the time you finish getting through that thick head of hers."

Jamie barges in the room, shuts the door behind him.

I am beyond pissed now. My head feels like it is going to explode and I do not want to have this conversation with him. I take a deep breath and when I turn around, Jamie is chest to chest with me.

"You need to hear me out. What happened last night was a mistake." His voice is firm and final.

A gasp leaves my throat involuntarily. I push against his chest and he takes a step back. I need space to breathe. I can't have him this close to me. Not today, not after last night, not after he just said last night was a mistake.

"You're goddamn right it was." I turn around and walk over to my duffle bag on the bed. I need to get dressed and get the hell away from him. I am trying to find a pair of yoga pants and a tank top when Jamie comes up behind me. He puts his arms around my waist, pulling my body against his chest. I struggle to pull away, but he just holds me tighter.

"Calm down, Cami. I didn't mean it like that. You're only hearing what you want to hear."

I take a deep breath and let it out. I repeat this action several times, trying to calm myself down before I lose my shit. My head is throbbing, my heart is racing. His tight hold only pisses me off even more.

"LET. ME. GO. NOW!" I demand through gritted teeth. Trying to get out of his hold, I twist and turn, attempting to loosen the death grip that he has on me. This just infuriates him more, causing him to pull me against his chest again.

"Are you done acting like an ass?"

I close my eyes and continue to take deep breaths to calm down. I mutter to myself, "Breathe in, breathe out. Breathe in, breathe out."

Maybe I should try a different route. I am still naked and this should buy me some time.

"Can you please get out? I need to get dressed. I'm naked under this towel, in case you haven't noticed." I grab my towel by my left breast to keep it secure around my body.

"Oh, trust me, I've noticed you're only in a towel. It's driving me fucking crazy. But I'm not leaving until you hear me out," Jamie says firmly.

"I heard exactly what you said, Jamie. You said that last night was a mistake. I heard you loud and clear just like last night. I'm not an idiot, although you made me look and feel like one."

I don't have it in me to fight with Jamie. He must sense that I feel defeated and he turns me around to face him. He places his finger under my chin, "Camryn, please look at me."

When I don't look up, he applies a little pressure against his finger, forcing me to stare in his eyes.

"Last night wasn't a mistake. Me not answering your question was a mistake. You caught me completely off guard. I wanted to answer you, I just couldn't find the words. They were on the tip of my tongue, the words have just been kept under wraps for so many years that I didn't know how to voice my feelings for you."

My heart is speeding up even more because of what he is saying.

He takes a deep breath. "When I tell you how I feel, I want the words to be perfect. Ones you'll remember for all your life."

Tears build in my eyes. I am trying my hardest not to let them fall. But one by one they begin to stream down my cheeks. I quickly try to bat them away. "Jamie, I don't know why I asked you that. I should have never put you on the spot."

Jamie lets out a deep sigh. "There you go again, you're not listening to me. You didn't put me on the spot. You had a question that you wanted an answer to. Yes, I am attracted to you, Cami. You know that I think you are the most beautiful woman I have ever laid eyes on."

He cups my face tenderly in his warm hands. Slowly and seductively, his gaze drops from my eyes, to my bare shoulders to the swell of my breasts. He leans in, his lips brush against mine. His tongue traces the softness of my lips. My knees weaken as his mouth descends down my jaw, burying his face in my neck. From just his kiss, my body aches for his touch.

The sound of the smoke alarms and the banging on the door

makes me pull away from him.

We both turn and stare at the door, which then flies open. Christian looks between Jamie and me with wide eyes. His eyes going back and forth between the two of us, taking in the scene before him. Jamie still has his arms around my waist. Christian has a bewildered look on his face, then smirks at us.

"Sorry for all the noise. I sort of burned breakfast. But I managed to not fuck up the coffee. There are bagels in the cabinet, the bacon isn't edible." Christian turns to leave but stops and looks at us. "I don't even want to know what was happening in here." Then continues to walk out leaving the bedroom door open.

Jamie looks down at me. "This conversation isn't over. We'll talk later when he isn't around, okay? That way there won't be any interruptions."

My voice is hoarse with frustration, I murmur, "Sure." My lips are still warm and moist from his kiss. I raise my fingers to them, wishing the kiss would have lasted longer.

He sighs then lets me out of his embrace. Jamie leaves the room in pursuit of my pain-in-the-ass brother who has the worst timing in the world. I flop down on the bed, throwing my hands over my head, praying that this day doesn't get any worse.

I hate fighting with Jamie. The only good thing that came out of our fight was he just confessed that he does see me as more than a best friend.

I can sense Jamie needing to tell me more. I saw it in his eyes . . . felt it when his fingers dug against my skin. I even felt it in the pulsing bulge between his legs as he held me tight against his chest. This is definitely not over between us and we just need time alone to figure this all out.

CHAPTER

Seven

Jamie

WALKING OUT OF CHRISTIAN'S BEDROOM, the smell of burnt bacon turns my stomach. A cloud of smoke hangs in the air. Christian is rushing around, opening up the windows in the kitchen, so I help him out by opening the ones in the living room.

"How did you manage to fuck up breakfast, dude? You make breakfast for us almost every weekend, and you never manage to screw it up." Christian is acting odd, so I know he is up to something.

Avoiding looking at me, he walks over to the cabinet and grabs the bagels and pops one in the toaster. He takes a few mugs from the cabinet and heads over to the coffee pot, "I wasn't paying attention."

I walk over and snatch a mug from the counter. Christian turns around and fills my mug with coffee. "What do you mean you weren't paying attention?"

Looking sheepish, he chuckles, "Do you really want to know?"

Raising my eyebrows, "Yes, please do tell, I am dying to know."

"I was eavesdropping outside of the bedroom door." Laughing he walks toward the fridge to grab the coffee creamer.

I walk over and snatch the coffee creamer out of his hand and pour some in my cup. Turning around to face Christian, I say to him, "Let me get this straight. You fucked up our breakfast, because you were being a nosey shithead? Dude, that is a new low, even for you. You could have just waited and made us a kick ass breakfast. I would have filled you in later when we were at the gym."

Christian shrugs his shoulders, "The two of you seemed pretty heated, I just wanted to make sure that everything was okay."

Glaring at him, "Are you kidding me? You wanted to make sure everything was okay? When have things between me and Camryn ever not been okay? We argue, we get over it. We bicker, we move on. You, of all people, should know that." I walk around the counter and pull out a stool to sit on. After I take a sip of my coffee, I continue, "There was a misunderstanding last night and I needed to clear it up with her. I didn't want her being pissed at me all day."

The toaster pops and Christian slides the bagel on a plate in my direction. I spread on some cream cheese and take a bite.

"Cami, do you want a bagel?" Christian yells down the hall.

She responds, "Sure, I'll be out in a few minutes."

"Did the two of you settle this *misunderstanding?*"

Taking another sip of my coffee, I look at Christian over the brim of my cup. "I think we did. Only time will tell."

"Don't hurt her, dude, I'm warning you," he says as he leans back against the counter, crossing his arms over his chest.

"I would never hurt her." I bite out and take a calming breath. "I just need to figure out how to tell her how I feel."

He glares at me. "You have been in love with my sister for years. Pull your head out of your ass and just tell her. You get one life, Jamie. Make sure you live it with the one you love. Every minute you waste is a minute you don't get to spend with my sister. Make every second count."

Christian turns his attention to the hallway when he hears his bedroom door open. Camryn walks into the kitchen, gets herself a cup of coffee, and steals the bagel as it pops up from the toaster. Both of us looking at her in awe, knowing we won't say a word as she munches on the bagel that was meant for Christian.

The three of us eat our breakfast with small talk. Christian goes over the schedule for the studio this week. While I should be concentrating on him, Cami's eyes continue to flicker over to me. We share a smile as Christian rambles about his two new clients coming in.

I am beginning to see things with more clarity. Christian is right. I am wasting time by not telling Camryn how I feel. I need to lay it out there and let the pieces fall where they may. It's going to be her decision on where we go from here. I can only hope that she feels the same way. God, I sound like such a pussy in my own head. No wonder Christian sees what a mess I am with having Camryn back home. It's like dangling a carrot in front of Bugs Bunny and telling him he can't have it. Pure fucking torture and it's time to end this and in order to *end this,* I have to *start this* between us, and that scares the ever loving shit out of me.

♪ ♩ ♪ ♩

ONCE CHRISTIAN IS SHOWERED, THE three of us head to the gym. Christian and I hit the weights while Camryn heads over to the cardio equipment. I'm shocked she is doing cardio after the amount of alcohol she consumed last night. She must be trying to sweat the alcohol out of her system. Camryn catches me stealing glances while she's on the elliptical and she smiles at me. She has her earbuds in, probably listening to one of her old playlists she used when she trained for softball. Maybe one day this week before Camryn has to travel for work, the two of us can head to the batting cages.

Guys' heads turned to her the minute she walked into the gym wearing her yoga pants and fitted workout tank. The tank is skin tight and leaves nothing to the imagination. Every guy in here can see every curve on Camryn's petite body.

Christian clears his throat getting my attention, "Are you done drooling over my sister, or do you plan on standing there looking like a dumb ass all day? Let's get our work out in. I want to head back upstairs and watch the game today."

I shoot him a death stare. "You sure do know how to make me feel like a complete ass, you know that."

He holds his hands up in surrender. "I am just pointing out the obvious, dude."

Trying to focus on my workout, I turn my attention to the bench press. "Fuck you, just spot me."

As always, Christian laughs and stands over me to make sure I can handle the weight. As I push the bar off my chest, Christian continues to spout his advice. "You know you have some time to work on Camryn. She's home for three months. Now is as good a time as any to tell her how you feel. She's heading to Boston this Saturday, I'm pretty sure she is going to Aces on Friday night for your show. If you don't have anything planned, why don't you take the trip to Boston with her? She's only gonna be gone for two days. I'm sure she won't mind."

After doing twenty reps, Christian helps me set the bar back on the workout bench. I grab my towel and wipe my forehead, taking a drink of my water. Trying not to be obvious, I steal another look in Camryn's direction. She's moved to the treadmill now. "I'll see if she asks me to go with her. She may ask one of the girls to tag along."

"Just wait and see. The week is young, my friend." Christian takes his place on the bench, and I lift the bar off for him. We continue our workout, while discussing this weeks' meetings and what our plans are for tonight, all while my eyes are on Camryn and trying to keep my hands off of the dicks who are ogling her on the treadmill.

THE FOOTBALL GAME WAS EXCITING right down to the last second. After Penn State beat Temple, I head upstairs to my apartment to relax before I get showered for tonight. The clock shows it's only seven o'clock. Lincoln is swinging by to grab us at ten, so I have plenty of time. Going through my closet, I look for a particular light blue Henley shirt. The one Camryn loves. I'm going for a casual look tonight, a Henley shirt, a pair of dark jeans and my Kenneth Cole brown shoes. The question of the night, do I plan on taming my unruly hair or just throwing on my Red Sox hat? My hair is longer than usual and I am in desperate need of a haircut. After ironing my outfit, I make my way to the bathroom to hop in the shower.

While I wash by body, my mind begins to wander to Camryn and what it would be like to have her in the shower with me. What would it feel like to lather her body and have my hands all over her? To feel every curve of her body under my fingers. *Fuck*, just thinking about Camryn has my dick hard. Trying not to think of what it would feel like to be inside of Camryn, I squirt some shampoo in my hand and scrub my head. After washing my hair for what seems like forever, I'm still aroused. Looking down at myself, I'm standing at full salute. Shaking my head knowing there is no controlling where my brain goes next, my hand slides down my stomach. The image of her mouth on me while my fingers tangle in her silky long brown hair flashes before me. Three minutes later I've rubbed one out in the shower, all the while wishing it was Camryn's hand or mouth stroking me when I reach my climax.

THERE'S A KNOCK AT MY door around nine-thirty, but Lincoln didn't text me letting me know he was downstairs. When I open the door, my jaw damn near hits the floor. Camryn is standing before me in a tight ass, black, strapless dress and those black fuck me heels again. Her dress sits about two inches below her ass. From the look of it, she doesn't have a bra on either. I can only pray that she has panties on underneath that dress. Otherwise, every time she bends over, I'll be right behind her to make damn sure no one sees anything.

Without thinking, I blurt out, "You do have panties on under that dress, right?"

Camryn pushes me aside and walks into my apartment while Christian laughs his ass off in the hallway. With an evil look on her face, Cami turns and faces me. "Wouldn't you like to know, Mr. Banks?"

I take a deep breath and remind myself to keep breathing. Christian finally pulls himself together and walks over to the couch to sit down. "You got anything to drink in this place?"

I look at him like he has lost his mind. "You know where the fridge is, help yourself. What do I look like, the damn butler?" Camryn walks over to the kitchen and pulls out three bottles of Miller Lite and hands us each one. When I take the bottle from her, our fingers graze and the hair on my arm stands up. Camryn knows what she did and there's no hiding my reaction to her, she simply laughs and walks over to sit next to her brother on the couch.

"You look very appealing tonight. Did you wear that shirt on purpose because you know it's my favorite?" she says in a flirtatious voice.

"Wouldn't you like to know?" I laugh, giving her a taste of her own medicine, then turn and walk in to the kitchen just to avoid eye contact with her. I holler over my shoulder, "I didn't know this was a favorite of yours, but thank you for the compliment." *Touche, two can play this game.*

My phone chirps. "Hey, that was Linc, he's downstairs, are you ready?"

I was expecting a cab, but a Mercedes stretch limo is waiting by the curb. When I open the door for Camryn, I notice Karsen and Lindsey are already in the limo. Hopefully tonight will not be a repeat of last night. I cannot handle a second round. Camryn slides into the limo and sits next to Karsen. Christian climbs in and grabs the seat next to Lindsey, leaving me the seat closest to the door. The limo is massive. There is a row of seats lining the entire length of the car, and along the front and back there is another set of seats. The divider is up, so the driver can't hear or see in the back. Lincoln hits the intercom and advises the driver to head to Redemption while I busy myself as bartender for everyone.

The ride to Redemption isn't long at all. Thirty minutes with traffic, which is surprising for a Saturday night.

"Nice ride. What was the occasion?" I turn to Lincoln after we step onto the sidewalk.

"A buddy owed me a favor, so I called it in." He shrugs as though it's no big deal. If I'm reading between the lines correctly, someone probably owed him money and they offered up their limo for the night to settle the score.

We follow Lincoln and Morgan to the side entrance and he swipes his keycard through the scanner. On the other side of the door a bouncer is standing with his arms crossed and an earpiece in his ear. He is talking to someone and gives Lincoln a nod. The loud music filters throughout the club to the hallway that leads to a private set of stairs where the private rooms are located. Camryn said Morgan has a private room reserved for us. I make a mental note to tip the waitresses and bartenders well since our bar bill is covered.

When we enter the private room, music is filtering through the speakers. The room overlooks the dance floor below where the DJ is set up near the main stage. Frosted glass windows stretch the entire length of the one wall so we can see what is happening downstairs, while still allowing us privacy. The waitress comes in and takes our drink order. I plan on taking it easy tonight and order a Miller Lite.

Our drinks arrive and the girls gather over near the glass to see what's happening on the main floor. Christian, Lincoln, and I talk about our upcoming show this Friday and the new clients that Christian has lined up this week in the studio.

The girls decide to head downstairs to the dance floor, so we walk over to the glass to keep an eye on them. Morgan has her earpiece in tonight so she is in constant communication with her staff. Even though Lincoln owns the club, this is Morgan's baby, too. Lincoln lets Morgan handle everything except the security, that is where he draws the line. He needs to know that his patrons and Morgan are safe.

Not Myself Tonight by Christina Aguilera starts to play and the girls throw their arms in the air and swing their hips to the tempo of the music. Once again, Cami and Morgan are dancing rather provocatively and Karsen and Lindsey are following close behind.

Seeing the girls so carefree makes me smile. I scan the crowd looking to see if I recognize any familiar faces. I'm also making sure there aren't any creepers looking for an opportunity to get too close to my friends . . . and my girl.

When the song ends, Maroon 5's *Love Somebody* starts up and I know that Cami is going to go nuts. She's a huge fan of theirs. Camryn dances in the middle of the girls, moving her hands above her head. Her hips sway back and forth with the beat and she sings the words to the song along with Adam. Morgan eggs her on acting like she has a microphone and holds her fist in front of Cami's mouth as she sings her heart out. These are the moments that I live for. To see the smile that is spread across Cami's face, and how much fun she is having. I want to make her mine. I want to experience everything with her . . . and not just as a friend. I want to wake up next to her every morning and kiss her goodnight every night before I pull her body close to mine to cuddle before we fall asleep. This is what I have been waiting for. For Cami to be mine.

When the song finishes, the girls walk over to the side and stand by a high top table. Cami grabs a napkin to wipe her forehead and I see a waitress approach the girls and hand them each a drink. They look shocked since they didn't order any. Lincoln nudges me and points in the direction of the girls, "Did you have the waitress deliver their drinks?"

"I didn't send anything to the girls." Camryn and the waitress are talking, when the waitress points in the direction of the bar. Camryn looks in the direction where she indicated, and a guy holds up a drink and smiles at her.

I strain to see who the guy is, to see if I recognize him. He's standing with a group of guys. None who look familiar. There is a buzzing in my brain and the sharp pain ends in my chest. I'm restless now as an uneasy feeling works its way into the pit of my stomach. I'm overwhelmed with the sudden feeling of jealousy. She's my girl.

"Who the fuck is that?"

"I have no idea, but I'm about to find out in a second." Lincoln walks away and takes the back stairs leading to the main floor. I watch as Lincoln approaches the girls at the table. Morgan and Lincoln are talking but the other girls are just standing there. Camryn waves the guy over to their table, which immediately pisses me off. The guy leans in and kisses Camryn on the cheek.

"Dude, do you know him?" Looking over my shoulder, Christian watches the same scene I am.

"I have no idea who he is. Do you?" As I watch the guy pull Camryn into a hug, my body tenses. Lincoln sticks his hand out and the guy shakes his hand. The guy talks to Lincoln and Morgan, and Camryn points up to the VIP area. The guy waves his friends over, now there are five of them standing there at the table with them. Another guy pulls her in for a hug. He must have said something to her because she leans back to look at him and laughs. Camryn and Morgan begin to walk away, and the rest of the group follows. "What the hell is she doing bringing them all up here? Has she lost her mind?"

Christian pats me on the shoulder. "Calm down, man. Obviously she knows them. Wait and see what she says." The words no sooner leave Christian's mouth, when the door to our private room opens and everyone comes in.

Lincoln walks over to where we are standing and pulls us aside. "She knows them. She saw them perform last year in California and wrote a piece on them. Believe it or not, she actually sat next to the lead singer and the guitarist on the plane yesterday."

"I saw the way he watched Camryn down there. That guy was way too into her for my liking." My jaw clenches, and my eyes narrow toward the guy standing on the other side of the room. The one who seemed to be a little too interested in Camryn.

Camryn walks over to us and leans into my side. I raise my brow at her.

"I see that look in your eye. Shall I ask?" She stands on her tiptoes to get closer to my ear. "Are you being protective, or are you jealous?" she asks in a seductive purr.

I scoff at her accusation. Knowing all the damn while that she hit the nail on the head.

"Don't act like this, Jamie. I know them, they're nice guys."

"Nice guys, huh?" *Oh shit. She's right. I'm jealous. I can't believe I am jealous of some tool I have never met.*

"Stop it. We met last year when I wrote a review about them for my column. I sat next to Chad and Buffer on the plane yesterday. I had no idea they were going to be here tonight. Chad gave me his business card, but I never gave him my number." *That little bit of information makes me smile.*

Nodding my head, but I don't take my eyes off of the guys. "What's the name of their band?" Christian walks over to join our conversation, when Cami says their name, Troubled Pasts, Christian's eyebrows shoot to his hairline.

"They're Troubled Pasts?" Christian asks with a look of recognition on his face. I am completely lost on what is going on here. Looking at Christian, "Do you know them?"

Cami eyes the two of us as if we have three heads. Christian pulls me closer to him by putting his arm around my shoulder, "They, my friend, are our new client. We have a meeting with them at the studio on Tuesday morning at ten o'clock."

I turn to face him. "You have got to be shitting me," I mutter with complete surprise on my face.

"Nope," Christian replies with a shit-eating smirk on this face.

Camryn calls Chad over. With his cocky swagger, he approaches us.

"Guys, this is Chad. He is the singer in the band, Troubled Pasts." Cami introduces.

Christian shakes his hand, then I do the same. Christian speaks up first, "I'm Christian Townsend, Camryn's brother, and this is my best friend and business partner, Jamieson Banks. We own Townsend and Banks, LLC. We have a meeting set up with your band on Tuesday morning. It's nice to meet you . . . small world. I had no idea you knew my sister, Camryn."

"It's nice to meet you too. I had no idea that Camryn knew you. Our managers set this meeting up for us. I only met Camryn last year when she did a piece on us for *Key Notes*." Chad calls the rest of the guys over and introduces them. We all shake hands, Camryn walks away and heads over to be with the girls. Lincoln stands with them, keeping a watchful eye on everyone. Lincoln is one who takes everything in. I thought I was tough on welcoming newcomers into our group, but Lincoln is who you need to get past in order to be in our close circle. Lincoln gives me a look, as if I got this covered. *Mingle with your clients. I'll keep an eye on the girls.*

CHAPTER
Eight

Camryn

I GRAB MY CELL OFF the nightstand to look at my calendar for the next three months, I'm booked solid. This was the only week that Shelby didn't have events scheduled, so I took advantage of spending quality time with my family and friends. I didn't realize just how much I needed this down time to relax and enjoy myself.

This week has blown by in the blink of an eye. I spent Monday at the spa with my mom and every night my mom has shown me a new dish to prepare for dinner. She thinks I don't cook enough being that I live alone, so she is showing me quick meals that I can make. Our house has been a revolving door this week with different guests stopping by to visit or stay for dinner.

Karsen and the girls were able to come to dinner on Thursday, which was Karsen's only day off from the hospital.

My cell vibrates in my hand. I look down and see a text from Morgan.

Morgan: Hey. What time are you heading to Aces tonight?

Me: Not sure yet, I'll definitely get there before Jamie starts. Will

Karsen be there? I know she works a lot of hours at the hospital.

Morgan: Being an ER nurse will do that. Not sure if she is or not. I haven't talked to her. Are you excited to finally see Jamie perform?

Me: It's been ages since I've seen him perform, so YES, I am excited.

Morgan: Aces should be packed. Side Effects pulls in a decent crowd.

Me: I'm looking forward to it. C-ya tonight.

Morgan: C-ya.

There is something about seeing him on stage, commanding the audience's attention that I find undeniably hot. The way he interacts with everyone is what makes his performances memorable.

Tomorrow night I have an event in Boston, so Christian and Jamie are going with me. Christian was a little reluctant at first, claiming he didn't want to go. But I played the guilt card since I will be traveling a lot while I am home, and won't get to see him as much as I would like. So after persuasion, they both agreed to make the four-hour ride with me.

I shower and slip on a pair of skinny jeans, my Boyce Avenue t-shirt and a pair of chucks when Morgan texts me that she's reserved us a table. Morgan said that she isn't sure if Lindsey and Karsen are coming. I am hoping tonight is low key since we have an early morning. I send a quick reply to Morgan that I'll meet her there at nine o'clock. I apply a minimal amount of makeup and blow dry my hair into loose curls, then pull it back into a ponytail.

My phone rings and I hurry out of the bathroom. Christian's name flashes across the screen and I slide my finger to answer. "Hey, brother, what's up?"

All I hear is Christian laughing. "Hey . . . Cami . . ."

"It's me. I said hello, what's up?"

He must have stepped away from the crowd, because the line quiets, "What time do you plan on getting to Aces?"

Checking the clock on the nightstand I see it's only eight o'clock. "I'm finishing getting ready, then I'm meeting Morgan there at nine. Why, are you there already?"

"Yeah, I got here a little while ago. Jamie needed help setting shit up. Parker had something to do and won't get here till right before they go on. I just wanted to check to see if you needed a ride."

I smile knowing that my brother always worries about me. "Thanks, but I'm good. I have dad's Range Rover. We're going to need it to head to Boston tomorrow, so I figured I would save us a trip back home in the morning to grab it. I'm just gonna park it near your place and catch a cab over to Aces."

"Okay, call me when you are on your way and I will meet you outside."

"Sounds like a plan. See ya in a little bit." Once I hang up with Christian, I gather what I need for the weekend and throw it in my small suitcase.

CHRISTIAN IS WAITING OUTSIDE OF Aces as he promised when my cab pulls up. I pay the driver, and walk over to meet him along the wall. Christian nods his head in the direction of the bar, "It's pretty packed in there, good thing Morgan saved a table for us."

The music booms outside before Christian even opens the door. There is a line outside half way down the block of people waiting to get in. Once Christian opens the door, it is mad chaos before my eyes. He was right, the place is packed. Most of the high top tables are now placed along the outskirts of the room allowing more room in front of the stage.

Christian leads me toward the table where Lincoln is talking with Morgan. When Morgan notices me by Christian's side, she walks over and hugs me. "Tonight should be a blast, Jamie has a great set lined up," she yells over the loud music.

Knowing that we can't have a conversation with how loud it is, I just nod my head acknowledging that I heard what she said. I look around the room to see if I recognize anyone when I spot Jamie on stage. He's talking to the band members. Lincoln walks away and heads toward the bar along the back wall. I notice that he sends a waitress in our direction to take our order. I'm keeping it pretty simple tonight and order a vodka and cranberry.

When the waitress returns with our drinks, I pull out one of the stools to sit next to Morgan. Christian is working on the soundboard and I see Jamie walking over in my direction. He carries himself with confidence. He is built like a sex god. He has muscles in places that I didn't know muscles existed.

He looks absolutely gorgeous tonight in his black, fitted, long sleeve shirt and jeans. His shirt sleeves are pulled up showing off his arms of colorful tattoos. He has his Boston Red Sox hat turned backwards, which I love. I love Jamie's hair whether it's under a hat or not.

I can stare at Jamie for hours and never get tired of looking at him. I have always thought he was attractive, but recently I have come to the realization that he is downright sexy. He is tall, rawboned, with a ruggedly handsome face. I would love to know what it feels like to have the weight of his body pressed against mine. To have his lips on mine. I squirm in my seat, when I realize I'm getting turned on just sitting here thinking about all the things I want him to do to me. As Jamie walks toward me, we never break eye contact. His hazel eyes are mesmerizing. Hazel like mine, flecked and ringed with gold. Sometimes it's like Jamie and I can have an entire conversation with just our eyes. I'm just really glad he can't read my mind right this minute.

When Jamie reaches my side, he pulls me into a hug and kisses my temple. "Like what you see?" he wiggles his eyebrows at me and his smile instantly shifts into a devilish grin.

Laughing, I smack his chest. "What's not to like? With the way this place is packed tonight, you're like my very own Rock God."

Jamie squeezes me closer to his chest, leaning in so he is right next to my ear, "Well, when you say it like that, I can be your full-time Rock God, if you'd like?" He leans back, winks, then reveals his signature smile.

Goosebumps immediately shoot up my arms, which Jamie doesn't fail to miss. He rubs his hands up and down my arms. "You would like that wouldn't you, Cami?" Pulling away, he kisses the side of my neck, sensually licking as his lips move over my skin, instantly making my panties wet. "You know you want me," he whispers seductively in my ear. Once those words leave his mouth, he turns around and walks back to the stage. He looks back over his shoulder raising his brows at me, knowing the effect he is having on me. He's playing dirty now.

Side Effects takes the stage at eleven o'clock, once Parker finally arrives. Jamie screams into the mic, "Hello, everyone!"

The crowd roars, and the group of girls in front of the stage throw their arms in the air and jump up and down. "Are you excited to hear Side Effects tonight?" Jamie smiles as his voice speaks into the mic.

The cheers from the mass of people is deafening. Jamie waits for the crowd to go quiet, then he cups his palm to his ear. "I don't think I can hear you." He works the crowd into chaos again. My eyes scan the dance floor, which is packed with a sea of people.

Once they settle down a little, Jamie looks over at me. Butterflies are in my stomach. The cocky grin appears on his face just as if he's letting me know the effect he has on me as well as on this crowd. He turns his attention back to the audience, "I hope everyone is ready to have a hell of a time tonight."

All the lights in Aces shut off, leaving the bar black except for the lights lining the back of the bar. It is completely quiet when Isaac taps out a few thumps on the drums. Parker joins in with a few simple chords on his guitar. The crowd erupts, immediately recognizing the fan-favorite song. Jamie's voice fills the air with the first few words of the song and the goosebumps from earlier blanket my skin.

A spotlight focuses on Jamie and his gaze is steady as he sings, never breaking eye contact with me. This is a song I haven't heard him sing in years. It's one of the very first songs he wrote with my brother when they were in college. As he sings, *What About Me,* my heart pounds in my chest as I listen to the words.

The words hit me like a ton of bricks. Jamie is singing about a relationship between two friends. The guy is saying that he will always be there. That his love never went away, even when the girl did. That he could never find the right words to say, that there were always unspoken words between them. How he was afraid that things wouldn't work if he revealed his feelings. But rather than telling her that he loved her, he just stayed by her side as a friend.

When he gets to the chorus, I can feel the tears building in my eyes. He continues with how his love has grown for her over the years that no matter what happens he will never leave her. The time is right between them now, then he sings, "What About Me? Why can't it be me?" He is singing with so much love in his voice, but at the same time, I hear pain. His eyes never leave mine while he sings. I can't bring myself to look away either. After all these years, I never realized that this song *could* be about me and Jamie. That this song *was* about me and Jamie.

When the song ends, the lights go out and the mood is completely changed when Isaac starts the beat on his drums. Jamie's voice starts in singing *Crazy Bitch* by Buckcherry and the crowd goes wild. With every word he sings, the audience sings along with him. People have their hands in the air, rocking to the beat. When Jamie gets to the chorus, he holds the mic out over the group in the front near the stage and they sing into the mic. The crowd is loving this song and everyone is moving to the beat of the music.

Jamie looks over at me, nods his head, and smiles at me, "But you fuck so good, I'm on top of it." The smile in his eyes contains a sensuous flame. He turns away laughing, continuing with the lyrics. "When I dream, I'm doing you all night. Scratches all down my back." Girls are screaming at the front of the stage and Jamie just continues to work the crowd. He was born to perform. I love to watch him own the stage.

I get hit with a cherry, which makes me look away from the stage to see who threw it at me. Morgan is laughing, "Girl, I think Jamie popped your cherry tonight."

My eyes go wide and my jaw drops. "Shut up. I can't believe you."

Morgan is now laughing hysterically. When she composes herself, she leans into my ear, "Your cheeks are red as shit, and if I had to bet, he has your panties on fire. Girl, if I was single, I would do him. I don't know what the fuck you're waiting for. But if you don't snatch him up, some other girl surely will."

Pulling back from Morgan, I continue to look at her face. Not sure if she is going to continue to talk smack or not, I turn away and look back at Jamie. He is singing *I Won't Let You Down* by Static Cycle. He knows I am a huge fan. He's still watching me. Waiting to see what kind of reaction he'll get. I wanted to come out tonight for a simple night of music. A night out with my friends. I didn't sign up for this. Why did Jamie select these song choices for tonight's playlist?

My breathing becomes rapid. My chest tightens and my heart races. I know my face is flush. I need fresh air. Pushing back my stool, I get up and walk away from the table without saying anything. Working my way through the crowd, I continue to push my way toward the side exit.

"Hey, sweetheart, are you okay?" the bouncer asks me as I approach the exit we came in through. Nodding my head, I push the side door open and head outside. The fresh air immediately fills my lungs. My heart is still racing and I'm trying to catch my breath. *Breathe in, breathe out,* I recite over and over in my head. When my breathing starts to regulate, I lean over placing my hands on my knees. Not paying attention to my surroundings, I don't realize when someone walks up behind me, until their hand is on my back causing me to scream and jump away from the person.

"You know better, baby girl . . . don't ever come outside alone." Recognizing Lincoln's voice, I walk over to him.

"I need a hug." He wraps his strong arms around me. "Morgan said you headed in this direction. I figured I would check on you. You wanna talk about it?"

Lincoln always knows when I need a friend. He is always a great listener, and advice giver. Morgan is a very lucky girl. Lincoln is very attractive with his light brown hair. Lincoln's piercing, brilliant blue eyes are what attracts women along with his personality. It's just a matter of time until they get engaged. They have a very solid relationship, one built on trust. The love they have for each other makes me envious. I can only hope that I will have that one day. That someone will look at me the way Lincoln looks at Morgan.

Lincoln squeezes me, "Did I lose you there for a minute?" Realizing that I never responded to him when he asked me if I was okay and if I wanted to talk about it, I simply reply, "I'm okay. I just needed some fresh air. It was getting hot in there."

Lincoln laughs, "Is that code for Jamie shouldn't have opened up with that song or chose those songs for the playlist tonight?"

Leaning back so I can see Lincoln's face, "How did you know?"

"It was written all over your face, Camryn. You know I am always here for you, baby girl. Even if you just want me to listen."

Nodding my head, I whisper, "I know."

Lincoln tilts my chin up so I am looking at him, "Just know one thing. He will always be there for you, and nothing will ever change that. If you can remember that, everything will work itself out. Trust me." Lincoln kisses my forehead, "Come on, let's head back inside before everyone comes looking for us. I'm surprised Morgan hasn't busted the door down yet."

We both laugh at his comment, "You know your girl too well."

CHAPTER

Nine

Jamie

WE ARE UP AND ON the road early today. We didn't stay long at Aces last night once our set ended. Christian stayed with me to help break down our equipment, while Cami caught a ride back to Christian's apartment with Morgan. This trip to Boston couldn't have come at a better time. Cami kept pushing Christian to come with us to Boston, while I, on the other hand, was hoping he would have come up with an excuse why he couldn't tag along. I wanted some alone time with Camryn. Even if it is was just a few days.

We met with Troubled Pasts on Tuesday and they committed to studio time. Chad seems a little too interested in Camryn for my liking. He thought he was being nonchalant with his questions, but I caught on to him really quick. The guy has a set of brass balls to ask Christian for her phone number. Christian simply told him that if Camryn wanted him to have her number, then she would have given it to him. I totally can't stand this douchebag already.

Christian drove, so I got to relax in the back seat. For a good part of the ride, my eyes were closed and I just listened to the two of them. The events from last night keep going through my mind. I haven't had a chance to talk to Cami about why she left in the middle of the set. She was gone for a little while, then I saw her walk back to the table with Lincoln. Was she upset at my song choices? From the look on her face, I think she finally put two and two together with the lyrics of *What About Me*. She's heard me sing that song time and time again not knowing that I wrote it for her. The two of us need to talk this weekend. I am keeping my fingers crossed that I will have a chance to talk to her alone.

After four hours in the car, I am happy when we arrive at the hotel and our rooms are available. Christian called to book a room this morning for us. The hotel didn't have two rooms available, so Christian and I are sharing a room with two beds. Not exactly how I want to spend the night, but it'll do.

Cami opens the door to her room and we head in to check the place out. The door to the adjoining room is open, so Christian heads in there. Her room is spacious with the king size bed in the middle of the room, a couch in a sitting area and large flat screen television secured to the wall above the dresser.

I walk over to check out the other room, immediately I turn around and head back to Camryn's room with the king bed. I place my bag next to the bed, kick off my sneakers and climb onto the bed. Camryn lifts her eyebrows.

"What are you doing? You're staying in the other room with Christian."

Laughing at her, I place my arms under my head and cross my legs at the ankles "Are you insane, Tink? I am not sharing a bed with your brother."

Camryn gives me a look as if I have ten heads, "What are you talking about, there are two queens in the other room. Get your ass off my bed, and go to your own room."

"Go look for yourself. There is only one bed in there. I'm staying here with you. I'm not sleeping with Christian."

Cami must think I am joking as she just stands there glaring at me. "The two of you have slept together before."

Is she for real? Does she actually think I am going to share a bed with her brother? "Camryn, there is only one bed in there, and I am not sleeping on the floor. For the record, we haven't shared a bed together since we were kids and had sleepovers. Once we reached puberty, we NEVER shared a bed together, do I make myself clear?"

Camryn doesn't respond, she stands there looking at me, so I continue to plead my case. "Your brother snores like a bear in hibernation. Why are you making a big deal about this? You and I have shared a bed a million times. You love to cuddle with me, and if you choose not to, you can stay on your side of the bed. It's big enough for the two of us."

Camryn walks over and stands next to me at the side of the bed. "I have a better idea. Since you pointed out how big and spacious the bed is, you can stay here. Christian can come in here with you. If the two of you choose to cuddle, that is between the two of you." *She can be testy when she wants to. Not to mention stubborn.*

Christian sticks his head in the room interrupting our battle for the bed. "I got dibs on the room next door. You two can have this one." A smirk appears on his face. "Did I forget to tell you? There's only one bed next door?"

This motherfucker set us up. He knew damn well when he booked that room that there was only a queen bed in there. Fuck. Why didn't I think of asking him to do that? My boy is always looking out for me.

Camryn looks at me, then looks at her brother. "Are you kidding me? This cannot be happening."

Christian walks over and pulls her in for a bear hug. "Come on, sis. Don't make a big deal out of this. Yes, you asked us to accompany you on this trip. I think I am a little too old to share a bed with my little sis." He scrunches his nose. "Society would frown upon it, don't you think? Not to mention, I think it would be fucked up if you expect me and him to share a bed together."

Camryn looks back and forth between me and Christian. She folds her arms across her chest, which pushes her breasts up to show the perfect amount of cleavage in the v-neck of her shirt. I look down at my sweatpants praying that my dick decides to play dead and not react. I do not need to have an erection with Camryn and Christian both here discussing our sleeping arrangements.

Camryn sighs and looks directly at me, "Fine, you and I will share the king bed. But don't get any ideas." She cocks her head and an evil smile spreads across her face. "I felt the effects of you being close to me last weekend. Do you think you can refrain from poking me in the back while we sleep?" *Oh, hell no. She did not just throw my ass under the bus. She was right on board with me last week. This is her way to make me look like an ass for not answering her question. Touche.*

Christian busts out laughing. I throw him a look that screams 'Shut the fuck up'. Finally, after what seems like five minutes of him laughing, he composes himself. "Camryn, there's no need to call the man out on how his penis functions when you are around. What can he say, he has a hard-on for ya?"

Throwing my hands in the air, "Hello, I am here, ya know. In my defense, if you weren't rubbing your ass all up on me, it wouldn't have been hard. It was a natural reaction to the situation at hand."

It was now Camryn's turn to laugh her ass off. "Whatever you say, Mr. Banks . . . whatever you say."

♪ ♩ ♪ ♩

SEEING CAMRYN IN HER OWN element is such a turn-on. Christian and I are hanging at a table near the stage, while Camryn records the band's performance on her phone in front of the stage. The show ends and Camryn signals that she is going with the band to do her interview. Christian and I acknowledge her with a nod of our heads and continue downing our beers.

After about forty-five minutes, Camryn emerges from the back with the band members following close behind her. She reaches our table, and smiles at me. "I'd like to introduce you guys to the band." We shake hands with everyone and Christian and the singer immediately talk amongst themselves.

"What did you think of them?" Camryn asks me.

I look around at how crowded the place still is even though they wrapped up forty-five minutes ago. "I liked them. They were really good."

On cue, Christian reaches in his back pocket and pulls out a business card and hands it to the singer. He never leaves home without a stack of business cards. Christian constantly brings new clients into the studio. I look at Camryn, she is smiling at me. She leans close to my ear and whispers, "You're welcome. I thought they would work well with you guys. I know you and Christian can help them out." She pulls away, kisses my cheek and wiggles her eyebrows at me.

This girl brings me to my knees with just one look. I have to tell her how I feel before I lose my mind. She starts to walk away from me, and I grab her hand to pull her close. I place my hand on her hips to guide her between my legs.

I cradle her face between my hands, my fingers bury in her silky brown hair, and my thumbs caress her cheeks. Camryn is nervous, her cheeks are flush, and her body trembles. There is a pensive shimmer in the shadow of her eyes. As I stare at her, she becomes increasingly uneasy under my scrutiny.

Her tongue comes out to wet her lips, as she licks them nervously. She pulls her lower lip between her teeth, causing my dick to twitch. She bites her lip and that is my undoing. I run my thumb across her bottom lip and she releases it. I lean in slowly, kissing her softly a few times. I pull away, her eyes are closed and I whisper against her lips, "Thank you. Not for the business referral but for allowing me to kiss you."

Camryn gasps and opens her eyes. She just continues to stare at me with desire. I can't bring myself to look away from her. I'm nervous that she is going to freak the hell out. Maybe I shouldn't have done this in the middle of the bar. I don't know what made me do that here of all places. At least I know she won't make a run for it. Christian has the keys to the Land Rover, so she can't ditch us and head to the hotel.

We continue to stare at each other, without saying a word. I have so much to say to her, I just don't know when the right time will be. I don't want to scare her, but she needs to know how I feel. Camryn finally whispers, "You're welcome," and smiles innocently at me.

I pull Cami into a hug, securing her tightly against my chest. Glancing over Cami's head, I see her brother gawking at us. I am pretty sure he just saw what went down between the two of us. He simply raises his brows at me and nods.

I know what that look means. I see it all the time when I am around Camryn. He's waiting for me to make my move.

Christian tells the guys to give us a call so they can set up a meeting. Once Camryn says her goodbyes to the band, we head back to the hotel.

CHAPTER

Ten

Jamie

"I DON'T MEAN TO BE anti-social, but I'm exhausted. I'm gonna watch some TV before I fall asleep. What are the plans for tomorrow? Are we doing a little sightseeing or do you have to meet up with the band again?" Christian asks as he leans against the doorway separating the adjoining rooms.

Camryn is digging through her suitcase, looking for her pajamas as she answers him. "I have to meet up with the band in the morning for a little bit to go over a few things. I'm going to take a few pictures for the column and they forgot to bring me a demo of their latest album."

I toss my duffle bag on the bed, searching for a pair of Nike shorts and a t-shirt. I need a quick shower to get the smell of beer off of me. Since Camryn and I are sharing a bed, I want to make sure I don't smell like a bar. I turn on the shower and wait for the water to warm-up before I climb in. I'm not in there long and when I pull the shower curtain back, Cami is standing in front of the sink. I jump. "You scared the shit out of me. What are you doing?"

Hello . . . I am completely naked standing in the shower. Holding the curtain close to me, I give her a look telling her to get the hell out, get the hell in here with me, or at least hand me a towel. Cami shrugs her shoulders, "I was brushing my teeth. I figured I would jump in when you got out. Relax."

Pointing to the towel rack, "Can you hand me that, please?"

Laughing, Camryn says, "Don't worry, you don't have anything I haven't seen before."

What did she just say? My blood is boiling now. A wave of possessiveness works its way through my body. I do not need a visual of her with another dude.

Growling, I snatch the towel from her. Camryn hasn't seen me naked in years. The time she did, I was thirteen or fourteen, at most.

It was Christian and Camryn's fourteenth birthday and they opted to have a Hawaiian Luau-themed pool party that year. When we all got there, Cami's mom gave every one a lei around our neck as we walked out of the kitchen into the backyard. We all played in the pool, had races against each other, and played volleyball. Our dads were cooking on the two grills, while our moms were making sure everything ran smoothly with us kids.

When it got dark out, the entire backyard was lit up with lights. There were tiki torches placed all around the backyard, palm trees that had lights wrapped around them and lanterns that were strung around the fence. Once all of us kids were fed, our parents went inside and left us alone. We didn't need to be chaperoned. Christian had his stereo outside and was playing his CDs. Some of the kids were dancing around the pool, some were still in the pool, while others were playing night volleyball.

Christian walked over to us while we were all sitting on the lounge chairs around the pool. "I have an idea, why don't we go over by the shed, where mom and dad can't see us and play truth or dare."

Cami immediately speaks up, "Are you insane? If mom and dad see us, they will never let us have another party here."

"That's why I said, let's go over by the shed. Just take your beach towels and lay them out on the grass. They won't see what we are doing. Stop being a baby."

Camryn pushed Christian against his chest, "I'm not a baby. I'm the same age as you, you idiot."

Chuckling, I walked over and grabbed my towel and Cami's towel. "Come on, Tink, just ignore him. It'll be fun."

A group of about six go over by the shed and spread their towels out. Christian went into the house and came back out with a bottle of liquor, I guess he snuck it out of their cabinet. It's not like we were planning on drinking it, we just needed the bottle.

Christian spins the bottle first and it lands on Chelsea. Christian asks her, "Truth or dare?" Chelsea squirms in her seat, then answers, "Truth."

"Is it true that you have a crush on Jamieson?" What the heck? Where did that come from? Why is he putting me on the hot seat? There were a million questions he could have asked, and he had to ask that. Chelsea blushes answering quickly, "Yes."

The group all starts to hoot and holler. Chelsea spins the bottle and it lands on Morgan and she asks, "Truth or dare?"

Morgan is brazen and she doesn't have any secrets, so she chooses dare. Chelsea dares her to kiss Lincoln. I know for a fact that she likes Lincoln, but the two of them are just friends. They both say they are too young for a girlfriend or a boyfriend. Lincoln leans into the circle and puckers his lips, making kissing noises at Morgan. When Morgan laughs at him, he acts like he is making out with her, sticking his tongue in and out of his mouth. "You're gross, what are you doing. I hope when you kiss a girl, you don't kiss like that," Morgan says. She moves to the middle of the circle, and Lincoln moves in and kisses her on the lips softly and then pulls back and places another one on her forehead. He leans into her and says, "When I really kiss you, you'll know it." Morgan shoots Lincoln a dirty look and moves back to her towel. Lincoln spins the bottle and it lands on Camryn.

Raising his eyebrows at her, "What's it gonna be, baby girl, truth or dare?" Lincoln has called Camryn 'baby girl' since they met a few years ago. It's not like he is older than her, we are all the same age, but he started calling her baby girl and it just stuck.

Camryn looks around the group, trying to decide which is easier. I don't think Lincoln would embarrass her that much, but Camryn doesn't like people in her business, so I doubt she will pick truth. "Dare, but you better not make me eat something gross, Lincoln."

Laughing, Lincoln rubs his chin and looks directly at me. When he raises his eyebrows at me, I know I'm going to be part of Lincoln's dare. He never takes his eyes off of me when he addresses Camryn, "I dare you to make out with Jamieson. I don't mean a peck, or a kiss on the cheek, I mean a full-on kiss."

I never break eye contact with Lincoln, he knows I am going to beat the shit out of him when this is done. I can't believe he put us on the spot like this in front of everyone. Everyone teases us that we like each other, but we're just best friends. I have Cami's back and she has mine. I get up and stand in the middle of the circle. Our friends were hooting, and chanting, 'kiss him, kiss him'. Christian shushes the group, "Hey, keep it down, you're gonna make our parents come out."

Camryn got up and came to stand with me in the middle. I took her hand, feeling her shaking. "Breathe, Tink. It's just me." I try to calm her down. I don't know if she ever kissed a boy before. Not that I have kissed a ton of girls either, but I don't want her to be embarrassed. Camryn squeezed my hand letting me know she's listening to me. I placed my finger under her chin, gently guiding her to look me in the eyes. "I'm nervous too, but we'll do this together, alright."

Camryn nodded her head and continued eyeing me. I was gonna have to talk her through this, so I placed my hands on the sides of her face. I leaned in and whispered, "I'm gonna kiss you. Just follow my lead and do what I do, okay." She nodded her head again. It's as if she couldn't find the words to speak. Camryn closed her eyes, then I kissed her lips softly, once, twice, three times. I gently bit her bottom lip, then licked it slowly trying to soothe the sting. I kissed her lips again, this time moving my tongue across her lower lip. When she opened her mouth granting me access, my tongue moved slowly against hers. I tasted the grape soda that she was drinking just a little bit ago. Camryn moved her tongue against mine and mimicked my moves. She pulled away, kissing me tenderly. When she opened her eyes, I whispered against her lips, "Happy Birthday, Tink."

She cleared her throat, and whispered, "Thank you," so only I could hear.

When we both looked around after our kiss, everyone was staring at us. I walked back to my spot and sat down. Cami grabbed the bottle and gave it a spin. The bottle landed on me. Smiling at me, "Jamie, truth or dare?"

"I'll take the dare," I say smugly. Camryn laughed, "I dare you to do a cannon ball in the pool."

I had this, "You got yourself a deal. I'll even up your dare." I jumped up, started running toward the pool while stripping out of my bathing suit, then I cannon balled naked into the pool. Everyone in the pool started screaming. Most of them jumped out of the pool. I was naked, I couldn't get out of the pool, so I started swimming around talking to the few who stayed.

Camryn walked over to the edge of the pool, holding my bathing suit in her hand. "I think you might need these. There is already one moon out tonight, we surely don't need to see yours. Plus, your butt is Casper white, cover it up."

Laughing, I jumped out of the pool and snatched my swim trunks from her. She just stood there wide-eyed. I quickly put them on, then I looked at her "Pick your chin up, Cami, you're gonna catch a few mosquitos. Tonight has been a night of firsts for you. You got your first kiss, and you saw your first naked boy. I'm glad both of those included me." I leaned in and kissed her on her cheek and jogged off toward the house.

I know Camryn isn't a virgin, but I do not need a visual of her being with another guy. When I have the towel wrapped securely around my waist, I pull the shower curtain back. Camryn pulls the hairband from her ponytail and fluffs her hair. She is killing me.

I ache to touch her. I need her like the air I breathe. I'm a selfish bastard. I want to own her, claim her as mine. I know she is my best friend, but I want so much more from her.

I step out of the shower, grab my clothes and leave the bathroom. Camryn shuts the door behind me and I hear the water start to run again. I throw on my shorts then stick my head in Christian's room. Noticing he is sound asleep, I shut the door connecting the two rooms, hoping to talk to Cami tonight about how I feel.

I grab the remote control for the television and put on ESPN to catch the highlights from today's football games and hop in bed. I prop the pillow behind me, so I'm sitting up. I hear the water shut off, but Cami doesn't come out right away. I hear the blow dryer, so she must be drying her hair. When she finishes, she comes out in a pair of tiny pajama shorts and a tank top. It's obvious she doesn't have a bra on, as her nipples perk up when her warm body hits the AC temp of the room.

I pull the covers back, patting the bed next to me. Camryn stops dead in her tracks and stares at me. She doesn't move, she just keeps looking between the bed and me. I give her a look as if saying 'come on'. Seeing my facial expression, Cami rolls her eyes. "Don't be weird, Camryn. We have slept together a thousand times before. This isn't any different."

Cami points at me. My eyebrows raise immediately silently asking, "What?"

"You're naked in my bed. I am not getting in bed with you naked."

A deep laugh escapes me. "I am not naked, Cami. I have shorts on. I'm not sleeping with a shirt on. Get your sweet little ass over here. You've seen me without a shirt before."

Cami looks nervous, but she climbs in bed next to me. She grabs her two pillows and positions them behind her, so she can lean against them. Once she's settled, she turns to look at me. "Things are different, Jamie. For one, we kissed. Two, things seem like they are changing between us. Last week, when we danced together, it felt different. My body felt things that it has never felt before. The way the two of us have been flirting, it's different than it was before. I feel like there is meaning behind it. Hidden meanings."

I try to talk, but she presses her finger against my lips, essentially cutting me off. "Let me finish. You can talk when I'm done. If I don't say this now, I don't know when I will get the nerve to say it again. Jamie, we've shared a few kisses since I've been back. I don't know what this means, or where it is going, but I don't want our friendship ruined over this. You are my very best friend. I cannot imagine my life without you in it."

She keeps twirling her hair around her finger, a thing she does when she is nervous. I pull her toward me, wrapping my arms around her. She lays her head against my chest and I start drawing circles on her back with my finger. "Cami, I don't know what is going on between us, but something definitely is. I want to see where this can go. I'm willing to go as slow as you need to go, but I don't want you to push me away, or run from me. Is that clear?"

I pull my head back so I can see her. I place my finger under her chin and raise her gorgeous face up so she looks at me. "Do you understand me? No running, Cami. Last night you left the show after three songs. I saw fear in your eyes when I sang *What About Me*. If I'm guessing right, you freaked out when you really listened to the words. I saw it written all over your face, you were never good at hiding your feelings from me. Now you know the meaning behind it. I have to say, I'm a little surprised it took you this long to figure it out." I place a soft kiss on her head and take a deep breath. "You and I know each other's quirks, we know how each other ticks. We can make this work, Cami."

Camryn pulls back so she can look at me. She leans up, placing a soft kiss on my lips. My girl took the initiative to kiss *me*. "Last night scared me. When I heard you sing that first song it hit me like a ton of bricks. I couldn't bring myself to look away from you while you sang it to me. I've heard you sing that song a hundred times, I never realized it was about us . . . not until last night."

Camryn's hands make their way to my face. I never break eye contact with her. Her facial expression has now changed to serious. "I'm willing to give us a try, to see where this goes. Let's take it slow and see what happens, just promise me that if we don't work out as a couple, our friendship won't be affected. If you can't promise me that, then I can't give this a try."

I pull her closer to me and kiss her like I've never done before. It is laced with such need and hunger. I have been wanting to kiss her like this for years. Since the moment I realized that I wanted more of Camryn. I wanted her to be mine. Our tongues are entwined. I pull back and look at Cami. She looks at me with hooded eyes, biting her bottom lip. Growling at her, "Stop doing that, it drives me crazy."

I bite her bottom lip softly and run my tongue along it, then bite it again.

"Nothing will ruin what we have," I whisper against her lips.

Camryn whimpers, and climbs on top of me. She straddles me and the minimal amount of clothing we both have on is unnerving. I can feel her heat against me as she moves against me. It doesn't take long for me to get hard. I know in my heart that we are not sleeping together tonight. Her brother is in the next room, so we sure as hell aren't making love tonight.

I need to slow this down, so I place my hands on her hips to stop her from grinding on my aroused dick. "Trust me when I say that I want you, but we need to take this even slower. For one, your brother is in the room next door. We can't do this here. And two, when we do make love, when I make you mine, when I claim you, when I mark you, you will be screaming my name each time I make you come and I don't want an audience."

Camryn's beautiful hazel eyes are huge from what I just said. I see her swallow, but she doesn't say anything. She simply nods her head and climbs off of me and sighs as she puts her head back on my chest. She knows I am not rejecting her, this is just not the time or place for this to happen. After a few minutes she finally speaks, "I'm sorry. We said we'll take it slow, so slow it is. I have a question though. Can I sleep like this, here on your chest, in your arms?"

I pull her tightly against my body, and kiss her goodnight. "Don't apologize, Cami. We'll get there, sweetheart. Trust me, I'm not going anywhere. If I had it my way, you would fall asleep in my arms every night." With Camryn's head on my chest, I lean down, placing another soft kiss on her head.

Camryn pulls back looking me in the eyes. "I like the sound of that," she murmurs. Preparing for being wrapped in my arms tonight, she begins to soothingly run her finger lightly over the tattoo on my chest, following the tribal design with her fingertips. We lie there in each other's arms as we drift to sleep. This night could not have ended more perfectly.

CHAPTER

Eleven

Camryn

THE SOUND OF MY ALARM clock stirs me from sleep. I hear a groan next to me, then an arm reaches around my waist and pulls me closer. I feel light kisses on the back of my neck. My body is instantly wide awake, feeling Jamie's muscular chest pressed against my back. Slowly his right hand slips under the hem of my tank top, skimming my navel. Instinctively, my body arches toward him. His hand explores my bare skin. I moan softly as he continues to caress my body. The mere touch of his hand sends a shiver through me. My body is on fire . . . aching to be touched.

It's been a long time since I have been intimate with anyone. So long that I can't even remember when it was. I think I've had more orgasms, thanks to my trusty vibrator, than I have had at the hands of a man. To be honest, I haven't had many sexual partners, I've only been intimate with two guys.

Jamie nips my right earlobe, bringing me out of my daydream. He bites it again, then sucks it into his mouth to soothe the pain that he just inflicted. My voice is barely above a whisper, "Jamie . . . What are you doing?"

He buries his face against my neck, his voice rings with command, "Just relax, nothing is going to happen. I'm just touching you. Enjoying you."

His breath is warm on my neck. I can feel his heartbeat thudding against my back. The room is so silent, you could hear a pin drop. I'm sure he can hear my heart hammering against my chest. My breath catches, my body stills when he continues nibbling my earlobe, biting it gently. The mere touch of his hand is making me so very wet.

I can feel his uneven breathing, he is affected by this just as I am. Gently he eases me on my back and his hard body is atop mine. He places a series of slow, shivery kisses on my lips, along my jawline, my neck. Jamie works his way back to my mouth where his lips are warm and sweet on mine. Our eyes lock and our breaths come in unison. My cheeks redden under the heat of his gaze. I bite my lip nervously.

He asks, "Do you know how beautiful you are?"

I shake my head from side to side. Jamie kisses the tip of my nose, then my eyes, and, finally he satisfyingly kisses my lips again. I could stay in bed with him all day and do this. My body is calling for Jamie and I don't want it to stop here. I know we are taking things slow, but he has me so worked up, my body is screaming. My legs instinctively wrapping around his waist.

"I plan on telling you how beautiful you are all the time. You're mine, Cami. We're gonna make this work."

I smile, pulling his face to mine so I can kiss him. "You're right, I'm yours."

There is a knock on the door and I hear the jiggle of the doorknob. "Yo, why is this door locked?" Christian shouts before he starts knocking again.

Jamie rolls off of me, "You know, you should have left him home. This would have been a nice trip for just the two of us." Laughing, I get out of bed and unlock the door. When I pull the door open, Christian is standing there with his arms stretched out with his hands on the top of the doorframe. He has a shit-eating grin on his face. I'm sure my face is flush, and by the look on his face, he knows exactly what we were doing.

"Whatcha doing in here?" he asks. Without answering, I turn and walk over to my bag, gathering my outfit I plan to wear. I have to meet the band at nine o'clock to go over a few things.

Christian walks into the room and flops down into the chair, grabbing the remote control for the television. Neither Jamie nor I answer him. Christian looks at me, then back to Jamie who is lying in bed still with his hands folded behind his head.

"Hold up. Did I interrupt something?" That comment stops me in my tracks.

"Dude, you have the worst timing in the world," Jamie says as he shakes his head at my brother.

I cannot believe Jamie just said that. It's not like we plan on keeping our relationship a secret, but it's not like I was going to broadcast it either. I'm not even sure what we have is a relationship yet. We agreed to see where things go. It's not like I plan on seeing anyone else, but I need to make sure Jamie and I are on the same page before this goes any further.

Looking directly at Jamie, I say, "Excuse me. Can I talk to you in here for a minute? In private, please." I point to Jamie, then turn and point to the bathroom. When Jamie gets up out of bed, I damn near die. I can feel the heat on my face immediately.

Christian sees my reaction and busts out laughing. "Damn, I guess I did interrupt something, or do you wake up like that every morning? Can you say timberrrrrrr?"

Jamie adjusts himself, but it's pointless. "Shut the fuck up," and throws a pillow at Christian, hitting him in the face.

We walk into the bathroom and I close the door behind us. Jamie pushes me against the door, grabbing my hands, placing them above my head. He swoops down and captures my lips with his as he grinds his erection against me. His lips leave mine and he plants a tantalizing kiss in the hollow of my neck. Immediately, my sex is pulsing. His mouth grazes my earlobe. He lets go of my hands and grabs me under my thighs lifting me against the door. I wrap my legs around his waist as he grinds into me again. I whimper into his neck as I bite down to mask the sounds that escape me.

I can't disguise my body's reaction to Jamie. In just the few hours that we have been intimate with each other, he knows what my body wants. We haven't even had sex yet, I can only imagine what he will do to me when we do.

Remembering that my brother is on the other side of the door, I pull back, placing my hands against Jamie's shoulders. Once I have his attention, I place my hands on his face and hold it gently. "I need to ask you a few questions, before this goes any further between us."

His hazel eyes come up to study my face. He is trying to read me before I have a chance to ask him what I need to. I feel his body tense against me. He clenches his mouth tighter, causing his jaw to flex. "Calm down. This isn't bad. I just need to make sure we are on the same page. If we aren't, then this stops here before it even starts."

He releases his hold on me, placing my feet gently on the floor. I walk over and sit on the countertop. "Come here," I crook my finger for him to come closer.

When he walks over to me, he spreads my legs to stand between them. He places a loose strand of my hair behind my ear, looking at me with concern in his eyes.

"I don't like to share, but you already know that. I have shared you all my life with my brother, and I'm okay with that. But I refuse to share you with anyone else. If we are going to see where this goes with us"— taking my finger and motioning between the two of us—"then it's just you and me. No one else."

Jamie has a confused look on his face. "What do you mean exactly?"

I take a deep breath and let it out. "Let me make this perfectly clear for you, just so there isn't any confusion. I won't have you seeing any-one else while we are hooking up. I don't know what exactly is going on between us, but I won't share you. Bottom line. No one else, Jamie. You can't see any other girls, and I can't see any other guys. Not like they're pounding down my door or anything, but you get what I'm saying. I know we agreed to take this slow, but I need to know that it's just me."

Jamie places his large hands on the side of my face, raising it to meet his stare. "Listen to me. I will only say this once. I don't want any-one else, Cami. I told you last night that I want to see where this goes.

I meant that. I have no interest in seeing anyone else. You know me better than that. You of all people know that I would never hurt you. We agreed to take this slow. I don't plan on going anywhere." He leans down and moves his mouth over mine, devouring its softness. Slowly, I lift my arms around his neck, running my hands through his thick hair. I tug on his hair, not wanting this kiss to end. When he pulls back, he leaves my mouth burning with fire.

With a wicked grin on his face, he points to the shower. "I have to get out of here before I have my way with you. Your brother is out there waiting. Go get a shower, cool off, do what you have to do to calm yourself down. But if I hear moaning, I am gonna be all over you whether your brother is here or not."

I chuckle knowing what he is insinuating. Before he can move, I bite his lower lip, sucking it into my mouth. I release his bottom lip and place a soft kiss on it. "Mr. Banks, I will have you know, if I plan on moaning, it would be because you made me, it won't be self-induced."

I push myself off the counter, walking over to turn on the shower. When I look over my shoulder Jamie is standing there, his jaw clenched, his eyes slightly narrowed.

I am going to give him a show and drive him crazy. He thought he was cute when we were younger when he jumped naked into the pool at my birthday party, I am going to have a little fun with him today.

I pull the hem of tank top up and over my head, leaving me standing there topless. My back is facing Jamie, so he can't see my breasts. I slowly peel my sleep shorts off of my body, one leg at a time and toss them in his direction. When I turn around his muscle flicks angrily in his jaw. I fix my eyes on his. "Do you like what you see, Mr. Banks?" Knowing that he is going to lose his shit, I quickly get in the shower and shut the curtain behind me.

Peeking around the shower curtain, I squeal at the intrusion into my personal space as Jamie smirks at me saying so quietly that I'm not entirely sure I heard him, "You think you're funny, don't you? Two can play at this game. You better pray the next time I see you naked, your brother isn't in the next room. Cause if he is, he will hear what you sound like when I'm making you come with my mouth." He reaches out and pauses mid-air as he's about to stroke my breast. Instinctively, I lean toward his touch wanting his hand there, wanting him in here, knowing my brother is literally steps away from me grabbing him and pulling him into the shower with me. Inhaling a breath, never breaking eye contact with him, I moan, quiet enough that no one hears but he heard. Smirking at me with lust-filled eyes, he pulls his hand back, retreating the hand that was so close to the water beading on my nipple that my skin feels his absence and he never even touched me.

And he stalks out of the bathroom. Just like that.

Holy. Shit. I need to make this a cold shower after what he just said to me, after how he almost touched me. A smile spreads across my face as I hear the bathroom door shut. One for Cami, One for Jamie.

Why did I invite my brother with us again?

AFTER MY MEETING WITH THE band, I head back to the hotel to hook up with Jamie and my brother. Our plans today are to do a little sightseeing while we are here in Boston. Throughout my meeting with the band, I couldn't stop thinking about last night and this morning with Jamie. When I walk in my hotel room, Jamie is lying on the bed and my brother is lounging in the chair. Jamie has his journal on the bed next to him while he is trying to figure out a melody on his guitar. My brother is telling him the harmony is off, it doesn't match the lyrics. Jamie quickly closes his journal so I can't see what he is working on when I walk over to the bed to sit down. Which is odd, he usually asks for my opinion. If I think the lyrics fit the melody, if the lyrics tell the story that he wants told.

"What are you two working on?" Looking between the two of them.

Christian is the first to speak up, "Nothing, he's working on a new song. We're just trying to find the right harmony for it. He'll figure it out with the guys when we get back home."

Looking at Jamie, he just nods his head agreeing with my brother. They have this sneaky look on their faces. They're up to something.

Dismissing the two of them, I get up and start gathering my clothes and throwing them in my duffle bag. I head to the bathroom to grab my toiletries. Christian and Jamie's bags are already packed and sitting by the door. Once I am done packing, I throw the pamphlet on touring the city that I picked up in the hotel lobby at Jamie.

"We are doing a little sightseeing before we head back home later today. I want to go to the Cheers bar and have my picture taken outside of there."

Once we check out we load the car and head to Newbury Street. Newbury Street offers some of the best of Boston in restaurants and retail shops, small venues from hi-line shops to basic fresh food places. We spend a few hours walking around, shopping, and eating lunch before we head to Cheers and Fenway Park.

As we approach Cheers, I am all giddy in the backseat bouncing around. Christian looks at me in the rearview mirror, "Will you calm down. It's just a bar that was on a TV show. Relax, will ya."

My lips pucker with annoyance. "Remind me next time to leave your ass home."

Jamie laughs, "Don't worry, Tink, I'm excited to see the place, too."

Christian scoffs at the two of us and looks at Jamie, "You're such a kiss ass. Did she cut your balls off while you shared the bed with her last night?"

Jamie replies through gritted teeth, "Watch yourself, my friend."

Christian looks at him again before looking back at the roadway. "Have you lost your mind? What the hell has gotten into you today?"

Jamie turns and looks at me in the backseat, I simply just shake my head, telling him to drop it. I don't want us to bicker while we are here. Let's just enjoy ourselves. If I had to guess, Jamie is probably annoyed that my brother is on the trip with us now that he told me how he feels. Jamie nods his head understanding what I said without actually saying it.

We pull up outside of Cheers and I am the first to get out of the truck. Jamie gets out and walks over to hand his phone to my brother. He advances toward me, but rather than stand next to the sign, he positions himself behind me. He wraps his arms around my waist, pulling me tightly against his chest. My brother takes a picture.

Jamie leans down and kisses my cheek. I am praying my brother is still taking pictures of us. In one swift movement, he spins me around and places his hands under my arms and lifts me up, so that I am above his head looking down into his eyes. Swinging me around in a circle, I laugh out loud at what he's doing. As he lowers me, my body slowly glides down his, and he kisses me on the lips, before gently dropping me to my feet again. I laugh as we turn to look at my brother, whose eyes are sharp and assessing us. Christian's infectious grin appears, "It's about fucking time. You can thank me for this, you know."

"Well, thank you, my wise brother. What would I ever do without you?"

"The two of you would still be pussy footing around like you have been for years," Christian replies.

"I'm sure my awesomeness has nothing to do with it," I tease.

Jamie laughs, "Thanks, buddy. Maybe we can find you a love interest of your own and you can stop cock-blocking me with your sister."

I watch Christian's eyes widen. "Let's get one thing straight. I don't have an issue with you dating Camryn. But I don't ever want to hear the word cock and *my* sister's name leave your mouth in the same sentence."

Jamie laughs and raises his hands in surrender.

WHILE DRIVING BACK TO NEW York City, I am in the backseat not paying attention to Jamie or my brother while they talk about the studio time Troubled Pasts has scheduled over the next few weeks. Morgan and I are texting back and forth.

Me: You are not going to believe what happened while I was in Boston.

Morgan: Fill me in then, bitch.

Me: Jamie and I kissed. Like really kissed.

Morgan: WHAT!!!!!!!!!!!!!!! OMG !!!!!!!!!!!!!!! How did that happen? How was it? Was it everything you imagined it would be? Come on, give me the dirty details. Did you guys do the nasty?

Me: *Slow down there, girlfriend. You just shot off 100 questions. I don't know how it happened. He kissed me in the bar while I was there checking out the band. Then when we got back to the hotel afterwards, one thing led to another, and it happened again.*

Morgan: *One thing led to another??? What does that mean? Did you sleep with him? I am dying to know how he is in bed!!!! Give me details, bitch!!!!!! NOW!!!!!*

Me: *LOL ;)*

Morgan: *Why are you avoiding my questions?*

Me: *I am not avoiding them, you are just asking them faster than I can respond. NO, we did not sleep together, not in the true sense, at least. Not for my lack of trying. Jamie and I agreed to take things slow to see where things go. He was my first kiss when I was fourteen, but, boy . . . has he changed. The things he does with his tongue and his hands . . . My body quivers just from him kissing and touching me . . . GIRL . . . I can only imagine what it will be like when we do sleep together.*

Morgan: *Okay, I am fanning myself now. I want to know EVERYTHING when you get home. Don't forget we need to go look for costumes for the Risqué Halloween Masquerade when you get home. Any ideas on what you are looking for?*

Me: *Nah, when I see it, I'll know. But I want it to be something that will make Jamie's jaw drop. BUT nothing too skanky.*

Morgan: *Girl, then just stand naked in front of him, that will do the trick. Gotta run, I'm at Redemption tonight going through stock to get this week's liquor order together. Love ya, girl.*

Me: *Love ya, too. I'll text you tomorrow.*

CHAPTER

Twelve

Jamie

WE ARE BOOKED SOLID AT the studio for the entire next month. I need to figure out when I can squeeze practice in with the band. Troubled Pasts is scheduled for studio time every day this week. Great, that means I get to see that douche, Chad, more than I want.

I don't know why they are on the schedule again this week, I was under the impression they got the tracks that they needed in order to approach a few record companies hoping to sign a deal last week.

The more time I spend with Chad, he rubs me the wrong way. I can't exactly put my finger on why I don't like him, I just don't. He is paying for studio time, and every opportunity that arises, he is asking questions about Camryn. For someone who only met her once last year when she did a piece on them, and again by coincidence by sitting next to him on a plane, he acts as if they are long lost friends. Once again he asked Christian for his sister's number and as Christian said before, "If she wanted you to have it, she would have given it to you. You're here to work on your record, not inquire about my sister."

I just sat back and listened to the dude make an ass out of himself. The more he asked Christian about Cami last week, the more pissed off I got. I think Christian is becoming a little annoyed with Chad's persistence with Camryn. Christian usually lets shit roll off his back, but he is very protective of Camryn. I just sat back and watched the situation unfold before me, knowing that I was the one who would talk to Camryn before she closes her eyes at night, that my voice would be the last she heard before she falls asleep. Camryn and I have always talked on the phone, lately we talk into the wee hours of the morning.

My phone vibrates in my pocket. I shift in my seat and pull my phone out. Immediately, I am pleased with who the text is from.

Camryn: Meet me in your office.

Me: What? When?

Camryn: I didn't stutter. Meet me in your office. Hurry.

Me: I'm on my way.

I stand from my chair, straighten my shoulders and clear my throat. "I'll be right back. I have to make a phone call in my office."

Christian looks over from the sound board, "Sure, Troubled Pasts should be here at one o'clock. We've got time."

My footsteps thunder down the hall. With each step, my pulse increases. What is Camryn up to?

When I open my office door, my eyes widen. Camryn is lounged casually against my desk, in a tight grey skirt, a white blouse tucked in and those damn fuck me heels. Her feet are crossed at her ankles and her palms flat against my desk.

"Lock the door," she says seductively.

I do as I'm told, the click of the lock echoing in the silent office.

She straightens her body, curling her finger, "Come have a seat."

I walk over, spread Camryn's leg with mine and stand between them. My arms wrap firmly around her waist, pulling her body against mine. My mouth needs to be on her. I whisper in her hair "To what do I owe the honor of having this mid-afternoon visit?"

She leans in, her lips touch mine lightly. "I missed you. I wanted to see you."

My lips capture hers, more demanding this time. Searing a path down her neck, I nip her earlobe. It doesn't take much and my erection is pressing against my zipper. "Do you feel what you are doing to me?" My voice rough and raw with arousal.

Camryn laughs and her hand pushes against my chest, putting distance between us. She withdraws from my arms and shifts her ass off my desk. I reach out to her, "Where do you think you're going?"

She moves to the right dodging my grasps. She wiggles her finger at me. "Have a seat Mr. Banks." She motions toward the couch in the corner of my office. I like where this is going.

I make my way over to the couch. Camryn stops me before I sit down. Her shaky hands reach for my belt buckle, unfastening it. She doesn't waste time and unbuckles my pants. The sound of my zipper echoes through the silent room. The only other sound is my heart pounding against my chest and the hiss that escapes my mouth when her hand wraps around my hard cock.

After a few strokes, I am hard as steel. Withdrawing her hand from my cock she pushes my pants past my ass. "Sit," she says, pushing her hands against my chest. I do as I'm told.

Never undressing herself except for undoing her hair, letting it fall free around her shoulders, I am not prepared for what Camryn does next. She gets on her knees, wrapping her fist around my cock again. I'm not sure if I hoped she would climb on top of me and straddle me, but I surely didn't think she would be on her knees in front of me, in my office.

She licks her plush pink lips. Damn those lips, I am not prepared for what she is about to do. The moment her lips wrap around my erection, I just about lose my shit. Slowly her tongue moves around my head, while her hand massages my balls. It's not gonna take long for me to come. I try to think of anything other than her soft lips wrapped around me. The tingle begins at the base of my spine. My balls tighten to my body. My hips jerk up off the couch when Camryn hums against me. I push against Camryn's shoulder. "Baby, you gotta slow this train down. It's been a long time and I'm not going to last," saying this through gritted teeth, I continue, "I'm gonna come. Stop. Please."

She doesn't stop, she does the exact opposite. She sucks harder, her hand begins to work up and down my shaft. "Tink, you're gonna make me come."

My dick pops from her mouth, "Not yet, I'm not finished."

Her tongue slowly traces my head. She nips it lightly with her teeth. I lean my head back against the couch, I close my eyes, savoring this moment. She takes my entire length in her mouth. I hit the back of her throat and there's no holding back my orgasm. I moan and fist her hair as I move her mouth to the rhythm of my hips. Fucking hell, what she's doing to my dick is beyond my wildest fantasy. I feel her swallow around my dick as I swear she took me in even deeper and I damn near lose it.

I look down at her, her wide eyes staring back at me. Unspoken words pass between us. She's giving me permission to come in her mouth. When her tongue swirls my head, I growl. "Fuck, you look beautiful." My hands grip her hair tighter as her hand works its way over my shaft. She tightens her grip, sucking harder making my hips jerk in wild spasms. I can't hold it any longer. I see stars. Fucking stars as I come.

And this goddess takes every last drop, even when she's finished she slowly wraps her tongue around my shaft as she slides that glorious fucking mouth all the way up my dick.

Camryn sits back on her heels. "Mr. Banks, I hope you enjoyed that as much as I did."

I can't even speak, my chest heaves. Once I am able to get my bearings, "Tink, you have no idea how much I enjoyed that."

She smiles shyly.

"I don't even want to know where you learned to do that."

Camryn laughs. "I read a lot of romance novels."

I raise my brow at her. "What are you saying?"

"Read between the lines, Jamie."

"Was I your first?"

She nods, avoiding my eyes, she picks at the hem of her skirt. My Tink is embarrassed.

I've just fallen even deeper in love with her. "Baby, I love that I was your first."

I hear my phone vibrating. Camryn picks it up off the floor and hands it to me. "Shit, Troubled Pasts just got here. They have studio time scheduled." My eyes drop to Camryn who is still sitting on the floor.

"It's okay, Jamie. You're at work, so go work. I just wanted to stop by and help you relax for a little bit."

"Oh, trust me, I'm relaxed. I just wish I didn't have clients here. I would love to lie you on the couch and return the favor right now. I will be returning the favor. I wish you weren't staying with Morgan tonight."

I quickly tuck myself back in my pants and stand, extending my hand to Camryn, helping her up from her knees. My hands circle her hips, pulling her against my chest. I look down at my little Tink, "I missed you and thank you," I say and place a kiss on her forehead.

She leans on her tiptoes kissing me on the lips. "I missed you more. You can make it up to me another day. Now get out there, I'll be out in a few. I need to freshen up. I can't go seeing my brother, looking like I do."

"Yeah, I don't think that is a great idea. Your hair is a mess and your lips are swollen." Smiling I know I'm the reason she has that just fucked look. Just the way I want her to look.

"Then my job here is accomplished, Mr. Banks," she says as she walks into the adjourning bathroom in my office.

The door to the studio opens and in walks Chad like he owns the place. The band follows in shortly behind him. Christian tells them to get set up and we would be with them in a few minutes.

"I haven't seen Camryn, how is she?" Chad asks.

"Camryn isn't your concern." I say calmly, not letting this douche know he works my last nerve.

"She may not be my concern . . . right now, but I'd like to explore the opportunity."

"That won't be happening." This douche can't take a hint. Camryn is mine.

"Really? You seem quite sure of yourself," Chad says with a raised brow.

"Yeah, you could say that," I say firmly, as the images of Camryn on her knees in front of me not even twenty minutes ago flash through my mind.

Christian shifts his eyes from me to Chad, then clears his throat.

"Why don't we get started? We have a lot to get to today."

Chad walks into the sound room and places his headphones on.

I turn to Christian, "I can't stand that motherfucker. The quicker we can get his shit done, the quicker he can get the hell out of New York."

The door opens and I turn to see Camryn walk in. Her hips sway as she makes her way over to me. She sits on my lap placing her arms around my shoulders. She leans down, her lips meeting mine. "I'm gonna head out. I wanted to say goodbye."

"Hey, sis, what brings you here today?"

"I had a few things to *handle* with Jamie."

"Really what?" Christian asks curiously

"Nothing you need to be concerned about."

Christian looks between us and shakes his head. "I don't even want to know."

Camryn laughs. "Don't ask questions, if you don't want to know the answers."

I rub my hand up and down her thigh. "You're awful, you know that, right?"

She leans in and whispers in my ear "I'll be waiting on your return favor . . . or maybe I'll *handle* my own needs while I wait for you to get done." She stands from my lap, a sexy as hell smile on her face. I adjust myself because I am getting hard again thinking about her bringing herself to orgasm and knowing I most definitely want to watch her. What can I say, my girl has that effect on me. She turns to leave and I smack her on the ass. "You can stop by the office *anytime.* Call me when you get to Morgan's. Have fun with the girls tonight."

When the door closes behind Camryn, I turn back and see Chad glaring at me. Yeah, take that fucker, I told you she was mine. I raise my brows at him.

We spend the next six hours finalizing another song that they couldn't get right last week. So once that is squared away, I am hoping I never see this prick again.

"Are we finished here? I'm gonna head over to Parker's place to get a few hours of practice in for next week's gig."

"Yeah, I got this covered. I just need to make a few adjustments on this piece and I'm done for the day. Go ahead. I'll wrap things up here and catch you later."

I grab my bag to head out the door, but the hairs on the back of my neck are standing up. Something doesn't feel right. When I look over my shoulder in the direction of the band, I notice Chad is standing there glaring at me. I simply nod my head, and walk out the door.

RUNNING LATE SUCKS. I OVERSLEPT this morning after hitting my snooze about five times. I slept like shit last night, the last time I looked at the clock it read three-thirty. No wonder my ass is dragging today. After shooting Christian a text letting him know I would be a few minutes late, his reply suggested I grab us Starbucks on the way in.

There are at least fifteen people in front of me, so I am praying that the line moves quickly. I hear a laugh that warms me from the inside out. I would know that laugh anywhere. I look around the coffee shop and that is when I spot her. Camryn is sitting by the window with her earbuds in and her laptop open. I know she stayed with Morgan last night, so I knew she was in the City. I just didn't expect to see her up and about so early.

My skin crawls when I see that fucking douchebag, Chad, sitting across from her. *What the fuck is he doing here?*

I pull my phone out of my pocket and send Camryn a quick text.

Me: Good morning, beautiful! Whatcha doing?

I see her phone light up on the table. When she grabs her phone, a smile immediately appears on her face.

Cami: I'm at Starbucks. Trying to get this piece done to send to Shelby. Lincoln was at Morgan's, so I headed out early. Whatcha doing?

Me: I'm grabbing coffee on my way to the studio. I'm running late.

Cami: Really. If I would have known you were heading to the studio this early, we could have met for breakfast, or even just coffee. I miss you ☹

Me: Don't worry, baby, you'll see me soon enough.

Cami: I wish it would be sooner. I'm stuck here at a table with Chad from Troubled Pasts. I tried to blow him off. He didn't take the hint. I'm annoyed. Actually, I am pissed. I have work to do. Ugh . . .

Camryn puts her phone back on the table. She gives Chad a fake smile, then picks up her coffee to take a sip. I place my order and wait patiently for it, never taking my eyes off of Camryn. She hasn't noticed me yet. There is no doubt, by the look on her face, she's annoyed. I didn't need her to confirm it in her text, I know my girl. When I read the text that Chad just helped himself to the empty seat, that pisses me off. This guy doesn't give up. He can't take a hint. Once I have my coffees, I head over to Cami's table.

She doesn't see me approach the table, but Chad does. I can see his demeanor immediately changes. His lips thin in anger, his nostrils flare with fury. He gives me a hostile glare when I lean over, placing a kiss on Camryn's cheek. "Good morning, baby," I say with a smug smile. *Eat that, shit head.*

I don't bother to speak to Chad, I simply nod my head acknowledging him. Camryn jumps up from her seat, and throws her arms around my neck. She whispers in my ear, "You creep. You've been here the entire time. Rather than come save me, you were texting me?"

Laughing, I pull her tighter against my chest. My lips nibble on her right earlobe. "I was enjoying texting you. Don't ever worry. I will always be your knight in shining armor. I got your back."

Camryn pulls back to look at my face, I raise my eyebrows at her. Her lips slowly descend to meet mine. When she kisses me, all I can taste is the caramel on her lips. I kiss her lips softly, before placing another on her nose.

Nodding toward the table, my voice is low and smooth, "Get your stuff together, come to the studio with me."

Camryn gathers her notes from the table, closes up her laptop and grabs her bag. Chad is still sitting at the table looking at the two of us. Anger lit in his eyes. He looks at Camryn with a sardonic expression that makes my temper soar.

"It was nice seeing you again," Camryn says to Chad. "I'm going to head to the studio with Jamie." He doesn't respond at first. His anger becomes a scalding fury. He swallows hard. I can see he is trying to reign in his temper. My ass just cock blocked him. He needs to realize that Camryn is not on the market. She is taken. She is mine.

"It was nice seeing you again, Camryn. Maybe next time you can stay a little longer. Possibly finish your coffee before you have to run," Chad says.

She doesn't reply to his last statement. She gives him a small smile.

This dude doesn't get it. Camryn is not giving off the vibe that she is the least bit interested in him. He needs to give it up. Just because he happened to stumble upon her in a coffee shop doesn't mean she's interested in him. She is simply being kind. Camryn isn't a mean person, she would never intentionally go out of her way to be malevolent toward someone. In this case, she needs to be forward and set the record straight. Chad needs to know that she is not interested in him.

When Camryn finishes gathering her belongings, I place my hand on her lower back guiding her out of the coffee shop.

I turn to look back at Chad. He stands there, tall and angry. I shrug my shoulders at him while sending him a chilling smile that says the unspoken words he needs to hear loud and fucking clear. *That's right, asshole. She's mine.*

I hold the door for Camryn as she exits the coffee shop. Once we are on the sidewalk, I reach for her bag, balancing the carrier containing the coffees in my other hand. She leans into my side, so I place my arm around her shoulder as we walk the few blocks to the studio. She looks at me and says, "Can I tell you something?"

I turn my head to look down at her, "You know better than to ask me that. Of course you can tell me anything. What's on your mind, beautiful?"

Camryn looks up at me, then bites her lip. Now I know she is nervous about what she is going to tell me. "I don't want you to go all caveman on me, but Chad made me feel uncomfortable today."

Trying to play it cool, I ask, "What do you mean he made you feel uncomfortable?"

I tighten my hold on her, encouraging her to continue. "I was working with my earbuds in when he came up behind me. I didn't even know he was there until he started rubbing my shoulders. I jumped up not knowing who was touching me. He held his hands up as if surrendering, then apologized for startling me. He claims he didn't notice my earbuds. You think he would have realized that I didn't hear him talking to me when I didn't respond to him. I don't know him enough for him to think he can touch me like that. I met him a handful of times. We are not friends. We are acquaintances. Nothing more, nothing less. After he apologized, he just pulled out the chair and made himself at home."

We walk into the studio, placing the carrier on the floor I lean against the wall, pulling her into me. I place my arms around her waist securing her to me. "You are not overreacting, Tink. I knew there was something about him that rubbed me the wrong way. I have never liked him since I laid eyes on him. He has no right touching you. When I see him again, I will make that crystal fucking clear."

Camryn stands on her tiptoes and claims my lips with a slow, drugging kiss making me forget my reasons for even being here today.

I SPENT MONDAY AND TUESDAY night practicing with Side Effects, so I can spend tonight with Camryn. When I left the studio today, I ran to the grocery store to grab what I need to make her favorite for dinner, crab legs and shrimp scampi. She is working at the New York City office today with her editor, so when she is finished there, she is coming to my apartment.

Around six o'clock there's a knock at my door. She's had a key to my place for years. I specifically told Camryn to walk in when she gets here. When I open the door, the most beautiful set of hazel eyes warms my heart. I see her duffle bag on her shoulder and know that she packed to stay the night with me.

"I told you to just come in. Why did you knock?" Gesturing for her to come in, I open the door wider. From the gasp that escapes her throat, I know she was surprised by what sits before her. I have a fresh bouquet of lilies in a vase and a bottle of her favorite wine on the table.

Cami turns to look at me, then back at the display I have set up. "What do we have here, Mr. Banks? You did this all for me?" she questions. "I didn't want to barge in. I know I have a key, but I felt funny," she answers my question, then shrugs her shoulders.

I've never cooked for a woman before, this is a first for me. A first of many that I want to experience with Camryn. I walk up behind her, and pull her close to me. Her back is against my chest, and I breathe in her scent. I love how she always smells of lavender and vanilla. I kiss her head softly, "This, my dear, is dinner for two. You and me."

I motion her to the table and hold out her chair for her to sit. I bring the dishes that I have prepared in from the kitchen and place them on the table. Cami's eyes grow wide when she sees that I have king crab legs with extra drawn butter on the side and a bowl of shrimp scampi. I place the cheddar garlic biscuits on the table as well. I walk over behind her and tie a bib around her neck, which reads 'Kiss the Cook'. When she looks down and sees the bib, she busts out laughing. "You went all out tonight, didn't you?"

I lean back, taking a sip of my wine "I wanted this to be memorable. We have eaten together a thousand times, this is different. We have never eaten as a couple."

She leans her elbows on the table, rests her chin in her hands. "I don't know what to say. This is beyond amazing. Thank you."

CHAPTER
Thirteen

Camryn

"NOW I NEED TO DO what this bib says and kiss you for this amazing meal."

I push my chair back from the table and the look in his eyes as I walk toward him and lean down to straddle Jamie's lap, the expression on his face says it all. Pulling his face close to mine, my tongue traces his lips before I kiss him passionately. My tongue glides out and meets his in a passionate war of emotions, both of us wanting each other, both of us unsure of upsetting the waters. My lips press against his, then gently cover his mouth, deepening the kiss. He groans against my lips as I shift in his lap and rub myself against his erection. He lifts his hips grinding against me. A gasp escapes me. My hands slide up his neck, into his hair. His touch sends a shock wave through my entire body. His hands find their way to my hips, holding me steady, fingers grazing incendiary skin under my clothes.

I kiss him, linger, and savor every moment. Shivers of delight follow his touch. He moves his mouth over mine, devouring its softness.

His gaze travels over my face and searches my eyes. "Do you know how much I want you?"

"I'm pretty sure I have an idea," I say, jokingly, wiggling my ass against his erection.

Jamie groans a visceral sound escaping his lips as he rubs a hand over his face, letting me know exactly how much he wants this too. "Cami, I'm doing everything—and I mean everything—to not strip you down right now and take you on this table. We have to slow down before I'm unable to stop where this is headed."

A look of hurt crosses my features, like surely he knows that we both want the same thing and we are here, in the now, focused on just us and I want this to take us where it will lead.

He grabs my waist, shifting me back to my chair, as he gets to his feet. "I hate to be the one to stop this, but you want us to take it slow. I'm going to be a gentlemen and not attempt to make love to you the first time I cook you a meal."

My eyes go wide, the hurt apparent but an unspoken understanding divides us. "Jamie, you have to know how bad I want this too, we've been taking this slow long enough and I know that what we have is nothing short of amazing . . . how you make me feel each and every time we touch has left me wanting more. And walking away from this—without some release—well, are you prepared for me to take care of my own needs when I have you right where I want you?"

He laughs. "Welcome to my world, baby. I have been like this for weeks, hell, years!"

Damn him, he's slowly torturing me.

One for Cami, Two for Jamie.

Our unspoken resolve still withstanding, after we have a quiet dinner, we clean up the kitchen together. Jamie finds a movie on OnDemand for us to watch as we cuddle on the couch. Both of us accepting the fact that we'll know when it's the right time, when our minds and bodies connect without interruptions, without the knee jerk *have sex just to have sex* reaction. We've waited—and anticipated—this moment for so long and it should be perfection, a moment where time stands still and the two of us are the only ones who exist in the world.

CHAPTER
Fourteen

Jamie

AFTER SNUGGLING ON THE COUCH while watching a movie last night, Camryn fell asleep nestled against my chest. I didn't want to wake her up, so I carried her gently into my room and placed her softly on my bed.

I lean down to place a soft kiss on her forehead whispering "Good night, Tink."

My girl was out like a light and didn't wake when I tucked her into bed and pulled her tightly against my chest. I laid awake for a while once we were in bed, thinking how I should have told Camryn sooner how I felt. For years I've been struggling with my feelings for her. There is a possibility that she felt the same way. Time wasted but I refuse to look in the past and only focus on the future. Our future.

I sleep with my true love in my arms and sleep so peacefully knowing everything I've ever wanted is wrapped in my arms.

I love waking with Camryn in my arms. The sunlight is peeking in through my blinds. My hand slowly moves up and down her arm. Camryn begins to stir, swatting my hand away.

"Stop. I need more sleep," she says in a groggy tone.

"Wake up, lazy bones. Let's hit the gym before our day starts. I have a fun-filled day planned for us."

Camryn turns into my chest, cuddling into my side. "Do we have to?" she asks in a whiny voice.

"Yes, we do. Come on. Once you're up and moving, you'll be fine."

She throws the covers off her body huffing and puffing as she makes her way to the bathroom. "Fine . . . Give me twenty minutes and I'll be ready," she says before shutting the door.

I HAVE A LONG DAY planned, so I want to get my work out in. I am surprising Camryn and taking her to Watchung Reservation, which is the largest park in Berkeley Heights. As kids, we spent a lot of time there with our families, camping, fishing, walking the trails, and horseback riding. When we were able to drive ourselves there, we would spend the day there just to get away. A lot of memories were made at the reservation, so I am hoping to make some new ones today with Camryn. She has always loved horseback riding, so I reserved two horses for us this afternoon.

When we enter the gym, Camryn heads over to the mats to stretch before hitting the treadmill, while I walk over to the weights.

"You good over there?"

"Yeah, I'm fine," she responds.

"I know you are fine." As I wiggle my brows at her.

She laughs at my remark, then puts her earbuds in.

"Nice one liner, Mr. Banks."

While I am working out my chest, I am stealing glances at Camryn. As always, she is in her little tight tank and running shorts. The way her legs glide on the treadmill, she makes it look so effortless. Camryn has always been one who runs for enjoyment. When she is stressed, she laces her sneakers and hits the pavement or the gym.

After an hour or so, we finish up our workout and head back upstairs to my apartment to get showered. While Camryn is in the shower, I check my email and make a few calls. I still need to grab a costume for the party at Redemption tomorrow night. Nothing like waiting until the last minute.

Camryn won't tell me what she is dressing up as, and when I asked Morgan she told me her lips were sealed.

Parker has sent me a few changes for the song that we have been working on this week. I was able to get the majority of the song on paper while I was in Boston. Coming up with new songs has always been easy for me. I take life experiences and turn them into songs. After spending the weekend with Camryn, I was able to get some new lyrics down. Now we're just trying to find the melody to fit it perfectly. I'm keeping my fingers crossed Camryn loves the new song and it doesn't freak her out. I've always been good with expressing myself in my lyrics. With my feelings about us laid out in the words of this song, I have a lot to lose.

When Camryn gets out of the shower, I jump in so we can grab breakfast and go to the park. By the time I finish showering, I assume Camryn would be dressed already. To my absolute delight, she walks into my bedroom in a robe.

An open invitation for some quality time stands before me in all of her terry clothness.

The look in my eyes as I gaze up at her, lust taking over my features that gaze upon her, speaks volumes. I take Camryn's hand in mine and guide her toward my bed. Leaning down, my lips descending towards her mouth, where she is sucking on her bottom lip, staring at me with literal fuck me eyes. I pull back and swear harshly.

Guiding her back on the bed, I grab her hips and pull her closer to the edge of the bed. Slowly my hands move under the hem of her robe to skim her hips and thighs and I notice she isn't wearing any panties. My God, my every fantasy is laid bare before me in this moment.

Her eyes lock on mine as I disrobe her so she's on full display for me. She doesn't miss my obvious examination and approval.

She looks like an angel spread out on my bed. Her brown hair splayed across the light comforter. My finger finds her swollen bud between her legs and when I apply a little pressure, her body arches off the bed and her eyes close. She licks her lips, then gently bites down on the bottom one, eliciting a groan from me. "Jamie," Camryn says my name in between shaky breaths.

It's taking every ounce of restraint to not go down on her right now and finish her off as fast as I can. My excitement seeing the reaction I'm giving her is enough for me right now. I told her we'd take this slow, and by slow I mean I'm going to make her come as slowly as possible.

My eyes rake over her naked body as I join her on the bed, leaving her entire body exposed to my every wish.

Between each word I plant kisses on her shoulders, neck, and face, "You're beautiful, Tink."

"Jamie," she whispers my name. I love hearing my name come out of her mouth knowing that I am the one making her body want more.

Leaning down, I take one of her nipples in my mouth, it's already budded so tight yet I know I can make it tighter, just with the moisture of my mouth, my tongue, and my hands as I touch every inch of her skin in wanting.

She's gripping my hair as my mouth moves to her other breast, in between the journey I ask, "Is this slow enough for you, baby?" Judging by her arched back and moans I know that I'm taking her to the places that we will get to together. No words are needed in response, her body is doing enough talking for the both of us.

My hands slide across her silken belly and make their way down lower, pushing her thighs apart. Camryn grabs my shoulders, digging her fingers into my bare skin and moans out a 'yesssssss' as I begin to palm her clit before taking two fingers and escalating her writhing to an entirely new level.

"I'm going to make you feel good, Camryn."

Instinctively, her body arches achingly toward me, granting me deeper access. Every part of her body is gripping me so tight, begging me not to stop as she rides my hand. All the while I'm kissing her every chance I get and sucking on her tits taking her higher. After a few minutes, the stroking of my fingers, the wetness of my mouth everywhere, and this moment sends explosive jolts through her. She grasps the comforter as she cries out my name as she comes, "Jamie . . ."

Her sounds and the vision of her writhing beneath my hand are seared into my memory. I'm in awe at how fucking beautiful she is as she falls apart beneath me. Everything about this woman—my best friend—has been worth the years of waiting for her. Finally being intimate with Cami has come full circle, I'm experiencing this with her like it's my first time. I'm a virgin with Cami and I'd have it no other way.

WHEN WE PULL ONTO THE road leading to Watchung Reservation, Camryn is fidgeting in her seat like a little child. "Oh my God, I can't believe you brought me here. I haven't been here in years."

Glancing in her direction, I see how excited she is that we are here. I place my free hand on her left knee, squeezing lightly. "I wanted to do something special for you. It's not every day I get to take my girl on a first date."

Her slender hands unconsciously twist together. My girl is nervous. I cover her hands with my right hand, "Relax. We're going to have a nice time. The weather cooperated. It's a perfect day to spend the day outside." I lift her hand to my mouth and kiss her knuckles hidden within our entwined hands.

Nodding her head at me, indicating that she understands, she turns and looks out the window. I can see that she is trying to regulate her breathing. She is taking deep breaths in and then deep breaths back out. I smile knowing that I am making her nervous, but at the same time, it's just me. She has no reason to be nervous around me . . . ever. It's always been the two of us together, we just changed things up a little.

Once I park the car, I take her hand in mine. "Come on, let's head to the stables."

When we reach the stables, there are a few horses outside being brushed. She lets go of my hand and starts jumping up and down like a five-year-old.

"Oh, Jamie. Are we going riding? Please tell me we are going riding!" She is oozing with excitement. Shaking my head yes, next thing I know, she lunges at me and throws her arms around my neck, standing on her tiptoes, she touches her lips to mine. Her kiss turns urgent and exploratory.

When a throat clears behind us, Camryn pulls away and her face colors fiercely. Her cheeks burn with embarrassment. Camryn isn't one for public affection, I have never seen her be openly affectionate with anyone she was in a relationship with. Not that she has dated a lot and I'd rather not think of the couple of assholes she's been with in the past.

On the other hand, I am not one to shy away from a little PDA. I want people to know who I'm with. I don't flaunt it, but I want to keep the creeps at bay, so they know their place. What's mine is mine, and I do not share.

The guy who runs the stables is standing behind Camryn. "Good afternoon, welcome to Watchung Reservation. My name is Mr. Gorman. We'll go over safety precautions before we mount up."

I help Camryn with her helmet. I lean in to whisper in her ear. "That's one lucky horse you get to ride today." I pull back to see the blush flood her cheeks as she innocently asks, "Why?"

I help hoist her into her saddle, all while my hands graze her thighs as I help lift her up.

"I have to say, I've never been jealous of a horse before. I wish I could have your legs wrapped tightly around me." I whisper so only she can hear me. I want her as turned on as I am right now seeing her up on top of the horse while envisioning her sitting on top of me.

Camryn laughs, "You know the song, 'Save a horse, ride a cowboy'? Maybe today will be your lucky day." she says seductively, winking as she licks her bottom lip.

Her words shoot right to my dick, forcing me to adjust myself. "Damn you. You and that mouth of yours."

She laughs again. "Sorry, babe. Come here." She leans down on her horse, then suggests with her pointer finger for me to come closer. When I do, she says, "Just think of all the things that this mouth can do to you, I'm specifically thinking of a certain office and a couch that comes to mind." She leans in and places a kiss on my forehead. She leans back up, positioning herself on the horse. "Now, go get on your horse. I want to go riding, Mr. Banks." Then she gestures with her hand toward my horse.

A groan escapes my throat. "Thanks, babe, now I'm hard as a rock. This is going to be one uncomfortable ride." I smack her leg before walking over toward my horse to put my helmet on and saddle up.

Two for Cami, Two for Jamie.

This little game is becoming quite entertaining.

Mr. Gorman goes over a few more things with us and we set out on the bridle trail. Camryn is behind Mr. Gorman and I am following their lead in the rear. The horse ride is about a two-hour trip. Camryn has a smile on her face the entire time. Once we approach the stables, we all dismount the horses.

"Camryn, would you like to help feed and brush the horses?" Mr. Gorman asks.

"Sure, I'd love to," she replies.

We spend about another hour or so in the stables with the horses before we head out to the picnic area. I have a picnic basket packed in the back of the Land Rover. I have a turkey and cheese hoagie and an Italian hoagie, with bar-b-que chips and Camryn's favorite soda, Mountain Dew. I had them cut the hoagies into quarters because I know Camryn likes to share. She can never decide which type she wants, so she usually swindles pieces off of everyone so she has her own private buffet to choose from.

While I'm unpacking lunch, Camryn sits at the picnic table biting her lip. When I make eye contact with her, she looks away. Awkwardly, she clears her throat. Her voice wavers, "Uh . . . You put a lot of thought into this today. Even last night. I don't know what to say."

She looks away again. I walk over to her and sit down beside her. I take my finger and place it under her chin. Guiding her to look at me, once I have her attention, "You don't have to say anything, Cami." I place a soft kiss on her lips, then her nose, then her lips again. "Let's have lunch." I smile and hand her a plate. I don't want my girl to be nervous or uncomfortable, but I can sense by her body language that she is. This is a side of me that she hasn't seen before and I like that I'm letting her see how good we can be together. She just has to get used to the new us.

Her voice drifts into a hushed whisper, "Jamie, I need to tell you something." She avoids eye contact with me, while she takes a napkin, and the bag of chips to put some on her plate.

A shadow of nervousness slips up her face. Still avoiding my eyes, I take my hands and place them on both sides of her face. "Talk to me, Tink. What's going on in that head of yours? I can see the wheels turning a mile a minute. Tell me."

She hesitates before she speaks. "I've never done this before, Jamie." She points to the table and waves her hand over it. "I'm not experienced like you are. I have no idea how to date. The two relationships I have had were in college, and my number one priority was school and softball, not the relationship. Hence, my failed track record."

A smile appears on my face, which I'm trying my damnedest to hide. Camryn pushes against my chest. "It's not funny, Jamie, just because I travel all over doesn't make me a woman of the world, ya know."

I pull her back to me, placing my arms around her neck. "Come here. Look at me. I am not laughing at you. I just love your innocence. You are fine. Actually, you are more than fine. All you have to worry about is you and me. What memories we will make. What experiences we will have. I don't care how many relationships you have been in Cami. To be honest, I like that you haven't been with a lot of guys. That means I get to be best at it all, and you don't have much to compare me to." I wink at her, so she knows I am teasing with the last part.

As if she is choosing her words carefully, her brows furrow. She chews on her bottom lip. I quickly pull her lip free and lean in to kiss it. "Stop biting your lip. It drives me crazy. If anyone is going to bite on it, it will be me."

"You know . . . I have always been honest with you. I've never kept secrets from you, Jamie. You know everything about me. If I am going to put it out there, I might as well put it all out there. I have only slept with two guys, I'm just afraid that I'm not going to be good enough for you. Not experienced enough for you." She looks away.

My heart swells at her being this honest with me. I knew she was only in two relationships, but I never knew that those were the only two guys she slept with. Nodding my head, I take a deep breath. I can't believe my girl thinks she is inadequate. Cami is always strong and confident, but I see she has a weakness. I need to make sure that she never feels insecure with me. "Baby, you will always be enough for me. When you and I make love for the first time, I don't want you to think about anything but you and me. I want you to think about how good I make you feel and how good you make me feel. I've waited for this for so long . . . you have no idea how perfect you are. We'll figure it out, babe . . . together."

I pull her in for a kiss. Her lips are warm. I take her mouth gentle at first, then more forceful. She returns my kiss and parts her lips so that my tongue can meet hers. She kisses me savoring every moment. She closes her eyes, as my tongue explores the recesses of her mouth. When I pull away, her lips are wet. I nip her bottom lip and suck it into my mouth. I release her lip, place a feathery kiss on her lips, then her nose. She opens her eyes, and stares at me. It's as if something clicked in her mind, as she smiles at me, shaking her head up and down.

Her brows draw together, looking at me with uncertainty. "Can I ask you something?"

I smile at her. "You can ask me anything you want."

She looks away, uncertainty shakes her voice, "Have you been with a lot of girls?"

My eyebrows raise in an attempt to conceal my discomfort with her question. I will never lie to her, so I hope she can handle the truth. "You know who I dated over the years. You've met all of the girls, but there have been a few in between, sort of just hook ups. Cami, there wasn't a lot of girls. I can count on two hands how many I've been with. I've always used protection with them, so you don't ever have to worry about that."

Her smile broadens in approval. "I didn't want to be intrusive but it was something that I was always curious about. I just needed to ask you. Thank you for being honest with me."

Kissing her lips lightly I pull back to look in her eyes, "Nothing but the truth. You know you can always trust me, I will never lie to you. You may not like the answers that I will give you, but I will never be dishonest. Relationships are built on trust and honesty. You'll always have that with me."

"Ditto." A smile emerges on her face. "Let's eat, I'm starving." Breaking the tension, a laugh escapes her throat before she leans in and kisses my cheek.

CHAPTER

Fifteen

Camryn

AS I'M STANDING HERE LOOKING at myself in the mirror, I feel completely exposed. "I cannot believe I let you talk me into getting this outfit." I turn to look at Morgan who is behind me curling Lindsey's hair.

"What's wrong with your outfit? You look hot as shit. Jamie is going to freak out when he sees you." Morgan wiggles her eyebrows at me.

Pointing at my attire, "Hello . . . do you see me? Of course he is going to freak out. He's going to throw me over his shoulder and carry me out of there the second he lays his eyes on me. Not to mention it's the middle of October and freezing."

I swear, this is God's way of punishing me for allowing Morgan to pick out my outfit. She kept telling me that I needed to go sexy, since Jamie and I aren't sleeping together yet, that I need to give him a sneak peek. I feel like I am giving everyone who is going to be there tonight a sneak peek.

My outfit consists of knee-high leather boots that lace up in the front, and a one-piece black police officer dress shirt that hugs my figure. The thing barely covers my ass. I specifically wore black spandex running shorts underneath to keep from showing the world my goods. The dress has buttons up the front; however, it's low cut and stops in the middle of my cleavage, leaving my breasts on full display, thanks to the push-up bra Morgan provided. A thick black belt accentuates my small waist, which holds my baton and handcuffs. The shiny silver badge showing I am an officer of the law is displayed nicely over my left breast. The costume is complete with my sexy police hat.

Morgan curled my hair in loose curls, so I can at least try and have my hair over my shoulder to cover some of the exposed cleavage. My make-up is done heavy tonight. Morgan thought the smoky-eye look would be more appealing with the black outfit. I think I look like Cat Woman, but Morgan and Lindsey keep saying that I am rocking the outfit.

Because it is a risqué masquerade party, I also have a black sequin mask to wear, but I am praying that we don't have to keep it on all night. I prefer to see the faces of the people I am talking to. The idea of hidden faces freaks me out.

Lindsey is dressed as a racy firewoman, which screams sexy with her leather black mini skirt and has yellow and white suspenders attached to it. She has a black, leather tank top on with a yellow and white stripe strategically placed under the breasts to bring attention to how low cut the tank is. She's rocking a pair of black lace-up five-inch platform heel, patent leather boots. If the outfit and heels don't catch anyone's attention, the black fish net stockings connected to the garter belt surely will.

Morgan should have been a stylist rather than managing a club. When I look at how all three of us are dressed, I am speechless.

I ask, "Morgan, does Lincoln know what your costume looks like?"

She throws her head back laughing, "Girl, if I had to get his approval on everything I swear, my ass would be in sweats and a t-shirt all the time. I don't think he'll like that it reveals a lot, but he will love it when we get back home tonight." Tilting her head to the side like she is thinking, she raises her finger to her mouth and bites the tip of her nail, "or maybe I will have my wicked way with him on his desk tonight.

Hmm . . . decisions . . . decisions."

I can't control my laughter, "Girl, you are naughty."

Morgan is looking at me with a devilish grin, "I'm not the one with the handcuffs, now am I?"

I place my hands on my hips and raise my brows at her, "I didn't pick this outfit out, *you* did!"

Morgan presses her lips together and replies, "You are welcome. And Jamie will be thanking me later for it."

Lindsey gets up from Morgan's vanity and leans into the mirror. She grabs the lipstick and applies yet another coat to her already scarlet lips. She turns and puckers her lips at me. "Come here, let me put this on your lips. It will make your lips pop right along with your eyes."

I walk over to Lindsey and she outlines my lips in a red lip liner, then applies the red lipstick to mine. I feel like a hooker tonight. I have a feeling Jamie and Christian are going to freak out when they see me dressed like this. I would have much preferred to wear what Morgan has on.

♪ ♩ ♪ ♩

THE CAB RIDE ISN'T LONG from Morgan's apartment to Redemption, which is good because our driver had his eyes on the three of us more than he did the road. When we pull up outside, the line is out the door and around the block. Morgan told us that the event was heavily promoted, they even had a few shout outs on a few of the local radio stations this past week. Our usual group will be here tonight, with the exception of Karsen who is working at Mt. Sinai Medical Center. It was her rotation to work this weekend.

Morgan has us enter the club through the side entrance where Jason, the bouncer, is waiting for us at the door. Morgan called from the cab, so he was expecting us. Jason eyes us all up, "Damn, ladies, you are all looking sexy as hell tonight."

He hands Morgan an earpiece. She leans over close to him before saying, "You better hope Lincoln doesn't have his earpiece in tonight. He doesn't like the staff ogling what's his." The entire staff wears earpieces while on shift. This way they can be in constant contact with each other if they need anything.

A sheepish look passes over Jason's face. "The boss man has nothing to worry about. I know what is his and I respect what is his," he says with a sly smile.

Morgan pushes off of Jason's chest, and winks at him.

When we enter the club, the party is in full swing. Morgan turns around to look at both Lindsey and me. "Hold each other's hand. It's packed as shit in here tonight. I have the private room upstairs for us. The two of you head up there. I'm going to go check with the bartenders to make sure everything is okay before I head up, alright?" We both nod our heads and walk off in the direction of the stairs that lead to the private room.

Lindsey stops on the stairs, and turns to me "Why does she have an earpiece on tonight? She's supposed to be off."

I shrug my shoulders, "She told me that even though she isn't technically working tonight, with as many people as they are expecting, she wants to be in constant contact with her staff in case they need anything."

Lindsey and I open the door to the private room and my jaw hits the floor. Jamie is standing by the table in his costume. We didn't tell each other what we were wearing. As if Jamie senses my presence, he immediately turns in my direction. His tongue slowly glides over his lips, then his face forms a knowing smile.

I immediately laugh at the sight before my eyes. Our guys are our very own superheroes. Jamie is dressed as Batman, mask, cape and all. My brother is none other than his trusty side-kick, Robin. I have no idea how Jamie convinced my brother to be Robin. I can only imagine how that conversation went. "Oh, hell no," would be my brother's response. He must have lost a bet or something. I make a mental note to get the scoop on that story.

As my eyes take in my brother's costume, he has a red body suit on with bright green leggings. He has on his black mask, hiding his face. If I were him, I would keep that thing on all night. His costume leaves nothing to the imagination, I mean nothing.

Lindsey nudges me, nodding toward Parker. When I find him, he is dressed as Captain America. His outfit is less form fitting and leaves little to the imagination, unlike my brother's. He has a one-piece suit, and the top is padded where muscles would be, with a large white star on the chest.

Lincoln is dressed as Thor. He has black pants on, and the top of the outfit looks as if it is armor. His large hammer is sitting on the table next to Parker's shield. Lincoln doesn't have a mask on, which doesn't surprise me. Morgan mentioned that he refused to wear one, because it could obstruct his view and he needed to be able to see everything at all times.

As Lindsey and I walk towards the table, Lincoln lets out a loud whistle, then says, "Hot Damn. Look at the two of you. Is there a fire somewhere? Did I break the law? The two of you can serve and protect me anytime."

Christian adds in, "Hey, Lins, if I light myself on fire, would you come to my rescue?" Then he wiggles his eyebrows at her in a provocative way. Lindsey just pushes Christian's chest before putting him in his place. "Please, you wouldn't know how to handle me. Men burn for me all the time. And not just on Halloween! I sure as hell don't need a costume to make guys any hotter."

The guys all hoot and holler at Christian, who is just sitting there shaking his head back and forth. "Did you know that women firefighters are professional hose handlers?" then he leans over and kisses Lindsey on the cheek. If I didn't know better, I would think that Christian has a thing for Lindsey.

"Rumor has it, you don't have a long hose, but I hear you're one hell of a pumper," she whispers.

"You're on a roll tonight, next thing I know you'll be telling me you scream like a siren." Christian adds.

"That is something you'll never have the pleasure of knowing, my friend." Lindsey replies then tilts her head at my brother.

I look over at Jamie, who hasn't said a word since we approached the table. I look at him, then at Lincoln, who has a huge smile across his face. Lincoln leans in and whispers in my ear, "You look sexy, baby girl. You know you're going to drive him nuts tonight in that outfit." He leans back and raises his brows at me, then he leans in and continues to speak, "Morgan told me your outfit was hot as shit, but I had no idea this was what you were showing up in tonight. You are going to have the man panting by the time the two of you leave."

I pull back to look at Lincoln's face. He grins and nods his head in Jamie's direction. I turn to look at Jamie and all I see is the rise and fall of his chest as he is breathing hard. With the mask on, I can only see the stare being drilled in my direction. His mouth is firm. I'm not sure if he loves or hates my outfit. I smile at Jamie and blow him a kiss.

Bringing my attention back to Lincoln, I smile. "Have you seen Morgan yet?"

He leans down close to my ear so I can hear him over the music. "Nope, she said it was a surprise. But if the outfits you and Lindsey are wearing are any inkling, I know I am in for quite a shock."

"Well, Jason was a fan of our attire this evening," I respond.

"Oh, really? What exactly did Jason say?" He raises his brow inquisitively, "Please, enlighten me."

Laughing, I lean in close so he can hear me, "He just said we were looking sexy as hell tonight." I pat Lincoln on his chest, "Don't worry, Morgan already told him he better pray that you didn't have your earpiece in to hear what he said."

Lincoln's head tilts to the side as he continues to look me in the eyes. "That little shit has one job and one job only . . . keep my patrons safe. Not to admire the outfits you ladies are wearing. Especially not Morgan." Lincoln's body stiffens and his gaze focuses on something over my shoulder.

I turn to see what has his attention, noticing Morgan at the door. She has her hand still on the doorknob as she scans the room, probably trying to find Lincoln. When her eyes land on him, she lets go of the door knob, waving her hands down her body, as if saying, 'do you like what you see?'

Morgan sways her hips as she walks over to us, in her beautiful peacock costume. The top is a black bustier that laces up the middle, pushing her breasts up. At the top of the bustier where the swells of her breasts are, it is outlined with gorgeous colorful turquoise, gold and black peacock feathers. Her skirt is very short, barely covering her ass. It is turquoise pleated satin with a black tulle underlay. She has black heels on with black fishnet stockings. To finish her outfit, she has black satin gloves up to her elbows and a mask with turquoise and black sequin. On each side of the mask, there are small peacock feathers. She looks stunning.

Lincoln pulls Morgan into his arms as his lips capture hers. His mouth covers hers hungrily. When he finally breaks the kiss, he smacks her ass, pulling her closer to him. "Girl, have you lost your mind? I get the idea it's a risqué masquerade, but I don't like the idea of every man in this place seeing what's mine. Do you understand? It is one thing to have a party, but it's another thing to put what's mine on display."

Morgan looks at Lincoln devilishly, placing her hands on his chest. "You are the only man who has *ever* seen the goods and you will be the only man who *will* ever see the goods. Nothing can be seen with this outfit. You are mine, baby, and I am yours."

She leans in and kisses him letting him know that he has nothing to worry about. Morgan tells us to help ourselves to the buffet that they have set up on the far side of the room. There are chafing dishes set up on the table with a variety of food such as hot wings, pulled bar-b-que pork, roast beef, roasted potatoes, chicken fingers, mozzarella sticks, and fries. There are several huge buckets filled with ice with different bottled beers and bottled drinks. A small bar is set up in the corner with a bartender making mixed drinks.

I walk over to Jamie and place my hands on the sides of his face. With my heels on, I still need to stand on my tiptoes to be eye level. I lean in, removing his mask so I can get a good look at that gorgeous face. I place a soft kiss on his lips. His lips immediately kiss me back, no longer hard as they were moments ago. He pulls me into his chest and really kisses me. This kiss sends the pit of my stomach into a wild swirl. I've missed his lips; I haven't seen him since our date. He showers me with kisses around my lips and along my jaw. He pulls me into him, crushing me against his chest and places a tantalizing kiss in the hollow of my neck. Kissing me tenderly while making his way back to my lips, when he reaches mine, he bites my bottom lip before sucking it into his mouth. It's as if we are in the room alone. He pulls away, then leans his head into mine. His voice is husky, "You are killing it in this outfit tonight. I may not survive the evening or I'm going to have to kill anyone who looks at you."

I try to hold back the smile that emerges on my face, but it's useless. I bite my bottom lip while looking up at him. "Does that mean you like it?"

"It means I fucking love it, but you are not leaving my side," growling at me. Jamie bites my chin, then kisses my lips. He takes my hand leading us toward the buffet. I get chicken fingers and fries. I need to eat something before I start drinking. I didn't eat lunch today because I was nervous about what Jamie would think of my costume. But seeing the lust in Jamie's eyes when I walked through the door was well worth my hunger pains.

CHAPTER

Sixteen

Jamie

I CANNOT BELIEVE CAMRYN IS wearing that outfit. It is so outside of her comfort zone. My girl has never been one to flaunt her body. She is more on the conservative side, unless pushed to be a little riskier by Morgan. Camryn has always been one to dress for comfort, rocking a pair of worn jeans, a t-shirt and her chucks or Nike's. It's the norm to see Camryn with a baseball cap on with her ponytail pulled through the back. That is one of the many things that I love about her. She never tries to impress guys. She is the 'what you see is what you get' kind of girl.

When Camryn walked through the door to the private room to-night, I knew she was there before I had even turned around. It's as if I can feel her inside of me when she is near. There is a current that runs through my body making me aware of her closeness. It's a feeling that I will never get tired of.

Jerking my head back, I stare at her costume. A burst of arousal tingles through my body. My mouth immediately begins to water. My pulse races and my heart rate increases. There's satisfaction in her eyes. She knows she would get a reaction from this outfit tonight. She notices that I am watching her intently until she walks over to me. The hand-cuffs on her hip have caught my attention. We agreed to take things slow, but my mind begins to think of the naughty things we can do with those tonight. With the visions of Cami cuffed to my bedpost, I can feel myself becoming aroused. Trying to clear my head of those images, I adjust myself hoping that no one else has noticed my sudden discom-fort. This outfit won't hide a damn thing if I'm walking around here with wood.

Once we are finished with our meal, we all head down stairs to the dance floor, with the exception of Lincoln and Parker who stay in the private room.

My hand is intertwined with Camryn's as we push our way through the crowd to find an area on the dance floor. Redemption is packed to-night. Everywhere you turn, it is wall-to-wall people. Most of the girls have fancy masks on, where the majority of men either have some sort of Halloween mask on or their face is painted with make-up.

Camryn is already moving to the beat of the music before we even find a spot to dance. Morgan has Lindsey's hand, navigating her through the crowds. Looking over my shoulder, Christian is right be-hind Lindsey. Shaking my head, thinking of the trouble he may get into tonight with Lindsey. The attraction between the two is evident, but neither one of them have said anything. Christian claims he isn't ready to settle down with one girl. He hasn't found that special someone who has piqued his interest enough to make him want to. With the studio's business growing, the countless hours he puts into it, he says he doesn't have time for a relationship.

When we find a clear spot, the music changes. *Down on Me* by Jeremih & 50 Cent blares through the speakers. Morgan yells over to Camryn, "This shit is my jam." Morgan instantly starts grinding up against Christian. Her little body is moving a mile a minute, as her hips do not miss a beat. The way she sways those hips should be illegal. Hot damn, Lincoln must be losing his shit up there. Although the more I think of it, he knows his girl is safe with us. Christian loves Morgan like a sister. They have been friends since they were five. There isn't any sex-ual tension or history between the two.

Camryn looks at me, raising her eyes to mine. She starts to move to the music. Camryn moves closer to me, where she has one leg between my legs so she can dance without any space between us. Her hands are slowly making their way up my chest. She runs her fingers through my hair at the base of my neck. She continues her assault on me, moving her hands down my back, cupping my ass, pulling me closer to her. My hands are on her hips while we are dancing, guiding her to the beat. Camryn breaks away from me. Turning herself to me, her back is now against my chest as she grinds that tight little ass against me. The outfit she has on is driving me nuts. The tiny skirt she has barely covers her ass. When she bends over, I can see her tight black shorts under her outfit. Thank the Lord, my girl was smart enough to wear those. If she didn't, and she did that little move on the dance floor, I would have thrown her over my shoulder and carried her out of this place.

While the song plays, Camryn continues to work my body over. Glancing over her shoulder, I see Morgan and Lindsey with Christian in between. With a wicked grin on his face, he raises his eyebrows, throwing his hands in the air, letting the girls do whatever they want with him. Hope he has the willpower to reign his shit in wearing those green tights.

All of us dance a few more songs. Lincoln makes his way down to the floor and stands by one of the tables. He motions for the waitress, who already has a tray filled with drinks. She places the bottles of beer on the table, so the girls will either have to drink those, or head back upstairs to the private room to grab their fruity mixed drinks or whatever bottled drinks that Morgan has set up for them.

Leaning down, I tell Camryn that I need a drink and point over to where Lincoln is. She nods her head and crooks her finger for me to lean down. She cups her hands around her mouth as she yells over the music in to my ear. "I am going to stay here and dance with the girls, okay?"

Pulling my head back so she can see my response, I nod. Cupping her face between my hands, I place a soft kiss on her lips, then her nose.

When I approach the table, Lincoln asks, "What's your poison? Beer or shots."

Taking the shot on the table, I toss it back. The liquid burns my throat as it goes down. Leaving a warm trail behind it, I shake my head, exhaling a deep breath.

Grabbing the beer, I take a long swig to ease the burning sensation. Lincoln pats me on the shoulder. "You should have asked what was in each shot glass. You had the choice between vodka, tequila, or fireball."

Laughing I say, "Sure, now you tell me."

Lincoln and I stand there for a little while watching the girls dance. Lincoln puts his hand to his ear, listening to whatever is being said in his earpiece. He nods his head in the direction of the bar, "I'll be right back. There is a problem at the bar in the back."

Nodding my head to acknowledge that I heard him, I turn my attention back to the dance floor. Christian is walking in my direction. Leaning to the side, looking around Christian, the girls are all dancing. Each of the girls has an infectious smile on their faces. Lindsey is working the crowd of guys that have formed around her since Christian left. Lindsey is in her own little world out there. Her arms are in the air, then she slowly runs her hands down her body, giving everyone around her a show. When one man attempts to get a little too touchy feely for Lindsey's liking, she reaches for Camryn's belt taking the baton. When she turns around to face the man, he is quite surprised by what stands before him. Lindsey has the baton pressed against his chest. Seeing her give him a few jabs to the chest makes me laugh. The man retreats, taking a few steps back, holding his hands up as if in surrender.

Morgan throws her head back laughing as Camryn just shakes her head at what Lindsey just did. Lindsey turns to face the girls, innocently shrugging her shoulders, handing the baton back to Camryn who, in turn, returns it to her belt. Laughing at what I just witnessed, all I can do is shake my head at my group of friends. They are an amazing group of people whom I have known almost my entire life.

Christian and I drink a few more beers while the girls continue to dance. Feeling a tap on my shoulder, I turn around and see Tabitha, my ex-girlfriend, standing in front of me. She pulls me in for a hug before I even realize what she is doing. When we broke up, it was mutual. Neither of us walked away with ill feelings toward the other. Tabitha wanted things that I wasn't able to give her. She wanted the happily ever after, with a huge wedding, big house, white picket fence and children. When realization hit her that I wasn't that guy, that I didn't have those feelings for her, we decided to go our separate ways, wishing each other happiness in the future. I pictured a petite brunette with hazel eyes, a girl who I have known for most of my life. She is who I want to spend the rest of my life with.

I hate drama, so having an ex-girlfriend who wasn't going to go all psycho on me whenever we ran into each other was great.

Tabitha releases me from her lingering embrace, leaning back she takes in my appearance. A huge smile emerges on her face when she notices that Christian is my trusty sidekick, not just in life, but as my bud in costume as well. She points a finger at Christian, then smacks her hand across her mouth trying to contain her laughter.

"Oh my goodness. You're in green tights . . . which are showing off your balls. Why in the world are you wearing that? You could have opted for a pair of green sweatpants, or something . . . other than those." She gestures with her hand up and down Christian's body.

Forcing a smile to his face, "It's nice to see you, too, Tabitha. Oh, how I have missed you," Christian murmurs, his disdain evident.

Raising her brows as if his comment insulted her, she replies, "I'm only speaking the truth. It is probably what every girl in this place is thinking, but none has the courage to say anything. Hey . . . I'm not complaining. You look hot. I always thought you had a nice body." Raising her brow at Christian when she finishes her sentence.

Christian looks at me, then back at Tabitha. I shrug my shoulders at Christian. Hey, he can say whatever the hell he wants to her. She isn't my girlfriend anymore, he owes me nothing.

"Thank you, Tabitha. It's nice to know that you were ogling my body while you were dating my best friend. It's a good thing, that the two of you didn't work out, now isn't it?"

Laughing at his comment, I look at Tabitha to see her reaction. She isn't fazed at all. She simply laughs and shrugs his comment off.

"So, boys, what have you been up to lately? I haven't seen or spoken to either one of you in months."

At the same time Christian and I reply, "Working."

Tabitha helps herself to one of the bottles of beers that are sitting on the table that the waitress dropped off a few minutes ago. The three of us stand around the high top table, having small talk.

After what seems like forever talking with Tabitha, my eyes drift toward the dance floor. Not seeing Camryn or Lindsey, my eyes dart around the room, trying to see if they are near the bar. Where the hell did they go? They left the dance floor and didn't even come over to where we were standing? That's odd. At least Lindsey and Camryn are together. They probably went upstairs to the private room to get a drink, or something quick to eat.

I throw a beer cap across the table hitting Christian in the hand. Nodding my head up toward the private room, I yell, "The girls aren't on the dance floor anymore, I'm gonna head upstairs to see if they're up there. You coming with me, or are you staying here?"

"Nah, I'll head upstairs with you. The music is loud as shit down here. I could use a break. Plus, I wanna grab some wings. My ass is starving."

"Alright, boys, it was nice catching up with you," Tabitha says before making her way over to her friends in her naughty nurse outfit.

The two of us make our way through the crowd. Once we get to the stairs leading to the private room, my stomach clenches. A strange feeling washes over me. Taking two steps at a time, I reach the top fast. Walking down the hall quickly, I push open the door. Parker is sitting at a table with Lindsey who has her feet kicked up on an empty chair next to her. Licking her fingers of the sauce from the chicken wings, she says, "Hey, boys. You have got to try these. They are crispy just like I love them and not to mention, delicious."

Looking around the room again, Camryn is nowhere to be seen. "Lindsey, where is Camryn? Weren't the two of you together?" As each question passes my lips, I grow annoyed that Camryn left the dance floor without telling me, and she is wandering around this massive club without one of the girls.

She shrugs her shoulders, "Camryn said she was going downstairs to meet up with the two of you. I asked her if she wanted me to come with her. She told me to stay and eat, that she would be back in a few minutes. She was heading downstairs to tell you and Christian that we were going to hang up here for a while."

She caught me off guard with that statement. Camryn never came to our table. I gave her a sidelong glance. "Why? Why are you looking at me like that? Didn't she come to your table?"

Lindsey wipes her hands on her napkin, slowly pulling her feet off of the chair next to her. She looks at me, then at Christian. When I don't respond. Christian says, "No, Lindsey. We haven't seen Camryn since the two of you were dancing. Tabitha, Jamie's ex, came up to the table. We were bullshitting with her. We didn't even notice the two of you leave the dance floor."

My temper flares, why would Camryn leave Lindsey up here and come looking for us by herself. She knows better than that. This place is packed tonight. Curses fall from my mouth. I shake my head giving Lindsey a hostile glare.

With sudden anger in her eyes, she shouts, "What, Jamie? She's a big girl. She told me to stay here, and she would be right back. Stop looking at me like I did something wrong!"

Without saying anything, I walk out of the room in search of Camryn. Hearing my name being called behind me, I don't bother to stop. Hopefully she is at the bar with Lincoln and Morgan.

CHAPTER

Seventeen

Camryn

WHEN I GET HALFWAY ACROSS the dance floor to meet up with the guys, I see Jamie at the table with a girl's arms thrown around his neck and pressed up against him. Who the hell is that? Her back is toward me, so I can't see her face. I am not usually a jealous person, but when it comes to Jamie, something fierce inside of me ignites. Jamie and I just started seeing each other. We agreed to be exclusive while we tested the waters with us as a couple, so why is he allowing this chick to touch him?

In order to avoid a scene here at the club, I turn my attention toward the bar. While heading in that direction, I debate on what drink I will order. As I try and squeeze my way to the bar, Lincoln spots me.

Waiting for me to reach him, he wipes the bar down in front of him. "Hey, baby girl. What's up? Why are you down here? The bartender up there could have made you anything you wanted."

Shrugging my shoulders, not really wanting to go into the real reason why I was at this bar, rather than upstairs. "Lindsey and I were heading upstairs, I was going to tell the guys where we were when we left the dance floor. Then I saw some girl with her arms around Jamie's neck. He didn't remove himself from her hold, so I bailed and headed over here."

Nodding his head in understanding, "You know it was probably nothing, baby girl. That man only has eyes for you. It's been that way for a while now." Lincoln raises his brows at me as if asking, 'you knew that, right'?

I don't respond to his declaration. Lincoln must realize that I had no knowledge of what he just disclosed. Changing the subject, he asks, "Have you seen Morgan? She's around here somewhere. The last I saw her, she was trying to get one of the security guys to run in the back and grab a few bottles of liquor from the storage room."

I shake my head. "I haven't seen her since she left us on the dance floor. She said that she would be busy tonight running around, making sure everything ran smoothly. It's no big deal, she'll stop upstairs when she has a free minute."

Lincoln asks what I would like to drink. When I reply, a watermelon martini, he laughs and shakes his head. "One watermelon martini, coming right up."

He walks away to prepare my drink, leaving me standing there by myself. I turn around, leaning my back against the bar. Glancing around the room, I take in all the costumes. There are a few guys dressed as Superman, a fighter with a robe on with "Rocky" displayed on his back. His makeup on his face shows several black and blue marks portraying he was fresh from a fight. I notice a man at the end of the bar wearing a *Phantom of the Opera* mask staring in my direction. I can't really tell if he's staring or not because of his mask, but it's freaking me out.

My attention is drawn to another man wearing a bright white mask with his eyes cut out. With the black lights in the club, his face is glowing. He has a huge condom on his head, with a large "C" on an emblem on his chest. When he turns around, I spot "Condom Man" written across his cape. Immediately, I start laughing. Feeling a tap on my shoulder, I turn my attention toward the bar.

"Here ya go, baby girl," Lincoln says as he places a napkin in front of me then placing my drink on the napkin. My drink is in a fancy margarita glass, rimmed with sugar, with a small wedge of watermelon, placed nicely on the side.

Stirring my drink slowly, then placing the stirrer on the napkin next to my drink, I gently, lift the drink to my lips, and try to avoid spilling any. I close my eyes, as my taste buds relish the sweet flavor. The perfect amount of alcohol mixed with sweetness. Opening my eyes, I see Lincoln with his head tilted to the side and his infamous crocked smile plastered on his face.

"Are you enjoying that, Camryn? By the moan that just left your mouth, I think you gave the guy standing next to you a hard on. He adjusted himself and quickly walked away when I gave him a look to beat it."

Placing my drink down. I laugh at Lincoln's comment. "I did not moan, you are exaggerating."

Lincoln laughs, "Whatever you say, baby girl, whatever you say."

I spend a few minutes at the bar talking with Lincoln. Every now and then he walks away to take a few drink orders. He is helping the bartenders out tonight since Redemption is so crowded. There are three bartenders covering this side, with an additional three on the other. The bar is set up in an L-shape. Since I have been standing here at the bar with Lincoln, the bar backs have filled the coolers with fresh ice and beer two times.

My eyes are drawn to the *Phantom of the Opera* mask again making its way through the crowd. I'm not sure if it's the same guy that was at the end of the bar earlier, or my mind is playing tricks on me?

Once I finish my drink, my body feels warm. A slight buzz hits me from the martini. While attempting to make my way through the crowd, I decide I should go to the restroom before I make my way over to Jamie and Christian.

Weaving my way through the crowd, I reach my destination. There is a line at least twenty girls deep. Sighing, knowing I am going to be here for a while, I pull out my phone to check my email. I respond to a few while I wait. Before I know it, I walk through the door to the bathroom.

After taking care of business, I dig through my tiny wristlet, and find the red lipstick that Morgan used earlier on my lips. I reapply a coat, and throw it back in. I do a once over in the mirror. Happy with my appearance, I turn to leave.

I weave my way through the line of girls in the hallway. Right before I reach the opening to the club, a set of strong arms wrap around my body, guiding me away from the bathroom, and toward a door labeled storage room. Taking a deep breath, I inhale his scent. Exhaling deeply, knowing it's Jamie. I would know his smell anywhere. The whole time walking toward the door, soft kisses are being placed on my neck. Leaning my head back against his chest, giving him more access, he plants kisses from my ear to my collarbone. His mouth continues its attack on my neck, and lightly bites it. My body immediately reacts to his touch, thereby pushing my ass into his groin. He growls near my ear, igniting my body even more.

Once the door is open, he pushes us in the dark room, letting the door shut behind us. He forcefully pins me against the wall. "Do you like how that feels?" he murmurs.

I freeze. My body tenses on high alert. It isn't Jamie's voice. Who in the hell is it? I need to get out of here.

I push back against the body behind me, then throw my elbow into his stomach. He groans, pulling back some, then slams my face into the wall. Tears run down my face as I scream, "Someone help me! Help me!"

A punch hits the left side of my mouth. Pain immediately floods my face. Tasting copper, I know I am bleeding. He grabs my hair and pulls it back against his chest. He leans down close to my ear. "Shut the fuck up. No one can hear you over the music. This can be easy, or it can be rough. It's your choice."

"Someone help me! Help me!" I scream as loud as I can. My throat burns as if someone has set it on fire. Struggling against his hold, I throw my head back, striking his face with the back of my head. I learned that move in a self-defense class I took in college.

"You bitch, this is going to be rough now." He growls.

He slams my face against the wall again, and spots form in my vision. I feel trickles of blood running down my face. Trying to open my eyes again, something sharp presses against my neck. *How can this be happening? He is going to rape me. Where are my friends? Where is Jaime? I* rack my brain on what to do. I refuse to allow this to happen without putting up a fight. I will fight with all I have before he gets what he wants. Hopefully, I can last long enough for someone to come looking for me.

His body presses against my back, forcing my body against the wall. Due to the darkness of the room, I can't see his face. I can only feel his breath against my neck. "Why are you going to fight me? I saw the way you were looking at me out there. You were begging me with your eyes to come dance with you, to touch you." *What the hell is he talking about? I didn't look at anyone while I was dancing with Jamie or with the girls.*

"Why are you doing this to me?" I plead in between sobs, trying to breathe.

He grabs at my dress to pull it up. Pushing back from the wall, I'm able to lift my left leg giving me just enough room to kick him, striking his shin. I throw my left elbow back, making contact again. I have to get out of here. There are hundreds of people in this club. The other side of the door is my salvation.

"You, bitch," he growls as he pushes himself against me. I gag when I feel his arousal against me.

I continue to scream at the top of my lungs. Any sound, any words, if I stop screaming then I feel like I'm giving up and allowing this to happen. This can't be real though. There were people in the hall, *how can they not hear me* is all I keep saying to myself in between my shouts.

He tries to clamp a hand over my mouth and I bite down, hitting air but letting him know that I won't go quietly and not caring about the repercussions.

I struggle to get free, but he slams me against the wall again. His right forearm is now around my neck, holding the knife along the left side of my throat. I grab at his arm with my right hand, trying to pull his arm away from my throat. It doesn't budge, it only tightens against my throat. Taking my fingernails, I dig them into his forearm and scratch him. He jerks his arm from the pain I just inflicted. Instantly feeling pain, I gasp from the sharp pain on my neck. This crazy fucker just cut me.

He leans down to my ear, "Look what you made me do. You made me cut you. Are you happy now? You were perfect, now you are flawed. I expected to mark you but not in this way. This is your fault. If you didn't fight me, this could have been easy."

He grabs a handful of hair, jerking my head back toward him. He licks the side of my face, then kisses the side of my mouth. I throw my head back again, colliding with his head. I see stars from the impact. His left hand comes up to punch me in the face again. I feel my lip split on that punch. He tries to turn my face around so he can kiss me on the lips, but I spit in his face. "Fuck you," I scream, which only infuriates him.

He throws my limp body against the wall again, striking my head against it in the process. My head is pounding and my vision blurs. The weight of his body is pressed flush against my back. His breath is touching my neck. Bile rises in my throat, and I start to gag. He wraps his left arm around my body, groping my chest. He then begins to pull at my dress tearing at the buttons to gain access underneath, leaving me exposed. His hand squeezes my breast roughly. I let out a cry as the pain shoots through my body. The knife is still pressed firmly against my throat, as he removes his hand from my breast. I feel him pulling at my shorts under my dress. I try to pull away from him, but that only makes his hold around my throat tighten. He takes his right leg, pushing my right leg farther part, giving him more access. Tears are running down my face as I continue to sob, the screams lessening as my energy and self-preservation wane. *This cannot be happening. Why is this happening?*

I feel my black shorts being torn from my body. I hear something being torn behind me. "Be thankful, I'm using a condom," he says in my ear. When he steps away to put it on, I try to turn around to see his face. He quickly shoves me back into the wall face first. He curses under his breath, "You stay right there, sweetie." He pushes his erection against my bottom. I'm going to be sick.

"Your boyfriend is one lucky guy. He gets to touch this body all the time. He doesn't know how lucky he truly is," he says against my ear as he grinds his erection into me.

With his left hand, he shoves my legs apart even more. He takes his finger, shoving it into my mouth, saying, "lick my finger." Instead, I bite down with the force I put behind the bite earlier.

"You bitch," he yells withdrawing his finger from my mouth. He punches me in the side, immediately feeling like he fractured a rib, I can't breathe. I gasp for air, feeling like my lung won't expand.

He takes his finger, shoving it violently into me. I whimper as he moves his finger around inside of my body.

"Oh, baby, you are sooooo ready for me. I know you've been wanting me all night, I could see it every time you looked my way. Get ready, cuz I'm about to give you the best time of your life."

He removes his finger, then thrusts his penis inside of me. My stomach churns and I close my eyes, sobbing. What did I do that would make him want to do this to me?

"You're tight, baby. Just like I imagined you would be." He grunts against my ear.

My body hurts with every thrust . . . so badly. I feel so broken. I try to fight more, but the more I fight, the harder he pushes himself into me. I feel his breath on my neck. He kisses my neck as he jerks himself in me. He thrusts so hard, my feet are lifted off of the ground. My entire body is shaking as I sob. I want to die. I wish he would just kill me. Move the knife against my throat, slice my carotid artery, anything. I would rather die than live through this.

He thrusts a few more times, then grunts as he reaches his climax. He withdraws himself from me, but not before kissing my cheek. I fall to the floor, curling into the fetal position.

"Now that's how it's done, sweetie," he says, and tucks himself inside zippering his pants.

I can't see out of my one eye. I try to look up at him to get a glance of the monster who did this to me. When he opens the door, I see that he is wearing all black, a black cape and what appears to be the *Phantom of the Opera* mask. One side of his face is covered. The only thing I see is a smirk across his lips. He turns and walks out of the room, and leaves me lying on the floor. It's the guy I saw that was watching me at the end of the bar.

I don't know how long I've been physically and emotionally dying here, before the door opens. I tighten my hold around my legs, praying it isn't him again. The light flicks on, blinding me. I hear a gasp, then my name. "Cami, oh my God."

I recognize the voice immediately, it's Lincoln. He kneels next to me. "Cami, who did this to you?" I don't answer him, I just shake my head back and forth. I hear him talking to someone, "Call a fucking ambulance, Jason. Now!" he screams.

I flinch away from his touch to my arm. "I'm so sorry, baby girl. I'll get you help. Don't move, Cami, your head is bleeding really badly."

I hear Lincoln talking again. He is telling Morgan to get her ass to the storage room and bring a blanket from the office. Morgan burst through the door moments later. Glancing in her direction, I see her hand immediately cover her mouth. She walks over to me, gently placing the blanket over me. Lincoln barks, "Go get Jamie and Christian now." Morgan nods her head and runs out of the room.

"Baby girl, I am so sorry. This is my club, you were supposed to be safe in my club. I am so sorry," he murmurs, and I think I hear tears threatening his words, him bearing the weight of what occurred in this tiny room. I see him looking around the room to find something to cover me with, my clothes ripped much like the tatters that my very soul is in now.

I see a tear run down his face. "Jason called 911, the police and ambulance are on their way."

Morgan quickly returns to the room. She comes over and kneels next to me on the floor. She goes to wipe my hair from my face, but I stop her. "Please, don't touch me. You can't. He touched me everywhere."

She covers her mouth with her hand, tears running down her face. Her body shakes as she sobs. "Camryn, I am so sorry. So sorry," she repeats.

The door is shoved upon, Lincoln jumps to his feet. Jamie and my brother are in the doorway. Jamie sees me on the floor, and hollers my name, "CAMRYN!" The way my name is said, will haunt me forever. The pain in his voice is so raw. He sounds like a wounded animal.

Jamie lunges toward me, but Lincoln stops him. Jamie tries to push

Lincoln out of the way, causing Lincoln to wrap his arms around him. Jamie struggles to get out of Lincoln's hold. "You can't touch her, man. You can't. You have to wait for the paramedics to get here."

"Why can't I touch her, she's my girl. Get the fuck off me, now!" Jamie screams. I see Lincoln lean in to Jamie's ear whispering so I can't hear. I am guessing he told him I was raped. Watching this scene unfold in front of me is so surreal, like I'm an observer watching the chaos. Jamie gets his arm loose, shoving Lincoln out of the way. He runs over to my side, coming down to my side on the floor.

He lifts his hands to touch my face but stops. "Oh my God, Camryn." His voice weak.

I can't even acknowledge his words. Looking past Jamie, I see my brother standing next to Lincoln by the door. Unabashed tears stream down Christian's face. He doesn't try to wipe them away. Lincoln didn't need to tell my brother what happened. He is piecing it all together. His hands are fisted at his side. This is the first time that my brother hasn't been there to protect me. Looking my brother in the eye, I can only watch him, the effort too much to do anything in this moment.

Christian doesn't speak, he just shakes his head back and forth. I can see the anger in his eyes. I know my brother better than anyone. He's gonna blame himself for not being there to protect me.

Bringing my gaze back to Jamie, I lean my body toward him. He wraps his arms around me, cradling me against his chest while telling me how sorry he is.

My head is cloudy and everything hurts. What seems like hours, probably has only been minutes, when I notice the paramedics are in the room. The female medic asks if she can examine me. She tells me they need to try and control the bleeding on my head before they transport me to the hospital. I didn't realize how bad I'm bleeding.

Looking at my hands, they are covered in my own blood. There is blood pooled on the floor where I was lying. Seeing all the blood, my hands begin to tremble. Their hands on me suddenly feels terrifying. I don't want them to touch me. I can't handle another person touching me. I need to get out of here. I squeeze my eyes shut and scream. "Get off of me! Don't touch me! Get off of me!"

"Camryn, they're the paramedics. They are here to help you. It's okay. They aren't going to hurt you. Let them help you," Jamie murmurs next to me.

Shaking my head back and forth, tears streaming like rivers of pain, "I don't want to be touched. Not by anyone. I want to go home and take a shower. I need to get him off of me. I need to wash him away."

The paramedics step back while Jamie comes closer to me. With his finger under my chin he tilts my head up to look at him. "I know you want to go home, but we need to get you to the hospital. Please, let them look at your injuries, baby." His voice is filled with so much emotion, my heart shatters into a million pieces. He is trying to be strong for me. Panic is rioting within him, but he is trying his best not to show it. As I look into his eyes, I see it. The despair, the hurt, the anger.

Sheer panic is in his eyes. I see Jamie breaking right in front of me. I know I will never recover from this, and by the look on his face, I don't think he will either.

As if holding all his raw emotions in check, he looks at the paramedics, "Can I go with her? In the ambulance?"

The medic says, "Yes, but we need to stabilize her first. Once we do, we will load her up and head to Mt. Sinai Medical Center."

Jamie brings his attention back to me. "Did you hear that? They're going to let me come with you, okay? Let them do what they need to now, so we can get you to the hospital. I won't leave your side, baby. I promise."

I nod my head, telling them they can touch me. I don't say anything, while they press a gauze pad to my forehead. I flinch when they apply pressure to my head. One after another, I see them remove the bloodied gauze, replacing it with a fresh one. I feel them lift me onto the stretcher. When they fasten the straps over my body, I wince from the pain. A sense of desperation almost overtakes me as I feel trapped, like I did in that room. I focus on Jamie, and the fact that he can see me and hear me, his breaths are my anchor in this maelstrom, enough to get me through the torrent of emotions that are threatening to overtake me. After what feels like forever I am rushed out the back door to a waiting ambulance.

CHAPTER
Eighteen

Jamie

"EVERYTHING IS GOING TO BE okay, Camryn," I keep repeating to her, while I hold her hand tightly. I can't believe this is happening. This is something you see on TV or the news or something. I can't wrap my head around what's happening. Maybe it's a defense mechanism to help me make sense of . . . of how someone could do this to my Camryn. The paramedic is working on her head wound, trying to control the bleeding. She lets out a painful cry. Her eyes are closed, her emotions in check, her face strained with pain. Camryn isn't fighting the paramedic anymore as she allows him to tend to her head wound.

I feel like I'm going to vomit. I can't control the shaking in my hands. I don't want Camryn to see me like this. I need to hold it together for her. Stay strong for her. The pain in my chest won't go away. I feel like I am suffocating. The sound of the siren echoes through the ambulance. When we arrive at the hospital, Camryn is immediately ushered into the back, leaving me standing here behind the doors that read 'PERSONNEL ONLY, DO NOT ENTER'. I hear Camryn crying out my name from the other side. Seeing the nurses' station, I run over to it. "Excuse me, why can't I go back there with my girlfriend. Why do

I have to stay here?"

The nurse advises me it's a restricted area and she will be taken care of. Someone will be out to talk to me once she has been evaluated, pointing for me to have a seat. I slam my hands on the counter, and I yell, "This is bullshit!"

Christian hasn't arrived yet, so I pace the waiting room by myself. I fight the urge to vomit as bile keeps working its way up my throat. I clench my fists as I continue to wait for Christian and his parents.

He also called Karsen, as well, to see if she was working tonight and, thankfully, she is. She told Christian that she would be in the ER waiting for our arrival, which she was. Karsen walks through the doors they just took Camryn through and guides me to a nearby waiting room for families.

When the door closes, she pulls me in for a hug. When she releases me she asks, "How are you holding up?"

"I'm a fucking mess. It's my fault this happened. I should have never left her on the dance floor."

Turning to look at Karsen's face, all I see is shock. She walks over to me, placing her hand on my arm. "Jamie, this is not your fault. Do not blame yourself. Do not let Camryn hear you say that. She needs you to be strong. You need to be her rock. She cannot see you beating yourself up over this."

Not knowing what to say, I just nod my head.

Karsen takes my hand in hers and squeezes it. "Stay here. I need to get back there with Camryn. I promised her I would stay with her for the exams. I'll keep you posted on her condition as soon as I hear something, okay?" I nod my head to acknowledge that I heard what she said. I can't speak past the huge knot in my throat.

A few minutes pass and the door opens again. Karsen walks in with scrubs in her hands. "Here, go get washed up and changed. Camryn doesn't need to see you with her blood on you."

Nodding my head, she points to the bathroom on the other side of the waiting room.

I take the bag from her and walk over to the bathroom. Once I exit the bathroom, I toss my costume in the trashcan. I never want to see that thing again. It will only remind me of this sordid night.

It seems like I have been waiting here forever. Checking my watch, it's only been fifteen minutes. I pinch the bridge of my nose trying to relieve some of the pressure. My head is pounding. My heart is racing. I am going to lose my shit if I don't hear something soon. I punch the vending machine. "What the fuck!" Christian comes up behind me wrapping his arms around me to settle me down. I didn't even hear him walk into the waiting room.

"Dude, don't do this. Camryn doesn't need you getting arrested tonight. Calm down. She's a fighter. She'll get through this. We'll be here to make sure she does. Do you hear me?" Christian says behind me. Nodding my head, he releases his hold on me, knowing I won't lash out again.

Christian guides me toward the row of chairs and demands me to sit.

I sit in the chair, and lean my elbows on my knees. I look toward Christian who is now pacing the room. "I am going to kill the mother-fucker who did this to her. I will kill him with my bare hands and not feel one ounce of remorse."

Christian turns to me, "I know you will, that's the part that scares me. You can't do shit, Jamie. You need to let the detectives do their job."

"How can you be so calm about this, man? Your sister was attacked tonight. Raped at our best friend's club for fuck's sake!" I say through gritted teeth.

Christian walks over to stand in front of me. He squats down so that we are at eye level. "Let me tell you one thing. I am not fucking calm right now!" he practically screams at me. I flinch at the anger in his tone.

"I am hanging on by a thread to keep my shit together. You and I show our feelings differently, Jamie. We always have. You show your emotions. I, on the other hand, never do. I am just as pissed about this as you. But we can't do shit about it. The detectives will talk to Camryn when they get here. The only thing we can do is make sure this doesn't destroy her. Do you hear me? We can't let this destroy her."

Not knowing what to say, I sigh and put my face in my hands and cry for the first time since I was a child. I cry for what Camryn is going through, for what she is feeling, for what that bastard robbed her of. I cry knowing that this may destroy my girl. I cry for not being there to protect her. I promised her that I was her knight in shining armor. I failed her. I didn't protect her. What the hell kind of boyfriend am I?

I sure as hell blame myself. Why did she not come to the table like she told Lindsey she was? Why did she go to the bathroom by herself? We had this discussion over and over. It was a rule that she always followed. Ever since we were younger we always made sure the girls went to the bathroom with a partner. I made sure to tell Camryn that time and time again when she was away at Stanford. Never go to the bathroom or walk at night by yourself. There are creeps out there just waiting to prey on girls. When I knew she was going to parties when she was in college, I would ask her to text me to let me know she got home safely, no matter what time it was.

I should have been there. This should have never happened. How could I have been in the same fucking place as her, and not know what was happening? How the hell did she end up in that room? Lincoln said it should have been locked. There are so many questions running through my mind. But most importantly, I need to know that my girl is going to get through this. I know I need to be strong for her. I need to be there to get her through this. I love her. I have loved her for years. I need to see my girl, to make sure she knows I love her. I'm not going to let this destroy her. I can't. I won't.

"Here," I say, handing Christian the pair of scrubs.

"Karsen left these for you. Figured you'd want to get changed too." Christian grabs the scrubs and heads in to change, discarding his costume as well when he exits.

A hand is placed on my shoulder. Looking up, it's Camryn's father, Mark. I can see in his eyes that he's on the verge of breaking but knowing what I know about his personality, he'd never let anyone see that even if it did happen.

With an emotionally choked voice, he says, "Come here, son. She'll get through this," before pulling me in for a hug. Looking over at Christian, he is holding his mom while she cries against his chest. I can't see her face, all I can see is her body shaking with sobs. Christian rubs his hand up and down her back, trying his best to console her as he repeats, "It's gonna be alright. She'll get through this, you know she will." He must have repeated that same sentence ten times before she pulls back to look her son in the eyes.

Shaking her head, she says, "How can you say that, Christian? We have no idea what she endured. What sort of trauma she suffered. Have you seen her? Have the doctors come out to talk to you yet?"

Christian pulls her back against him. "I saw her at the club before the paramedics got her in the ambulance." Shaking his head as if he is trying to rid his mind of the vision of Camryn, he continues, "No one has come to let us know any updates since we got here. When the medic told me what hospital they were bringing her to, I called Karsen to see if she was working. I filled her in on what happened and she promised she would be waiting for her when she arrived. Karsen put Jamie in here. She assured us that she would let us know something as soon as she knew anything."

Christian didn't tell his mom how bad the situation was at the club. She didn't need the visual of what we saw. Camryn looked broken as I cradled her bloody, limp body in my arms while she cried hysterically. The pain and guilt will haunt me for the rest of my life.

I will never forget the look on Camryn's face as they put her on the stretcher. They began to work on her immediately, obstructing my view of her. I could only hear her cries, which tore my heart into a million pieces. There was nothing I could do to console her. I stood back while they tried to control the bleeding from the cut on her head and neck. Shaking myself from those memories, I rake my hands over my face in frustration.

My nostrils flare with fury. I'm numb with increasing rage from the onslaught of visions of a broken Camryn that continuously play like a movie reel before my eyes. Adrenaline rushes through my body. I clench my fists to avoid hitting something. Seeing Camryn the way she is, seeing what that bastard did to her. He not only robbed her, but he robbed me.

I'm so furious I can hardly speak. What the fuck is taking so long?

We should have heard something by now. It's taking everything in me not to go search for Camryn. She needs me. I *need* to be with her.

A short while later, the door to the waiting room opens and a petite brunette with her hair pulled back into a ponytail walks in wearing scrubs. I'm not sure if she is a doctor or a nurse on duty. She shuts the door behind her, approaching us slowly. "Are you Camryn Townsend's family?" she asks.

Gwen quickly responds, "Yes, she's my daughter. Can you tell me what's happening? Where is she?"

The woman guides her over to the chairs. "Ma'am, please have a seat. My name is Dr. Megan Crosby, I'm the attending physician on duty tonight. I have some news."

Christian and I sit next to his parents. Mark has his wife's hand in his and Christian places his hand on her knee. The doctor pulls a chair up and sits in front of us. She takes Gwen's other hand in hers, gently squeezing it.

"Your daughter is a fighter. She put up quite a fight while I was trying to examine her, not wanting anyone to touch her. Karsen was able to calm her down. She is back there with her, she hasn't left her side since she arrived."

Gwen wipes her face with a tissue as her tears roll down her cheeks. Mark pulls his wife against his side, placing his arm around her shoulder.

"I want to warn you, so you're not alarmed when you see her. Your reaction could frighten her. She has been given medication for the pain, but her face is quite bruised from the trauma she suffered. Her right eye is black and completely swollen shut."

"Oh my God, Mark. How could this happen to our baby girl?" she sobs.

Dr. Crosby places a consoling hand on her knee to comfort her as she continues to update us on Camryn's condition. Raising her brows at Mark, the doctor asks if she should continue. Mark doesn't respond verbally, but simply nods his head.

Again, I feel bile working its way up my throat. Trying to focus on something to avoid vomiting, I lower my head into my hands taking deep breaths in and blowing them back out. When I look back up at the doctor, she has a pained look etched on her face. I can sense the infor-mation she is about to deliver to us is going to gut me to the core.

"Your daughter was sexually assaulted tonight. The forensic nurse is in with her now examining her and gathering any evidence she can."

A gasp escapes Gwen. Her hand covers her mouth to try and sub-due her sob. Her body trembles as she stares wordlessly between her son and me. I thought Christian told her what happened on the phone, evidently he didn't tell her everything. She jumps up from her seat, pointing her finger at us. "Why didn't you tell us she was raped?"

Christian stands by his mother "Mom, please don't do this here. Can we talk about this later?"

Shaking her head no, she says, "Why didn't you tell me when you called?"

Looking down at her, his eyes are saying so many things without even speaking. Finally finding the words, he says quietly, "How could I tell you that over the phone? The two of you needed to get here in one piece. I couldn't risk losing my parents tonight because they were too distraught to drive." Putting his head down, he walks back over to sit next to me, shaking his head back and forth, "I'm sorry."

Mark stands, pulling his wife into his arms. Holding her close, he whispers in her ear, "Don't be angry at our son. He did what he thought was best to get us here." Taking his wife's hand he motions for her to sit again.

Dr. Crosby looks over all of us. "Do you want me to continue? I know this is a lot to process, I wish I had better news."

Mark motions for her to continue. "She's banged up pretty bad. The plastic surgeon was called in to evaluate her. He determined stitch-es weren't required for all of the cuts, however, Camryn sustained a deep laceration on her head which did require several stitches."

"Like I said, Karsen is there with your daughter. She is walking her through everything step by step to help keep Camryn calm. Once the nurse is through, I will give her something to calm her down. She is also complaining of a headache from the trauma to her head, so she will be taken down for a CAT scan of the brain to make sure there isn't any swelling. The police have also arrived. They will want to speak with her when she gets back from her scan."

"Oh, Mark," Gwen cries out as she leans into her husband's chest, continuing to cry. He rubs his hand up and down her arm, trying to soothe her.

"I will come out and get you when she is back from her scan. Camryn will be placed into a private room until the results of her diagnostic testing comes back." Dr. Crosby stands from her chair returning it to the original spot where she found it.

When I hear the door close from the doctor exiting the room, I stand from my chair and walk towards the window. While staring out the window, the night sky is still dark. Not knowing how long I've been standing there, I feel a set of arms wrap around my waist. Looking down, Gwen has her head against my back. She whispers, "Our girl is going to need us, Jamie. More now then she ever has before."

I turn around in Gwen's embrace. I run my hands up and down her arms, I don't speak right away. There is a knot in my throat the size of a softball. My mouth is dry and I feel like if I open my mouth to speak, I am going to lose it right here in this waiting room. When I say lose it, I mean either lose the contents of my stomach here on the floor, or mentally break down. Trying to control my emotions, especially in front of Camryn's mom, two words leave my lips. "I know."

That is all I could say. My heart is broken for Camryn. Nothing I can say or do will change what has happened to her. There is really nothing any of us can say to console her. None of us know what she endured. What that animal did to her. We can only pray that she allows us to help her heal.

Gwen stays with me over in the corner for a while. Looking across the room, Christian and his father are both sitting with their elbows on their knees, their faces in their hands. Seeing Christian's body shake, I know he is crying. His father puts his arm around his son's shoulder pulling him against his side. The two of them cry together for Camryn.

CHAPTER

Nineteen

Camryn

KARSEN'S FACE IS THE FIRST thing I see through the one eye that actually opens, as they push me through the emergency room doors. The sadness in her eyes is evident.

"I'm here, Camryn. I'll stay with you the entire time, okay?" Karsen's voice shakes.

All I can do is nod my head as I'm wheeled through another set of doors. This time they are labeled 'AUTHORIZED PERSONNEL ONLY'.

"Jamie," I scream and reach out for his touch, but he's gone. Loneliness envelops me without my Jamie—my security.

"He's not allowed back here, Camryn," Karsen explains. "I'll update him on what's going on once things back here have settled."

My left eyelid winces from the fluorescent lights beaming down in the hallway. The ache in my head intensifies, and my fingers twist the sheets from the panic rapidly rising through my body. I take slow, deep breaths in and out to regulate my shallow breathing.

My gurney is maneuvered into a quiet, secluded room. Karsen rolls a stool over to sit next to my bed. She grabs my hand and interlaces our fingers. "I'm not going to leave your side. I'll walk you through this every step of the way, okay?"

I'm thankful that Karsen is by my side. I'd never be able to get through this alone.

A knot clumps in my throat and I nod my head. My mouth is dry from screaming for help.

My body trembles when I hear the click of the door from a doctor and nurse entering the room.

"Look at me, Cami." Karsen ducks down into my line of vision. My eyes lock on hers as she tries to reassure me. "You're safe now. No one is going to hurt you." I quickly look away from her, finding a sign on the wall to focus on. As much as I want to believe Karsen, I can't. Safe . . . isn't a word in my vocabulary at this point. Karsen is doing her best to help keep me calm, but she can't do anything to help ease the pain that I feel inside.

Every muscle tenses when the doctor walks closer. "My name is Dr. Megan Crosby. I am the attending physician on call tonight." I don't respond, so she continues. "I'll be as gentle as possible, Camryn."

The snap of Dr. Crosby's latex glove echoes through the small room and I attempt to prepare myself for the unknown. "Relax. I'm going to remove your bandage on your forehead first to see if I need to call a plastic surgeon in for stitches."

She leans over me and touches my head. Panic washes over me. "Don't touch me! I can't have you touch me!"

Karsen squeezes my hand but that doesn't stop my body from shaking uncontrollably. "Look at me, Camryn. Focus on me." It takes every ounce of energy to look over. "Keep your eyes on me for now. Dr. Crosby is only going to remove the bandage to see how bad the cut is, okay?"

I flinch from the doctor's fingertips. "You're safe, Camryn." There's Karsen with that word again. I'll never be safe again. Not with that monster still lurking out there.

I lie in the hospital bed, and attempt to emotionally morph myself somewhere else. A happier place. A time when all I could do was smile. The night my team won the State Championship game my senior year when I threw a no-hitter comes to mind. I was invincible on the mound. Every pitch was perfect, right down the center. With every strike-out, a feeling of euphoria.

Now, I'm dirty from his touch, and broken with no reality of myself.

"It appears that you are going to need stitches here and I also want a CAT scan of your head," Dr. Crosby's voice pulls me back.

Dr. Crosby advises the nurse to notify the plastic surgeon that I'll require stitches on my head and to let the forensic nurse know that she can come in. She turns to leave the room, then stops by the door.

"The wounds will be cleaned once the nurse is able to collect any evidence. I'll also request that a rape crisis counselor come down as well," Dr. Crosby states.

I nod my head once, acknowledging I heard her.

The mention of a rape counselor is all I need to hear. I begin to cry uncontrollably. My pulse begins to race. The sound of my heartbeat thrashes in my ears. I begin to gasp for air. A panic attack is just on the horizon and I'm not sure I can control it.

"Breathe, Cami, take a deep breath. Look at me. Breathe in . . . breathe out. You can do this."

My eyes lock on her face, and the rhythmic tone of her voice as I follow Karsen's instructions.

Dr. Crosby and the nurse file out of the room and I turn to Karsen, "Why did this happen?"

She squeezes my hand. "I don't know, Camryn. This isn't your fault, do you hear me? You did nothing to warrant this." She says with a look of implacable determination on her face. In her head, she truly believes that.

I want to believe her. The rational side of me is agreeing, but I can't allow myself to actually believe her words. That monster killed the rational side of me.

A little while later, a soft knock sounds at the door and Karsen says come in. Two women enter my room.

"My name is Claire. I'm the rape crisis counselor." She points to the woman standing next to her. "This is Marci. She is the forensic nurse who will conduct the exam and collect any evidence. She will need your consent to perform the exam."

Finding my voice, "It's fine. I want to get this over with so I can go home. You have my permission to examine me. But I don't need you here, Claire. I'd rather have Karsen stay with me."

I know Claire is here to help. I know this is her job and she is a trained professional who deals with this sort of thing all the time. But I can't bear to have another person in here while I endure the violation . . . the poking and prodding.

"Are you sure, Camryn? I can stand over there in the corner in case you have any questions."

I shake my head. "I'm positive."

"Are you sure you don't want her in here with us?" Karsen asks. "I think it would be a good idea to have her in here."

"I just want to get this exam over with, get my head stitched up and go home to wash him off me." My hands ball into fists beside me. "When I have to tell the police what he did, I don't need an audience, Karsen. I don't need another set of pity eyes looking at me."

Karsen's face is etched with concern and understanding.

"I'll leave my card with Dr. Crosby. Please call me if you need anything or if you change your mind and would like to talk."

"Thank you, I appreciate it." Claire nods her head then exits the room.

Taking a deep breath, trying to control my emotions, I sigh. "I just wish this night was over."

The forensic nurse clears her throat. "I'm going to be examining you tonight. I'll explain step by step as the exam is taking place. Your friend can also walk you through this and answer any questions, if you feel more comfortable with her, rather than me."

She grabs a pair of gloves then places a large piece of the exam table paper on the floor. "Can you please come stand over here for me?"

When I stand, I grip the side of the bed for support before I collapse on the hard linoleum. Karsen rushes over and grabs a hold of my arm. "I just got dizzy," I tell her, letting her know that I'll be fine in a moment.

Fine, is that even a word I can fathom right now?

"I'm right here, Camryn."

"I'm going to need you to disrobe while standing on the paper. This is to catch any fallen debris, hair, or fibers to avoid contamination. Step one is please take off your dress and place it in the bag in front of you."

I unbutton the few buttons that are left and my dress falls into a pile at my feet. "I can't bend over to untie my boots, can you help me?" I ask of Karsen.

Karsen rushes over. "Of course." She unties my right boot and removes my foot. She places it in the bag, and proceeds to do my left.

I vaguely hear Marci say, "I am going to evaluate you . . . trauma to your mouth, throat . . . swab the areas for any fluids."

I look away as I feel the swab against my throat. My body trembles uncontrollably as tears run down my face. I'm depleted of energy, too drained to even wipe them away.

The words DNA quickly snap me out of my trance. "He used a condom. But . . ." my voice wavers, "he licked the left side of my face."

"Perfect, Cami. Thank you." Marci gives me a small smile. I guess this is uncomfortable for both of us.

I stand there numb watching as the Q-tip swabs she is using to wipe under each one of my fingertips are gently placed in tubes. I hope that fucker left his mark. I scratched him so hopefully there's some type of genetic marker in there to find this criminal.

I can't help but count the ceiling tiles as I stand there cold and naked with my legs spread open while Marci examines my thighs with a lamp.

My body shutters each time the camera flash goes off, documenting every bruise and cut that asshole gave me.

All I can think during this entire thing is that is it not enough he robbed me of my womanhood, that now I'm also being stripped of my dignity in front of witnesses?

"I need you to lie back on the bed, place your feet in the stirrups, so I can perform the pelvic examination."

"Do you know how much longer this will take? I want to go home and take a shower. I can smell him on me," I speak in a broken whisper, tears running their course down my cheeks, feeling just as lost as to their destination as I am in this moment.

"I know you want to go home. We're almost through here. The plastic surgeon needs to stitch your laceration and you still have to be taken down for your scan. We'll do our best to get you out of here as quickly as possible."

Marci hands me a hospital gown, helping me put it on. I'm relieved to finally be covered up, although this next part will be the worst, emotionally, for me. I slowly walk back over to the bed, sitting my butt on the mattress, then gently lift my legs up. Despite the intense pain. My ribs on the left side are killing me with every breath I take.

Karsen resumes her place on the stool next to me, holding my hand and whispering incoherent things . . . a distraction, if you will. I go back to counting ceiling tiles and let her do what she needs to get this over with. The quicker the exam is done, the quicker I'm home.

I grip Karsen's hand from the burning when Marci enters me, scraping the last of my dignity with every swab. Fuck the ceiling tiles. "Karsen, talk to me about something else. Anything." Trying to hold the tears back becoming an almost futile effort. "How was work going? Were you busy?"

Karsen squeezes my hand. "Work was slow for a Saturday night. We had a few car accidents, some patients with colds, stomach pains, nothing too out of the ordinary."

Unable to shelter the tears anymore, a wet drop falls down my face and into my hairline. "Thank you for staying with me."

"I love you, sweetie. There isn't any other place I would want to be than right here with you."

Karsen leans closer. "Marci is almost finished just a few more minutes."

Shortly after Marci exits the room, the plastic surgeon comes in and stitches my forehead.

"Cami, can I go talk to Jamie? I'm sure Christian and your parents are here by now."

Glancing back over my shoulder as I'm being pushed out of the room, "Yes, please. Tell them I'm going for a scan."

Good, anything to keep them from here. I don't want anyone to see me. I'm broken, destroyed and dirty. I don't know how to go back to who I was before this. That bastard ruined me.

CHAPTER

Twenty

Jamie

THE SILENCE IN THE ROOM is unbearable. I pace the worn down carpet. From what I can tell, I'm not the first. There's a clear tread line in front of the windows. Where the hell are the people who took Camryn? The love of my life disappeared through those doors and they expect me to sit in a damn chair and let my mind take me to very dark places.

I begin to shake as the sordid images of the unknown build in my mind. My body fills with impotent rage and fear. Rage for what Camryn endured. Fear that she won't recover from this. Anger sweeps through my body, as my fists clench my hair until they are probably white knuckled. I'm not sure what's worse, *knowing* all of the details of what happened to her or *speculating* on all the ways Cami was violated. My mind is playing fucking tricks on me, causing me to question my sanity in this moment.

The lights from the skyline grab my attention and my palms grip the windowsill to remain upright. I pray it keeps me here instead of in those streets searching for the asshole who did this to my girl.

The glow of the building lights reminds me of our high school graduation party. The night Camryn's face beamed with excitement when I surprised her with a graduation gift. The night my life changed forever when Camryn delivered her shocking news.

Huge white tents were set up in the middle of the cul-de-sac where we all lived, another tent off to the side that housed all the food, drinks, and the DJ. The party started around two in the afternoon and lasted well past midnight. Most of the partygoers stayed under the tents while some made their way to the Townsend's backyard where the in-ground pool was.

Christian and I exchanged gifts, nothing big because I had saved all my money for Camryn's gift. My parents had offered to loan me the money, but I didn't want their money to pay for this. All winter I shoveled snow in our development and worked for a landscaper in the spring mowing lawns to earn the money.

I was nervous all day not knowing what Camryn was going to think of my gift. Things were going to change between us when Camryn left for the University of Maryland in August. I wanted her to always be able to look at the necklace that I got her and remember me.

When I saw the necklace I knew I had to get it for Camryn. The platinum necklace held a beautiful platinum heart locket. On the inside, I was able to get a picture from homecoming last year made small enough to fit. We were both smiling at my mom while she was taking pictures. She captured one of me placing a soft kiss on Camryn's cheek and knowing it was one of Camryn's favorites I knew I had to use that one. On the back of the locket I had engraved "I'm always with you, Cami."

When the party started to slow down some, I searched for Camryn. I hadn't seen her in the tent, so I went looking for her with the box tucked away in my back pocket. I finally found her sitting at her kitchen island with both our moms. I walked up, both our moms looked at me with sadness in their eyes. Immediately, I wondered what was wrong. Had something happened at the party that I wasn't aware of? Did someone hurt Camryn?

Looking between the three of them I needed to know what the hell was going on. "What's wrong? Why are the three of you in here and why are you all looking at me like something happened?"

Camryn spoke up immediately. "Nothing happened, Jamie. Everything is fine. I promise." Looking into her eyes I knew she was lying to me. I stepped up to the island. "Don't lie to me, Cami. I know you better than you know yourself. You were the one who said no more secrets, no lies between us. Did you not?"

Camryn looked away from me, she knew she was caught.

"Camryn Elizabeth, tell him. I told you that this was going to be a tough decision. He was going to find out eventually or hadn't you planned on telling anyone?" By the look on her mom's face and her tone, I could tell she was angry now.

Sighing, Camryn walked over to me. She took my hand in hers, walking in to the living room away from the kitchen. Pointing to the couch, "Sit, I need to talk to you."

Before I sat down, I reached behind me, pulling Camryn's gift out of my pocket, placing it on the end table. Looking up at Camryn's face, I could see this was something she was going to have a hard time telling me. My patience was running thin. Before my brain could think, the filter on my mouth gone, I spat, "Spit it out, Camryn! What are you not telling me?"

She sat in the chair across from me, her thin fingers tensed in her lap. She became increasingly uneasy under the scrutiny of my stare. Awkwardly, she cleared her throat. She looked away again before she spoke. "I don't know how to tell you this. But you need to hear me out before you freak, okay?" Raising her brow at me, she waited for my answer. I gave her a simple nod. I didn't even know what to say. I had no idea what was about to come out of her mouth. "I changed my mind about college." She began to speak, but her voice wavered. "I'm not attending the University of Maryland anymore. Stanford offered me a full athletic scholarship. They have one of the top journalism programs in the country and I couldn't turn it down. I would be an idiot if I did." Her voice drifted to a hushed whisper.

My head began to spin. Did she just say she isn't going to Maryland . . . a car ride away? Rather she is going to California, a plane ride away? I knew one day we were all going to go off to college, but I always pictured the three of us together. I never pictured Cami on the other side of the damn country. I took a deep breath, trying to gain my composure before I said anything that I may regret. "When did you make this decision? Am I the last to know?"

Camryn immediately jumped from the chair, grabbing my hand as she sat next to me on the couch. "No, Christian doesn't even know yet. Only my *parents and, well . . . your mom now. That's what we were talking about when you walked in."*

Nodding my head she continued. *"You know I was offered a scholarship to Maryland last year. I didn't even apply to Stanford. Coach told me that there was a scout at the playoff game. They came to the game to check me out. I didn't even know he was there. A few days after the game, the coach from Stanford called my parents, offering me a full ride, Jamie. I didn't accept their offer right away. I went back and forth for weeks struggling with it."*

She paused to catch her breath, her fears were stronger than ever. *"I never imagined I'd decide to go this far from home for school. I always wanted to be able to drive back home when I wanted to. After countless conversations with coach and my parents and weighing my options, I came to the decision that Stanford fit more with my ultimate goal. Their journalism program is one of the best in the country."*

I squeezed her hand, *"Camryn, I want what's best for you. Am I hurt that you didn't tell me right away, yes. If I said no, I would be lying to you as well as myself. You need to go after your dreams. Christian and I are heading to NYC chasing ours; you need to do the same whether it is in Maryland or in California. You might not be within driving distance for me to visit, but at least now I have a reason to vacation in Cali."*

She smacked me on the chest, laughing at my comment and gesture. She chewed on her lower lip and stole a look at me. *"I'm sorry I didn't tell you right away. I wasn't sure what I was going to do. I had to follow my heart, Jamie. It might not be the right decision, but my heart is telling me I need to go to California. If I hate it, I'll transfer, but I can't let fear keep me from going. My head has been spinning for weeks about how to tell everyone. My mind has been a crazy mixture of hope and fear and I can't go away with you being mad at me."*

Throwing my arm around Cami's shoulder, I pulled her close to me. *"Listen to me, I am only going to say this once. One, I could never be mad at you. And, two, I would never let you get on a plane with you thinking I was mad at you. You being in California is not going to change that. Got it?"* Lifting her chin to look at me. She just nodded her head and threw her arms around me.

Remembering I had her graduation gift, I grab the box from the table.

"Here ya go. I got you something."

She squealed, taking the box from me. She unwrapped it slowly, taking the lid off the box. She gasps as her hand covers her mouth. "Open it up."

Cami opened the locket and tears well in her eyes. When she looked up at me, they fell down her cheeks. She quickly tried to wipe them away, but they continued to fall. "This is beautiful, Jamie?"

Smiling at my girl, "Turn it over."

She turned the locket over to read the inscription then looked up at me. Tears streamed down her face, even harder now. She threw her arms around my neck and squeezed me tight.

I whispered in her ear, "Those words couldn't be more fitting right now. I will always be with you, Camryn, no matter where you go, I will always be with you."

The door behind me shuts and I'm propelled back into my nightmare. I release a breath and my heart calms when I see Karsen walk over. She pulls Gwen into a hug and the three of us rush to get any information about Cami.

Karsen sits in a chair across from us. She looks down at the floor, then back to us. I can see the sympathy and worry on her face. Gwen grabs Mark's hand. "Camryn was taken down for a CAT scan. When she's through there, they'll take her to her room, and the detectives will speak to her."

The door to the waiting room busts open. Morgan, Parker, and Lindsey rush in. Morgan takes the lead, "We got here as soon as we could. I had to give the detectives my statement. Lincoln's still there with them."

The group of us quietly sit in the waiting room while Cami's parents speak softly to each other. The eerie sound of the hands of the clock ticking by causes shivers up my spine. Not knowing how much time has passed, Karsen gets up from her seat. "I'm going to go check and see if Camryn is back from her scan and settled into her room."

"Thank you, sweetie," Gwen says.

Karsen returns about an hour later, advising us the detectives are through with Camryn and two of us can go back at a time. She's in a private room, waiting for the doctor to go over her scan results and discharge her. Her parents go back first. They were back there for a while before they return to the waiting room. Mark is holding his wife tight to his chest when they enter the room. Tears are streaming down his wife's face. With her face buried into his chest he says, "Our daughter will get through this. I know she looks bad, but those bruises will heal, Gwen. We need to focus on her healing emotionally, not the physical injuries."

Christian stands, "Do you mind if I go back alone?" he asks directing his attention toward me.

"Go ahead. Once I get back there, I'm not leaving her side."

I don't know how much time has passed when Christian sticks his head in the waiting room; his eyes are puffy and red from crying. "I'm gonna head home." Christian shakes his head, "I don't think she wants everyone to see her like this. She's pretty banged up. She told me to go home. You might want to wait till she gets settled at home and is up for visitors."

"I'm not going anywhere!" My voice harsh and raw. "I'm not leaving her. I need to see her."

Morgan nods her head. Parker and Lindsey raise from their seats heading out with Christian. Watching everyone leave, I follow after them heading down the hall to Camryn's room.

CHAPTER
Twenty-One

Jamie

MY GUT TWISTS AS MY feet slowly keep me moving down the hall-way. I've been waiting to see her for hours, but now, I'm scared shitless of what I'll find behind that door. One thing is for sure—I need to be strong for her. She needs all the support she can get. Knowing her, she won't accept anyone's pity. Most of all, mine.

My fist lightly knocks on the door and her voice quivers as she says come in. Pushing the door open, I slowly walk over to her bed behind the curtain. It's now or never. My eyes meet Camryn's, and the air in my lungs dissipate. Bile rises in my throat as though the asshole punched me. Her small body looks broken as she lies in that bed. If I didn't see her beautiful eyes, I wouldn't recognize her. Even though I saw her at Redemption and rode with her in the ambulance, I still wasn't prepared for this.

As my eyes take in Camryn, I push back the tears wanting to burst. I silently remind myself to compose myself. She doesn't need to see me upset. I'll be strong for her.

Camryn's vision focuses on mine. She slowly lifts an ice pack and places it over her right eye and flinches.

There are bandages placed sporadically on her body, her swollen eye means that fucking bastard beat the shit out of my girl. My fists ball next to my sides begging to hunt him down and kill him with my bare hands. As I approach the bed, her monitors begin to beep louder.

I grab the chair in the corner, and drag it to the side of her bed. I take her cold hand in mine, placing a soft kiss on the outside of it. Cami turns my way so she can look at me. "Hi," she whispers.

"Hi, beautiful."

"Don't let all the machines scare you. They're monitoring me because I was on the verge of a panic attack. I'm hoping they'll discharge me once my results from the CAT scan are back."

As gut wrenching as this is, I can't bring myself to look away. God, I hope my imagination of what happened in that room is far worse than the reality Cami has to live with. Tension envelops the room. Cami's knuckles whiten from her fists clenching the sheet. "Don't look at me like that, Jamie," she whispers in a small frightened voice. Tears falling down her cheeks.

My heart thuds rapidly in my chest. "How am I looking at you? You have no idea how scared I was. I was freaking out in the waiting room . . . your brother had to calm me down before I put my fist through the vending machine. This is my fault. If I was paying attention to you girls on the dance floor, I would have seen you and Lindsey wander off. Instead, Christian and I were too busy talking to Tabitha."

I stand from the chair to sit on the side of the bed next to her. I slowly lean down and gently kiss her forehead. "Don't you get it? This is my fault, Cami!" I say harshly, averting my gaze from her. "I'm sorry. So, so sorry this happened to you, baby . . ."

Camryn holds up her hand stopping me mid-sentence. "I can't do this, Jamie. If you're going to act like that, I'm going to tell you the same thing I told my brother . . . go home. Leave. I don't want everyone blaming themselves and I sure as hell don't want everyone looking at me with pity in their eyes. I don't want that." Her jaw tenses as she looks up and stares at the ceiling.

Her expression clouds with anger. "I know what I look like. I got a good look at myself in the mirror when I went to the bathroom. I felt every punch he landed on me. Every time my head or body was slammed into the wall, I know what it felt like. I don't want to have to think about it over and over each time someone new takes in all the injuries on my face for the first time. I just had to relive it with the two detectives. Go back to the waiting room and tell whoever is out there that I don't want any visitors. Not tonight, not for a little while, not until I heal."

Nodding my head, understanding where she is coming from. "Everyone left when your brother came back to the waiting room. Your parents and Karsen are the only ones left."

"You can go to if you want," she says her voice sounding detached. "I don't know how long they plan on keeping me here."

I gawk at her, she can't be serious. "I'm not going anywhere, Camryn. Do you hear me?" My voice carries with a unique force. "When I said you were mine, I meant it." If she thinks she is going to push me away, I'll push back harder.

She clenches my hand in hers and her knuckles turn white. "You can't mean that after what happened to me tonight, Jamie. Every time you look at me all I see is the pity in your eyes and I don't want that." Her voice breaks. "You'll never be able to look at me the same way."

Neither one of us says another word. I run my thumb slowly over her hand in soothing motions, letting her know I am here. The motion eventually lulls Camryn asleep.

I'm channeling all my emotions until I'm alone. Seeing her so damn broken and helpless is killing me. Leaning over towards the bed, I fight back the tears and whisper softly, "I have loved you all my life. I wish I could take your pain away." My voice cracks. "I wish I could rewind tonight, so this never happened to you. I am so sorry, baby. We'll get through this together. I promise, Cami . . . together."

There is a soft knock on the door. Lifting my head from the bed, her parents enter the room. "How is she holding up?" Mark asks.

"I think the pain meds kicked in. She fell asleep a little bit ago. We're waiting for the doctor to come in with the result of her scan so she can be released."

There is another knock on the door and Cami's treating physician enters. Rubbing my hand over Camryn's, I murmur, "Cami, wake up. Dr. Crosby is here."

Camryn doesn't even stir, so I place my hand on her arm, and nudge her a little harder. "Baby, wake up." She gasps and her eyes widen in terror. Her eyes flicker around the room at lightning speed.

"Shh, baby. It's okay. You're safe." My heart rate kicks up a notch knowing she's not going to feel safe anymore and she shouldn't have to feel like that.

"Safe . . . I'll never be safe again," she says as she can't control the spasmodic trembles within her.

She takes a few deep breaths. "Can I go, please?" She looks right at Dr. Crosby. "I just want to go home."

My heart just shatters in a million pieces all over the floor. I've never in my life heard or seen Camryn act like this, ever.

"Yes, we are discharging you. You do have two fractured ribs though so you must take it easy for the next few days. The nurses are preparing your discharge papers now. They will give you the scripts for your medications." She pats Camryn on the knee. "I wish you the best."

CHAPTER
Twenty-Two

Camryn

AFTER HOURS OF BEING AT the hospital, I'm finally discharged. My parents take me back to their house. Jamie and I are in the back seat of my father's car, my hand held tightly in his.

My father doesn't even have his keys out of the door, and I push my way past him. I head to my old bedroom, immediately walk into the bathroom and lock the door. I don't want to see anyone. I don't want to talk to anyone. I just need to get the smell of him off of me. I wish everyone would just leave me alone.

The hot steam clouds the mirror while I strip the scrubs that Karsen gave me from my body. Pulling my shirt over my head takes some effort because my ribs are killing me. A shudder runs through me when I catch glimpses of the bruises and marks on my body.

If I didn't wear that slutty cop outfit, he probably wouldn't have noticed me. Time and time again, Jamie has told me not to venture off on my own at clubs and parties. That girls should never go places alone, that we should always buddy up. If I would have listened to him, this may not have happened. I grab the toothbrush holder and throw it against the wall, watching as it shatters into pieces. That's exactly how I feel . . . shattered.

The water scalds my body when I step into the shower. I wince as the drops hit my sore skin. His scent permeates around me, so I scrub and scrub to rid him off me. The memory of his hands touching me, his breath against my neck, and the smell of his breath won't go away. My stomach churns as the bile rises in my throat. I throw the sponge against the wall and give up the fight. My back slides down the wall as tears cascade down my cheeks.

I seethe with anger and humiliation. Why did this happen to me? I should have fought harder. I try to force the images out of my head, but it takes more effort than I can handle. My body trembles uncontrollably. I rock back and forth on the floor of the shower, as I try to regain control of my breathing. I'm fearful I won't get through this. Will I be able to recover from this?

Once my panic attack subsides, I manage to get up off the floor of the shower by holding my ribcage. I squirt some shampoo in my palms, and massage it into my scalp, trying not to get my incision wet. After carefully rinsing the shampoo out of my hair, I cover my face with shaky hands and give vent to the agony of what I went through last night.

Closing my eyes, I lean my head back, letting the water stream down by body. My chest tightens as I can feel him touching me. Forcing himself into me. Panic riots within me again. Tears begin to fall down my face. I cry for what he did to me. For what I am left to deal with. I feel like who I was when I went to the party no longer exists. A million different thoughts run through my mind while I shower that I don't even realize that the water is now cold.

Once I dry off and dress slowly, I crawl into bed. Voices from people downstairs float up through the vents. Unable to bear the pitiful eyes they all wear, I pull the comforter up around my neck, and bury myself from everyone.

THE LIGHT FROM MY CLOCK glows midnight. How can I have slept an entire day away? Stretching my arms above my head as much as I can without inflicting pain on myself, I toss the covers back. I can't believe I slept as long as I did. The last time I looked at the clock it was three-thirty this afternoon. I maneuver my legs over the side of the bed, and wait a few seconds before standing. If I thought my body was sore earlier, I was dead wrong compared to how it feels now.

Quietly, I pry open my bedroom door to complete darkness. I tiptoe down the stairs in search of one thing . . . my parents' liquor cabinet. Rummaging for something strong, I grab the bottle of Belvedere vodka and make my way to the kitchen. Pulling open the refrigerator door, I search for cranberry juice. I slide the stool out gently to sit down, and place the bottle of vodka on the countertop. Without thinking, I pour it and swallow the vodka cranberry concoction in one gulp. I pour and down another one without coming up for air. As the liquid makes it way down my throat, I turn numb as ice. Thank goodness, there's a way to erase the pain.

The lights in the kitchen illuminate. My head flips to the doorway where I find Christian leaning against the wall with his arms crossed over his chest. "Care for some company?" he asks.

Wanting to be alone, I don't answer him and return my attention to my empty glass. He pushes himself off of the wall, and stands next to me. "Let me rephrase that. Pour me a drink."

"Grab a glass." Christian walks over to the liquor cabinet, returning with a glass for himself. I make him a vodka and cranberry along with another for myself. He doesn't take a sip, just stands there holding it in his hand.

"I'm not going to ask you to talk about what happened. Just know that I am always here for you. When you hurt, Cami, I hurt. I love you, sis." He leans over, placing a soft kiss on my head by my bandage. "When you're ready, come find me, please."

Nodding my head, I acknowledge what he said, then I whisper, "I love you, too." The two of us sit there in silence, both sipping our drinks.

Christian's always been a good listener. He never judges, he only offers his opinion when asked. I see the pain in his eyes. I know I'm going to have to talk to him eventually. I figure I might as well start now.

Looking at Christian, I open up and tell him what that monster did to me.

"I wouldn't wish what I went through on my worst enemy. I'll save you the gory details. All I will say is that when he was touching me, I prayed that he would just kill me. I didn't want to live knowing what he was doing to me." Looking down at my hands trembling around my glass, I remove them from the glass, wiping them against my yoga pants.

"You don't have to do this, Cami." Christian mutters.

Shaking my head, no, I continue. "I saw him at the bar when I was talking to Lincoln. He was watching me."

I see the sadness in his eyes. "I fought back, Christian, I swear I did. I struggled against him. The more I fought, the more he became enraged." I suddenly feel weak and vulnerable. Why wasn't I strong enough to fight him off? I wipe the tears away with my sleeve.

"He slammed my head against the wall. Any opportunity I thought I could get away, I tried to hit him. Even when he had the knife against my neck. I kicked him. I clawed at his arm when he was crushing my throat, that's when he cut my neck." I didn't care whether he hurt me or not at that point, I just wanted to die.

I take another sip of my drink. Tears flow freely down my cheeks.

"I never got a look at him, he had a mask on like most of the guests did. He was dressed as the *Phantom of the Opera*. I told the police everything I know. I scratched him when he had his arm across my throat. The detectives said they will run his DNA through the system. Who knows, maybe they'll get a match."

Christian walks around the island, pulling me in for a hug. "I'm so sorry, Cami. I was there tonight. This should have never happened."

My body stiffens, Christian pulls back to look at me. "What?"

"Don't blame yourself. I told you that earlier in the hospital. I'm not telling you what happened for you to take blame. I'm telling you because I need to talk to someone. You have always been there for me. I can't tell Morgan this and I sure as hell can't talk to Jamie. I feel like I am dying inside, Christian. Every time I close my eyes, he is all I can see . . . all I can *feel*. The counselor left her card, but I don't want to talk to a stranger."

Pulling me softly against his chest, he kisses my head. "You can talk to me about anything. Anytime, but you know you are going to have to talk to Jamie. You know our bond is solid, but you have something special with Jamie. You always have. You can't push him away. Not now, not when you need him the most."

I bury my head against my brother's chest, and whisper, "I will. I'll talk to him when I'm ready. In time, maybe. Just not now. Promise me, you won't tell him, Christian. I can't have him look at me the way he was doing at the hospital, that'll be what breaks me."

"I promise," he murmurs.

"SOMEONE HELP ME! HELP ME!" I scream. Hoping someone will hear me.

A punch hits the left side of my mouth. Pain immediately floods my face.

"Shut the fuck up. No one can hear you over the music. This can be easy, or it can be rough. It's your choice."

"Someone help me! Help me!" I scream until my voice is hoarse.

"Look what you made me do. You were perfect, now you are flawed," he growls.

I struggle to get free, but he slams me against the wall again. His right forearm is now around my neck, holding the knife along my throat.

I feel my body being pushed. "Camryn, wake up. Camryn you're safe," his voice echoes in the silent room. "Wake up. You're okay."

I awake with a start and jolt upright in bed, my chest heaving, beads of sweat on my forehead. Trembles rake through my entire body. I look around the room quickly, feeling disoriented. I try to figure out where I am. The lamp on the nightstand is on. Christian is sitting on the side of my bed.

"You were having a nightmare. You're safe. He won't ever touch you again."

"How did you get in here? The door was locked." I stare at him confused.

"Once I knew you were asleep, I picked the lock." He points to the floor, where a pile of blankets and a pillow lay. "I slept on the floor. I was gonna leave before you woke up."

I stare at him wordlessly. I want to be angry that he snuck in my room, but I can't. He did it to make sure I was okay. To keep an eye on me, always trying to be my protector.

"Christian, when will they stop? When will the nightmares stop?" I plead.

"I don't know, sis. I wish I did. But I'll be here to make sure you feel safe enough to sleep."

Christian stands. He grabs the covers and motions for me to lie down. "Go back to sleep. I'll be right over there. I won't leave you."

I lie down, pulling the covers up to my chin. "Thank you."

CHAPTER
Twenty-Three

Jamie

THREE DAYS HAVE PASSED SINCE Camryn came home from the hospital and I haven't seen her once. These have been the longest three days of my life. Every attempt to see her has failed, but not for lack of trying.

I've sat outside of her room, talking to her through the door. She never responds or acknowledges that I am on the other side, just a few feet from her. Some days I have sat on the floor with my guitar in my lap singing some of her favorite songs. Songs that I think would make her smile when she hears me sing.

I know she comes down at night when everyone goes to bed. Christian told me they meet in the kitchen at night. I told him I want to join them, but he insists that I wait for Camryn to let me in. As much as I hate that she won't open the door, this isn't about my feelings or what I want. Camryn has to be the one to initiate this on her own terms. So much of the decisions were ripped from her in that room at Redemption that I know I have to allow her the power to make her own choices from here on out.

Today, just like yesterday and the day before, my back rests against the door with my ass on the carpet, staring at her door.

"Camryn, baby, will you please let me in?" My voice breaks.

Nothing . . . silence. The faint sound of music streams out the crack of the door. Gwen said she hasn't been downstairs during the day since she got home, but she finds dirty dishes in the sink in the morning. I unleash my frustration to Christian every day about how helpless I feel, and he keeps insisting to give her time. She will come around. My patience is running out. Camryn has never pushed me away. I wonder if things hadn't evolved between us and we were strictly just friends, would she be ignoring me.

"Baby, can you at least let me know you are okay?"

Nothing.

"Can you at least knock on the door to let me know that you hear me?"

A few minutes pass before there is a faint knock on the door.

I rest my head on the door, so damn thankful that she's at least on the other side listening.

Another day passes, where she won't let me in. As much as I want to break down the door, I have to respect her wishes. She was raped. She was violated. I can't force my way in as much as I want. I have to let Camryn be in control of this situation, as much as it is killing me.

I lean against the wall and slide down it until my ass hits the floor. Reaching over, I grab my guitar, and place it firmly in my lap. I guess it's another day of me singing to her from the hallway.

I strum the chords to one of her favorite songs from Boyce Avenue, *Every Breath*. She loves the acoustic version I play for her. The door rattles behind my back. A small smile appears on my face knowing that she is listening on the other side.

As I continue to play, each word that leaves my mouth is filled with despair, anguish, and defeat.

When the song ends, Camryn's cries ring from the other side of the door. Her tears shatter the last shreds of my control. A stab of guilt lays buried within my heart. I failed her. I should have been there to protect her. Tears slide down my face, but I quickly brush them away. She can't know that I am dying inside along with her.

"Don't give up on me, Jamie, please." A faint whisper embraces me.

"Never . . . I won't ever give up on you, I promise. I'll be right here, waiting until you're ready to let me back in." A hot tear rolls down my face. I pray that I sense a crack in her fragile control and she lets me in to take care of her soon.

IT'S NOW BEEN EIGHT DAYS since Camryn's attack. Every day I go to see her and every day she refuses to answer her bedroom door. I knock lightly at first letting her know it's me. When she ignores me, I knock harder. She still ignores me. Her ignoring drives me insane. I knock again on the door. Still no answer.

Sliding down the wall, I pull my knees up to my chest, and wrap my arms around them. I lay my head down on my knees. "Camryn, open up. It's me." She doesn't answer, not that I am surprised. I lay my head back, resting it against the wall. The events of the last week begin to run through my mind.

The source of most of our interaction comes in the digital form. I text Cami several times a day. Some go unanswered but most of them she replies. Although, usually short. My patience has run its course. I know she doesn't want everyone looking at her with pity in their eyes. But it's me . . . Jamie, her best friend, her boyfriend. A man who loves her unconditionally. I'm the guy who will never leave her side, no matter how much she pushes me away. I would never look at Cami with anything other than love in my eyes.

Last night Christian and I went to Aces after working at the studio all day. He told me that I should give her space, but how much space am I expected to give her? He's assured me she'll come around. This is more than Camryn being her usual stubborn self. My girl is shutting the world out. She is retreating, pushing everyone away.

Lincoln isn't handling things well either. He blames himself for what happened at his club. He looks like shit. Dark circles under his eyes from lack of sleep. Looks like he hasn't shaved in days.

Camryn's attack has affected all of us in one way or another. Somehow we all blame ourselves.

Shaking my head to clear my thoughts, I get to my feet and retreat to the kitchen where my mom and Gwen are sitting at the island. "She won't answer?" my mom questions.

Shaking my head, I pull the stool out. With my elbows on the counter, I lower my head into my hands. "I don't know what to do. I don't know what I am supposed to do to help her." I look over at Gwen. "Can you help me out here?"

"You keep doing what you're doing. She will come around. She let me in the room to take drinks and food up to her, but she hasn't spoken to me since the hospital. Christian said she talked to him the night she came home from the hospital. She hasn't spoken much since. All I know is that what happened to her is bad, Jamie. It's really bad. She hasn't opened up to me."

"The girls have been calling and texting her, but she hasn't allowed them to visit. Morgan has stopped by but Camryn refuses to unlock the bedroom door. Cami told her in a text that she doesn't want all the sorrowful looks."

"I've been here every day. I don't know how much longer I can take her ignoring me. I do what I need to do at the studio with Christian so I can head over here, hoping she will open the door. The band is being supportive of me missing practice. I don't know how much longer I can last before I knock the door down."

Gwen comes over to my side, and places her hand on my shoulder. "I know my daughter needs time. She will talk when she is ready. We are all being patient with her and giving her the space she needs. You, on the other hand, have never been one to sit back and be patient. Especially when it comes to her. Things are different with you, Jamie, they always have been." She raises her eyebrows at me, and places a kiss on my temple.

I get up from my stool and exit the kitchen. Taking the stairs two at a time, I knock on Cami's door. "Open up, Camryn. I'm not going away until you do."

Silence greets me as I stand in the hallway. Knocking again, louder this time, "I am going to count to three. If I get to three and this door is not unlocked, I am going to take it off the damn hinges. One . . . two . . ." I hear the lock click and the door opens. A disheveled Camryn turns before I can see her face. I walk in her room, and spot the flowers I sent her on her dresser. Camryn climbs back in her bed and pulls the covers up under her chin. Seeing how she looks crushes me into a million pieces. A suffocating sensation tightens my throat. The pain in my heart becomes a sick and fiery gnawing. I've never seen her look so destroyed.

My feet lead me to her bed without even thinking. Sitting on the side of the bed, I brush a piece of hair away from her face, placing it behind her ear. It breaks my heart when she flinches and then I realize the last man to touch her, other than the plastic surgeon, was that monster. "I've respected your wishes for as long as I can, I can't do it any longer. Camryn, please don't push me away. Let me be here for you. I don't know what it is I can do to help, but please don't push me away." Tears streaming down my face, my emotional pain just as prevalent as her physical scars.

Camryn looks up at me. Her eyes have a burning, faraway look in them. Raw hurt glitters in her hazel eyes. "I don't know what to do, Jamie. I thought pushing everyone away was for the best. I want everyone to remember the fun, energetic Cami. Not the broken, beaten Cami. Everyone knows I was raped. You know I can't handle that, Jamie. I just want my face to heal, then maybe I'll be able to face everyone. But right now, I know what I look like," she says with a wavering voice.

"Okay. Whatever you want to do, I'll respect, but please don't shut me out. I need to be here with you before they commit me."

She throws the covers back and climbs out of her bed. "We need to talk about you and me."

My heartbeat picks up. *What does she mean we need to talk about us?* I stand from the bed walking to her. I take her hands in mine, intertwining our fingers. "Look at me, please," I ask.

She brings her eyes to meet mine. "What do you mean we need to talk about us? What are you getting at, Cami?"

Tears form in her eyes. She looks up at the ceiling and when she meets my eyes again, the tears trail down her face.

"There is distance between us now. I know I'm to blame for that. I'm pushing everyone away. The thought of you touching me . . . scares me. I need you so badly. I yearn for your comfort. So many days that you were outside my door, I wanted to beg you to hold me, to make the memory of his touch to go away. But at the same time, the thought of having your hands on me terrifies me."

I pull my hands away from hers and gently wipe her tears away. She closes her eyes when I cup her face and tilt it up. "Please, look at me."

She opens her eyes to meet mine. "You are my girlfriend but you are my best friend. I will always be here for you, baby. I'm not going anywhere. I promise you, we will get through this . . . together." I say, my voice breaking.

Her chest rises and falls. I know this is not easy for her. With everything she is going through, our relationship should be the furthest thing from her mind.

"I can't promise you that. He robbed me of all my power and humanity that night. I struggle every day to try and figure out who I am now." She shrugs her shoulders, and tears puddle in her eyes.

With my voice barely above a whisper, "Do you need more time? Tell me what you want."

"I don't know what I want or even what I need."

Cami pulls away from me and paces the room. I don't say anything as she continues to wear a hole in the carpet. She turns to look at me, and my heart breaks. The pain in her eyes tells me everything I need to know.

She sits on the end of her bed and pats it for me to sit next to her. Her cold hands take mine. Her face clouds with uneasiness. She becomes more uncomfortable as the minutes grow.

Pain seethes in her eyes and I can't be the cause of any more pain she has to endure. "We just started seeing each other, Jamie. This is a lot to handle. And this is my burden to bear, not yours. It's not fair to you. I don't want this to end, but I understand if you do." A few tears run down her cheek. She ignores them and picks at the bed of her nails.

"Look at me, Cami, because I'm only saying this once. You are not a burden to me. You are my girlfriend and my best friend. Nothing, and

I mean nothing will change that. No matter how long it takes you to recover, I will be by your side. Do you hear me?"

She simply nods, but I continue on.

"Please, stop with the 'I deserve better' bullshit. I want you and only you." I lean in kissing her forehead, then her nose. She doesn't pull away, thank God.

A pained smile teases her lips. "Just please don't ask me to talk about it, Jamie. I can't do that yet. Not with you at least."

I lean down to look Cami in the eyes. "What do you mean you can't talk to me?"

The hurt and longing lay naked in her eyes. She looks away from me. Taking my finger, I gently place it under her chin. "Talk to me."

She bows her head, her body slumps in despair, unshed tears about to erupt from her well of sadness and pain. "I can't talk to you about what he did to me. Imagine the worst, Jamie. You know what condition I was in when Lincoln found me. If you knew what he did to me, you would never be able to look at me the same. Everything . . . would change." She wipes the tears away.

When she tries to speak, her voice wavers, "I can't handle that right now. I'm barely hanging on. I struggle with how you look at me now already. I can't promise you I'll ever be ready to open up to you." Her expression is grim as I watch her.

A suffocating sensation tightens my throat. How could she think that? I try to push my anger away, to see Cami's point of view. To see why she would say this. I take a deep breath in before I speak. My hand moves gently to stroke her cheek. "Nothing you say will change how I feel about you. Nothing."

MY MOM, GWEN, AND CHRISTIAN sit around the island, their eyes fixed on me as I come down to grab some snacks. "So . . . I'm assuming she let you in?" Christian says with raised eyebrows.

"Yeah, she let me in after I threatened to take the door off the hinges. She told me she can't tell me what happened yet. She's taking a shower. I told her I would grab some snacks, and head back up to hang out for a while. I figure I can work on the new piece with her and maybe get her mind on something else."

"Let me make the two of you a sandwich." Gwen digs through the refrigerator, placing the lunchmeat and mayo on the counter.

My mom pats my arm. "Be patient with her, Jamie. She will talk when she is ready. Don't push her."

"I know, Ma. I just want to spend time with her. Help her get through this. I just got her as mine, I refuse to lose her."

A huge smile emerges on her face. "I always knew the two of you would end up together. It just took you kids some time to figure it out."

Once Gwen finishes with our sandwiches, I grab my guitar, and throw it over my shoulder. The door to Camryn's room is still open, so I just walk in.

Camryn startles, standing with the towel tightly secured around her body, revealing the bruises on her chest above her breasts. The bruises are now a shade of light green with a yellow tint to them. I can only imagine what they looked like ten days ago. She stands frozen, surprise siphoning the blood from her face. As if she realized what I'm seeing, she lifts her arms to cover the marks on her chest.

Dropping my guitar on the bed and the tray of food on the nightstand, I break the distance between us. Taking her hands in mine, I gently pull her arms away from her chest and hold them out in front of me, noticing her arms are red with scabs I hadn't seen before. Taking my hand, I gently move them up her arms. She tries to pull her hands away, but I tighten my hold on her arms.

"Let go of me, please," she speaks in a suffocated whisper. I immediately let go. I don't want her to fear my touch.

"Cami, what did you do? Why are your arms bright red with sores on them?"

She averts her eyes so she isn't looking at me. "You wouldn't understand." Her voice barely above a whisper.

"Try me."

She lets out a sigh before she continues. "I need to scrub him off of me. I can feel his touch and smell him. I need that to go away."

I rub my hands up and down her arms. "Baby, you are clean. He isn't on you. He will never touch you again." I dip my head down to hers. "Do you hear me?"

"Baby. Come here." I pull Cami against my chest, caressing my hand up and down her back. Leaning down, I place a soft kiss on the top of her head. My heart swells with joy when she allows me to comfort her.

Cami stiffens and pushes me away. Her eyes wide. "Take your shirt off. Now!" She yells. Her hands shake as she lifts them to cover her mouth.

Not knowing what the hell is going on, I do as I'm told. With one swift pull, I grab the shirt from behind my neck, yank it over my head then toss it on the floor. Camryn's chest is heaving as she tries to breathe. She slowly walks over to me, leaning in to smell my chest. She pulls back, pointing to the bathroom. "You have to take a shower. Now."

I look at her dumbfounded, raising my hands in the air, questioning her, "Why do I need to take a shower?" She doesn't answer my question, rather she screams with tears soaking her cheeks, "Now, Jamie! Go take a shower!"

"Please?" When she says the word please, that was my undoing.

"I'll do it, I just don't understand why I have to."

With eyes wide, she takes a deep breath. "You smell like him."

Without asking anything else, I head to the bathroom, stripping off the rest of my clothes. I turn the shower on and jump in before the water is even warm. I grab the sponge lathering it with shower gel, then scrub my body down.

Camryn has the fight of her life ahead of her. She's been violated in a way no one ever should be. That bastard took something from her that she will fight to get back. My girl, my Tink, is a fighter. This will be the fight of her life, and I can only pray that she comes out the winner. This can't break her. I won't allow it to.

I can only stand by and support her anyway I can. Do whatever I have to to ensure she feels safe again.

I wash myself at least four times making sure the scent is off of me. She said her attacker smelled like me. Bile rises in my throat. I'll never wear that cologne again. Every time she smells it, she'll connect it to him. Camryn has always joked and said I smelled like home. Home is where we're supposed to feel safe. Will she ever feel safe again? Will she feel safe in my arms?

My fingers pull on my hair as I wash it. My body begins to shake uncontrollably. I lean down, placing my hands on my knees. Fury almost chokes me. My own anger and hurt can no longer be controlled. Tears are falling from my eyes. I've been holding it all in trying to stay strong for Camryn. I'm not sure how it's even remotely possible but in this moment I feel as helpless as she does.

Minutes pass, after I straighten, sighing loudly, I slam one fist against the other. I just got my girl, I can't lose her. I won't lose her. I couldn't be there for her then but I will damn sure be here for her now.

Once the water runs cold, I exit the shower, wrapping a towel around my waist.

Returning to Camryn's room, her step falters when she sees me. Drops of water are running down my chest still. Her eyes are wide as she stares at my chest. I see her eyes glance down at my abs, then work their way back up to my chest where my colorful tattoos are. Her cheeks have a tint of pink to them. My girl is embarrassed. She extends her arm out to me without looking me in the face. "Here, these are my dad's, but they should fit."

Taking the clothes from her, I return to the bathroom to dress. When I walk back in the room, Camryn is already in bed propped against the headboard with pillows behind her. She has the comforter pulled up around her chest, tucked below her elbows.

She pats the bed next to her. Walking over to the bed, I stand next to it. Tears fill her eyes and stream down her face. "Are you sure?" I murmur.

She nods her head. I climb in with her. I let her lead this dance because I don't know what will cause her to feel panicked. She lays her head on my shoulder. I put my arm around her, pulling her against my chest. She leans in, takes a deep breath, inhaling my scent.

"You smelled like him just now. That's why I thought it was you behind me in the hallway. When he came up behind me, he put his arms around me. He started to kiss my neck, then he nipped my ear. I didn't pull away because I thought it was you, Jamie. He smelled like you. He had the same cologne on."

Cami looks away from me before she continues. She looks down at her hands, then begins to pick at her fingernail. "He led me toward the storage room. That's when I put two and two together and knew I was in trouble."

She looks up at me. "I'm sorry, Jamie. When I left Lindsey upstairs, I told her I was going to let you and Christian know we were upstairs. But when I came down and saw you, I was pissed. I didn't come up to the table because I saw you there with a girl. I didn't know it was Tabitha. I thought some random girl was flirting with you and you were letting her touch you, so I headed to the bar where Lincoln was at. I had a drink over there and talked to Lincoln for a little bit, then headed to the bathroom. If I would have just walked over to you and Christian, this never would have happened."

I gently wipe the tears from her cheeks. "Cami, there is no one else I want. You have no reason to be jealous of anyone. I only have eyes for you, baby. What happened that night isn't anyone's fault. We can play the 'woulda, shoulda, coulda' game all day long. Nothing is going to change what happened. We can only make sure you get past this." Leaning down I look her directly in the eyes. "I promise you, you will. We will. I'll make sure of it."

I AWAKE WITH A START and jolt upright from the makeshift bed I made on the floor. My heart is pounding in my chest. Camryn is thrashing around in her bed crying for help.

I throw the blanket aside and rush to Camryn's bed. I'm afraid to touch her. I've always heard not to wake a person from a nightmare, but I can't sit here and watch this.

"Camryn, baby, wake up," I say, hoping she hears me.

"Someone help me! Help me!" she screams.

Fuck this, I have to touch her. I quickly pull her into my arms, cradling her against my chest. "Wake up, Tink. Please, wake up," I say softly near her ear. My hands move slowly up and down her back.

She yanks away from me. Her eyes darting around the room.

I hold my hands up. "It's me, Tink. It's Jamie. I won't hurt you."

"Jamie, he was there. He was touching me." Her voice fragile and shaking. She hugs her knees to her chest and begins to rock.

"I know it feels real, baby, but it's not really happening. You're safe now. He can't hurt you ever again."

"Not physically, at least," she whispers to no one in particular, unspoken meaning behind her words. She remains absolutely motionless for a moment. I reach out to stroke the damp hair from her face.

"Come here, Tink." I reach out to touch her hand and she clutches it.

Camryn scoots over into my lap, placing her arms around my neck. She nestles her head into my neck and begins to cry.

"Shh, baby. It was a nightmare. You are safe, you're in your room at your parents' house. He's not here. He will never touch you again, I promise."

Camryn lifts her head up, wiping the tears from her face.

"Thank you for staying the night."

"Is it okay if I stay the rest of the night in your bed with you? Just to hold you while you sleep."

"I'd like that," she whispers.

"You are not in this alone, baby. I'm not going anywhere."

I scoot up her bed, settling against the headboard. I hold open my arms, "Come here. Get comfortable."

She lays her head on my chest again. I pull my phone out of my pocket. I scroll through my library, in search of a particular song. I grab the earbuds from the nightstand.

"Here, listen to this song. This song says exactly how I feel."

She places the earbuds in her ears, repositioning herself on my chest.

I hit play on the song. *You Got Me* by Gavin DeGraw.

As the words play in Camryn's ears, she looks up at me with a small smile on her face. I will always be there for Camryn, even when she isn't strong enough to withstand the mind games that a trauma like this causes. Like the song reminds us both . . . when the demons try to get to her, she will never be alone. *She's Got Me.*

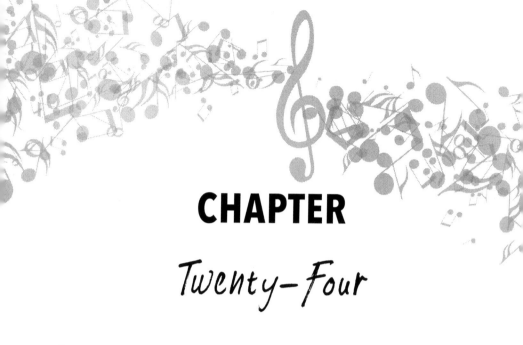

CHAPTER

Twenty-Four

Camryn

A LIGHT KNOCK AT MY door draws my attention from the romance novel I was reading on my Kindle. I open it and I'm not surprised to find Jamie standing before me with a huge smile on his face. His guitar hangs off his shoulder and he carries a bowl of popcorn.

"I thought you had practice tonight with the guys?"

He breezes by me and into my room. He makes himself comfortable by setting the popcorn on my nightstand and his guitar on my bed. "We got done early, so I thought I would stop by to see you. Maybe watch a movie or play a few songs that I have been working on."

"Let's hear the songs."

"I'm gonna start with one of your all-time favorites." Jamie nestles comfortably on my bed with his back against the headboard and his guitar across his lap. I plop down on the bed and wait patiently for him to serenade me. His fingers move effortlessly across the strings of his guitar and after a few chords I know exactly what song he's playing. *On My Way* by Boyce Avenue. This is my favorite song of theirs . . . Jamie knows this.

I'm stunned at how graceful his fingers strum the guitar strings.

The words to this song ignite goosebumps across my skin. Jamie reaches the chorus, and every word is sung with power. As though every word he sings is meant for me. A few tears trickle down my cheek. I love this man with every fiber in my body. Knowing that I have him, I'll be okay in this world. He is mine and I am his.

The last lines of the song spill from his lips, "Cause I'm on my way, on my way." This is one of my favorite songs and the words speak volumes. It's funny how Jamie knows the perfect song to help me heal.

"Thank you. That was beautiful."

"I'm glad you loved it."

IT'S BEEN TWO WEEKS SINCE my attack and I finally feel comfortable enough to see my friends. I've only texted them since the night at Redemption. My physical wounds are gone, but emotionally, I'm a wreck.

Nightmares continue to plague me most nights. A few times, my parents, Jamie and Christian witnessed me thrashing around in my bed. They comforted me when I woke up disoriented and terrified. Each nightmare is the same. Me trying to fight that bastard off. The first few nights after my attack, Christian hovered over me, watching me like a hawk after our nightly cocktail session. No matter what I try, every time my eyes shut, I'm transported to that night.

Karsen keeps insisting I should contact Claire, the rape victim counselor. But I don't feel comfortable talking to a stranger. Instead I have opened up to Karsen a little.

I sent an email to my boss, Shelby, a few weeks back, requesting a leave of absence. She assured me that my job is secure, and to take as much time as I need to recover. Thankfully, I have enough reviews submitted to cover me for a few more weeks.

I don't spend much time downstairs with the family. It's a ritual of mine to head down once everyone has gone to bed. Christian caught on to my habits early on and usually he joins me at night. He's been spending most nights here rather than at his apartment in the City. I have never been much of a drinker, but the alcohol helps me fall asleep.

Jamie has been over almost every day. He's a light in this turbulent storm. Times that I feel I am lost, drowning in my emotions, he makes me feel cherished . . . loved. Being in his arms makes me feel safe.

I'm brushing my teeth when a light knock hits my door. Shock hits me when Shelby walks into my room. I wipe my mouth with the towel, and walk over to her.

"Hey, sweetie, I have been trying to get a hold of you the past week. You haven't gotten back to me. I figured I would pay you a visit. I hope you don't mind?"

Shaking my head, I gesture toward my bed for her to sit. "How did you know where my parents' lived?"

"I went through your HR file. You have your parents' name and number as your emergency contact. After you sent me the email advising me what occurred, I immediately reached out to your mom to check in on you. I hope you don't think I am being too intrusive, but I was worried about you."

"It's okay. I'm not upset. My mom never told me she spoke with you."

"I asked her not to. I knew I would be in town, and hoped you'd see me as I need to talk to you face to face."

Tilting my head to the side I study her expression.

What do you mean you need to talk to me face to face? About what?

My heart rate picks up. "Oh, God, are you firing me?"

She shakes her head repeatedly, "No, no, sweetie. Your job with *Key Notes* is secure. You don't have anything to worry about there. Take as much time as you need. I have Kara covering your schedule until you tell me you are ready to return. Until then, you focus on healing. On getting yourself better."

Smiling at Shelby, I thank my lucky stars I have such an understanding boss. I'm not sure how many other employers would have given me this much time off.

"I don't want to pry or stick my nose where it doesn't belong." She takes my hand in hers and I look at her inquisitively. "You are not alone in this, Camryn. Your family and friends don't know what you are going through. They will never understand the emotions you are battling every day. I, on the other hand, do. I know *exactly* what you are going through."

My brows furrow as I try to process what she is telling me. The words come out before I can stop them. "What are you trying to tell me, Shelby?"

"I understand completely and wholeheartedly what you are going through. I was raped in college. I was a young and naive freshman. Never having lived in a big city before, I left a party alone after drinking too much. A man grabbed me and dragged me into the bushes behind my dorm building. I didn't know if I would survive what he did to me. I blamed myself for drinking, for leaving the party alone. I knew better . . . at least, I should have known better. I was ashamed of what happened, therefore, I didn't tell a single soul. Nightmares began to plague me and I withdrew from my friends, my grades were slipping. I would wake up screaming in the middle of the night. My roommate finally went to the resident advisor. She put two and two together. My RA sat me down. Once I was able to open up to someone, I felt better. I no longer felt like I was going through it alone. My RA put me in touch with her mother, who was a therapist here in New York City. After speaking with her, I was able to tell my parents what happened. My therapist, Gayle, never looked at me with pity in her eyes. She never made me feel ashamed, that it was my fault. She helped me get through the toughest time in my life, Camryn. A time that I didn't know if I could get through."

I swallow the large knot in my throat. "Shelby, I had no idea. I am so sorry."

She places her hand on my knee. "Sweetie, I didn't tell you all of this so you could be sorry for me. You don't want people feeling sorry for you, so don't you go feeling sorry for me. I told you all of this so you know that you are *not* alone. Let those who love you do exactly that . . . love you."

Shelby pulls me into a hug. "I am a survivor. You, too, will get through this. It will take time, just know that you are not alone, Camryn. Do you hear me?" She rubs my back.

She draws back to look at me. "I also have a few other things I would like to discuss while I am here. For starters, I want you to think long and hard on this one. I don't need an answer until January. There is an opening at the New York office. I am offering you the position. I know you love LA, but I think with everything that has happened, being close to your family will be good for you."

"What? Are you kidding me?" My heart sings with delight. I get to come home. I get to be closer to Jamie and my family. I could not ask for anything more.

She laughs. "No, I am not kidding you. The position is yours if you want it. It's actually a promotion with a salary increase. You will still have your column, but they are looking to add a few more reviewers to highlight more bands in each edition. Your column is hugely reviewed, and brings a lot of buzz to the magazine. All of the pieces would be submitted directly to you. You will have control on what bands to highlight. Well, that is, if you take the position." Shelby smiles at me.

I squeal and throw my arms around her neck. "Oh, my goodness, Shelby. My first thought when I saw you standing in my room was that you came to fire me. Now you're offering me a position here in New York . . . with a promotion."

"I don't want your answer today. I gave you a lot to process."

Shelby stands, and I do the same. She hugs me again and pulls out a business card from her handbag. "Here is Gayle's card." She places it in my hand and closes my fingers around it.

"I spoke to her the other day, I told her that I was coming to see you. I didn't tell her much, just that you were someone special to me, and you needed someone to talk to. What you tell her is completely up to you, Camryn. I am just a phone call away, as well. Anytime you want to talk, feel free to call me. Whether it is to discuss business, the promotion, or how you are feeling, or coping with everything."

Walking Shelby over to my door, I hesitate. Turning to look around my room, I walk out into the hallway with Shelby. This is the first time I have left my room during the day since I came home from the hospital.

With Shelby by my side, a sense of relief washes over me as I walk down the stairs. I know that I have someone who understands my feelings. Someone who knows exactly what I am going through. I have someone to talk to now when I feel panic squeezing the air from my lungs. I think I can make it like Shelby did. She is a survivor and I will be too one day.

My hand touches the card that Shelby gave me in the pocket of my sweatshirt. A smile appears on my face as I flip the card around in my pocket. The card is more than just a name and a phone number, it's the road to healing myself. A way that I can let go of this pain. A way that I can begin to move forward. I need to find myself again and regain my life back.

I am surprised to see my three girlfriends, my mom, and Jamie sitting in the living when I come down the steps. They all turn to find me standing there with Shelby. A huge grin lights up Jamie's face. A warmness fills my heart seeing my friends here today.

Yes, Jamie has entertained me, helping keep my mind off of things when he visits, letting me open up at my pace, but the smile on my face today is the first genuine one I have had in a long time. Knowing that I am not alone and that Shelby can relate to what I am going through lifts a huge weight off of my chest. I only hope that one day I feel like myself again. That I will be able to laugh uncontrollably rather than cry. In time, my emotional wounds will heal like my physical ones have.

And they'll heal with my friends, my family, my Jamie to help me every step of the way.

AFTER I SEE SHELBY OUT, I head into the kitchen with my friends. There's a spread of food on the island, courtesy of my mom. I think my mom is as excited as I am to have the girls over. She probably sees this as a step to my recovery. It may be a small step, but it's a step in the right direction.

"Gwen, thanks for putting this together. We could have just ordered something from Tony's. Sort of like old times when we all hung out here on Friday nights," Morgan says.

We all grab a stool around the island while my mom shuffles

around the kitchen getting everyone a cup filled with ice.

"I'm not going to ask you how're doing. I don't want to upset you today. I think I can speak for everyone, we just wanted to come hang out and laugh like usual. Just know we are here for you if you ever need us," Lindsey speaks first.

Smiling at Lindsey, I nod my head. I understand where Lindsey is coming from. I don't want to talk about how I am feeling, and I certainly do not want to talk about what happened.

"So, fill me in on what I've been missing?"

Morgan quickly responds. "I saw that guy from the band, you know the one you worked with before. I ran into him at Starbucks the other day. He was asking about you and gave me his card. He asked for me to give it to you. He said something about getting together with you for drinks."

Morgan slides the card across the counter. Jamie's eyes lock on the card. I notice he wrote 'call me' across the top.

Jamie walks over and reads the card over my shoulder. He picks the card up and rips it up into several pieces, then walks over to throw it in the trash.

When he returns by my side, he raises his eyebrows at me, as if inviting me to say something. The smile that emerges on Jamie's face does not go unnoticed. I lean up and kiss him softly on his lips and whisper, "I'm yours and only yours."

We all sit around enjoying the lunch my mom prepared for us. Listening to the girls talk about regular day-to-day things makes me realize how much I missed my friends. They love me. I know they would never judge me if I would have allowed them to visit sooner. But I love them even more for respecting my wishes and waiting for me to be comfortable with visitors. I am one lucky girl to have the friends I have and the family that God blessed me with.

MY KNEE BOUNCES AND MY eyes scan the room. I've picked the skin on my thumb so much, there's a pinhole of blood dropping. My stomach clenches tight and my heart races. I'm nervous as I sit in the reception area waiting for my name to be called. My appointment is for three-thirty, and, of course, I arrived early. I was uneasy when I called to schedule my appointment earlier this week, but I know I need to do this. I need to be able to talk to someone. I need to be able to find an outlet for the emotions that I am feeling. Shelby told me that Gayle worked wonders for her, so I am praying that I will be able to find a way to move forward with my life—and with Jamie. My fear of being able to be intimate with Jamie cripples me.

Jamie squeezes my hand and brings my mind back from my wandering thoughts. He's been my rock through this. I've been able to talk to him and he's never pushed me. He won't meet the therapist with me, but having him here with me is the support I need. The door to the reception area opens and an older woman, probably in her sixties, steps out from the doorway. "Camryn Townsend," she calls.

My legs feel wobbly as I stand. I follow the woman down a hall as she directs me to an office with a few leather chairs and a leather sofa with a couple of dark wood tables scattered around the room. The one wall is lined with bookcases filled with books. The other wall displays framed diplomas, which I assume are Gayle's.

After a few minutes of me observing my surroundings, a woman enters the room, shutting the door behind her. She is very attractive for being an older woman. I'd have to say she is in her late fifties, possibly early sixties. Her short, salt and peppered hair is styled very elegantly. She extends her hand to me introducing herself, "Good afternoon. I'm Dr. Gayle Cummings. Welcome."

I shake her hand, "Hi, I'm Camryn Townsend. Shelby Kemper referred me."

Gayle sits across from me in a chair, while I sit on the sofa. "Nice to meet you. Today we'll take things slow.

"Um . . . I'm not sure if you know the reasons why I'm here. But . . ." My voice catches in my dry throat. I cough to clear my throat, but it only makes it worse.

Gayle stands from her chair, walking over to the table where a pitcher of water sits. She pours a cup, returning to where I am sitting, still coughing. She hands me the glass. I slowly take a sip. Once I am able to speak again, I tell her, "I was attacked at a club about a month ago. I'm sure you can figure out the rest." Gayle doesn't speak at first. She reaches for her pad and pen on the coffee table, placing it on her lap. "I am sorry to hear what you endured." The room is filled with so many unspoken questions. Will she want the sordid details? Will she put the pieces together? I don't want to talk about what he did to me. I want to talk about what I need to do to get past this.

I've told the detectives exactly what he did to me. I told Christian and Jamie what they need to know. They saw me that night, they don't need the vivid details of what that monster did to me ingrained in their head.

Gayle watches me, waits for me to speak. When I don't, she asks, "How are you doing?"

I shrug, not knowing what to say. Do I tell her the truth or lie? Do I tell her at times I feel like I'm drowning? Do I tell her that during the attack, I wish he would have killed me? I'm supposed to be completely open with Gayle.

I take a deep breath. "I'm . . ." I pause a moment. "There are days that I feel like I'm dying inside, broken and devastated. I'm tired of crying. I'm trying to get back to normal."

"It will take some time for you to get back to normal. You suffered a tragic event. What you are feeling is quite normal for rape victims."

"I don't want to be a victim. I want to be strong, not feel weak. There are days that I am so angry, that I want to punch something."

"Having anger about the personal violation is probably the healthiest reaction, because you turn the pain outward instead of inward." Her tone solemn.

Lifting my head, I study her. "I have nightmares. I'm usually back in that room, where I can smell him. I can feel his breath against my neck. I'm alone, wishing someone would come."

I press my lips together, my eyes watering. I look at the ceiling willing the tears to stay at bay. I will not cry. I will not let that bastard make me cry anymore.

"You survived, obviously you did the right thing," Gayle says matter-of-factly.

"I blame myself for wearing that promiscuous outfit that I did for the masquerade. I blame myself for going to the restroom by myself. I knew better. We always do the buddy system, never go anywhere without a friend. But I was at my best friend's nightclub. Of all places, I thought I was safe.

"Camryn, this was not your fault," she says firmly.

This is not your fault. Everyone tells me this. I've even told others that it wasn't their fault. Sometimes it's harder to convince ourselves than others.

Gayle and I talk for the entire hour-long session. I like how she puts me at ease. She would ask a question, and allow me time to process my feelings and figure out how to express them regardless of how long it takes me to gather a response, formulate my feelings. Basically, figure out how to get through this so one day I can get past this.

My mood seems suddenly buoyant. I feel good as I walk back to the reception area where Jamie waits for me. I feel like there is hope at the end of the dark tunnel. This is not going to be my only session. I walk up to the counter and schedule my appointments for the next month. Knowing I have sessions with Gayle scheduled, I leave the office with a small smile on my face.

MY MOM AND I HAVE been up since the crack of dawn preparing our Thanksgiving feast. The turkey has been in the oven since six o'clock this morning. I am responsible for making my famous broccoli casserole and Stove Top stuffing. My mom cringes and refuses to make Stove Top, so it's left up to me.

Hours later, Jamie's mom walks into the kitchen with a pie in her hands. Jamie's dad, Christian and my father trail behind her each holding a dessert.

"What do you have over there?" I ask pointing to her hands.

She laughs. "You know exactly what I have. Keep your little hands off of it until after dinner." With a pointed stare, she continues, "The

top is perfectly smooth, so you can't sneak some without me knowing."
She smiles. Michelle's chocolate mousse pie is my favorite.

Holding my finger up to mimic scout's honor, "I promise to keep
my fingers off the pie. But I can't make any promises as to how many
pieces I will eat today."

A smile appears on her face. "Sweetie, you can eat the entire pie, if
you'd like. You know I make it special for you. Jamie was given instructions to bring the rest of the desserts over with him. I even baked double chocolate chunk-cookies and another one of your favorites, oatmeal
scotchies."

A squeal escapes from my lips and my hands flail like a little girl. "I
am going to gain a hundred pounds by the end of the day with all these
goodies."

My mom leans in placing a kiss on my cheek. "It's nice to see you
smile again, sweetie."

A smile radiates on my mom's face. I know when I hurt, she hurts.
Mom hasn't pushed me to talk about that night. She has given me the
space that I need to cope with it.

I fear leaving the house. My therapist visit was the first time I
stepped outside the safety of my parents' house—my childhood home.
I feel safe here. Like no one can hurt me while I am under this roof. I
have spoken to the detectives a few times, but there aren't any leads on
my case. I fear it will end up being another unsolved case on a shelf
somewhere. I think, deep down, that is another reason why I haven't left
the house. That monster is out there somewhere. He could be preying
on someone else. I don't know if I will ever feel one hundred percent
safe and secure knowing he could be walking right beside me.

CHAPTER
Twenty-Five

Jamie

IT'S A TRADITION FOR MY family to spend Thanksgiving with the Townsends. The women spend the day in the kitchen preparing the feast while the men watch football on the big screen. Mark and my dad offer to help, but they're ushered out of the kitchen. The women claim they get in the way, more than they help. I ran a few errands this morning, grabbing a few bouquets of flowers on the way home.

Walking through the Townsend's front door, my eyes ping around the room searching for Camryn. Glancing down the hallway, I spot her in the kitchen with our moms. I stand in the hallway admiring her appearance. It's nice to see the smile plastered on her face. I haven't seen it enough recently. Lately, when she notices me looking at her, she forces a smile, but it isn't a true one. To see my girl smiling, makes my heart beat faster. My girl is making progress.

Camryn and her mom notice me before my mom does. Walking over to both of them, I hand them their bouquet of flowers. Leaning down, I kiss Gwen's cheek. "Thank you for having us for dinner."

"Oh, sweetie, you are always welcome here, this is our tradition." She grabs the dishtowel to dry her hands. "You know my door is always open, even without an invitation," she says, patting me on the shoulder before she walks into the dining room, removing two vases from the breakfront.

Camryn walks over to where I am standing, tilting her head at me. "Are they for me?"

I laugh. "Maybe, maybe not."

She bites her lip to stifle a grin. "Well, if they are mine, they are beautiful. They are my favorite flowers. Whoever is on the receiving end of them is one lucky girl." She's barely able to hide the laughter from her voice.

I can't help myself. I throw my head back and roar with laughter. No matter the situation, she can always make me laugh.

Leaning down I place a soft kiss on her cheek, igniting a rosy color blush to spread up her neck. I think I embarrassed her by kissing her in front of my mom. I have kissed Camryn like that a thousand times but I guess knowing that she's my girlfriend now made her a little self-conscious.

DINNER WAS DELICIOUS, AS USUAL. I lean back against the sofa, my hand rubbing my stomach that is completely full. Between all the food and desserts, my ass needs to hit the gym hard this weekend.

A few hours pass, my parents have already left, Christian is getting his stuff together to head back to the City. With platters of food in his hands, he walks out of the kitchen toward me. "Hey, you want a lift home?"

Camryn walks out of the kitchen. She has a look on her face that I can't read. I walk over to her and place my hands on her cheeks. "What's that look for, baby?"

Her eyes veer away, but I hold her face firm in my hands. "Tell me. What's wrong?"

Cami's eyes peer over my shoulder to Christian, and then back to me. "I don't want you to leave yet. Can you stay for a little while?"

A smile appears on my face immediately and I pull her close to my chest. I'm happy she asked me to stay with her. Each day I see a little bit of the old Camryn. The Camryn that I fell in love with, my best friend. Squeezing her tightly, I whisper close to her ear, "I will stay as long as you want me to, baby." I place a soft kiss on the top of her head.

Turning to Christian in the foyer who is saying goodbye to his parents, I say, "Hey, I'm gonna hang here with Cami for a bit. I'll meet ya at the gym in the morning. Eight or so?"

"Sure. That works for me. Good night, sis. Your broccoli casserole kicked ass, as usual."

"With the pound of butter I used to coat the croutons and the four bags of Swiss cheese, you'll definitely need the gym in the morning." Camryn laughs, and grabs my hand pulling me toward the stairs.

I follow her to her room with her hand securely in mine. I rub circles with my thumb on the outside of her hand. She turns, giving me a genuine smile. When we reach her bedroom door, she turns, then leans up on her toes to place a soft kiss on my lips. I wait to see if she will take this kiss further. Camryn has been navigating this ship for the past month. I will not push her to do something she isn't comfortable with. Being in the same room with her is good enough for me. She kisses my lips slowly again, then feathers soft kisses along my jawline, to my ear. She whispers, "Thank you for staying."

Cami pulls back to look at me. A smile appears on my face the moment I see how happy she is. I would stay everyday if it would guarantee me that smile on her face at this very moment.

Hearing footsteps, I turn and see Camryn's parents coming upstairs. Mark walks toward his bedroom opening the door. He turns to look over at us, smiling at me before he enters his room. Camryn walks into the room with her flowers, then heads to the bathroom, closing the door behind her. Gwen takes my hands in hers. "You know that I love you like a son and you mean the world to Camryn. I want to thank you for always being there for our girl."

"You're welcome."

"You know as well as I do, she is a fighter and she'll make it through this, I know she will. We just need to be patient with her, but with you, it's always been different. You know exactly what she needs. You always have. I need to thank you for helping bring my daughter back to me. You did something that I couldn't do."

"I don't know what I did different from anyone else."

"Whatever you did, it worked. I know it will take time, but it was a blessing to see her smile today. I've missed her smile, Jamie. You make her smile, you bring that joy out of her. You always have. The relationship the two of you have is special. I want the two of you to hold on to that feeling. It is rare and when it comes along you have to seize the moment, hold on to it and fight for it. Thank you for not letting her push you away like she has the rest of us. I know in time, she will let the rest of us back in, but knowing that she has you eases the ache in my heart." She squeezes my hand.

I pull Cami's mom in for a hug and rest my chin on her head. "You know I love your daughter, I'm not letting her go. She can push, but she will never push me away. She's stuck with me."

She pulls back to look at me. "Cami is one lucky girl to have you." We hear the bathroom door open and Cami emerges in a pair of yoga pants, a tank top, her face is clean of any makeup, and her hair is piled on top of her head in a messy bun.

"Good night, sweetie," her mom says, as she walks down the hall to her room, closing the door behind her.

I turn and walk into Cami's bedroom, closing the door behind me. Cami is moving pillows around on her bed, piling them up by the headboard. "So, what shall we do? Are you in the mood for a movie or do you want to just hang out and talk?" I ask as I walk over and sit on the edge of her bed.

She turns toward me, a mischievous grin on her face. "I was thinking we could just cuddle and talk. If that's okay with you?"

I jump eagerly on the bed and position my back against the pillows. I open my arms to her. "Come here, I am totally up for cuddling and talking."

"Can you take off your shirt, so I can feel your skin?" she asks quietly. With one quick movement, I pull the shirt from behind my neck, tossing it at the foot of the bed. Cami crawls up the bed, settling next to me. She lays her left leg over mine, cuddling into my side laying her head over my heart.

"Did you know that hearing your heartbeat soothes me?" she says in soft whisper.

The tenderness in her voice makes me smile. "I had no idea."

Her fingertips slowly move over the intricate lines of my tattoo on my chest. With every move of her fingers, my skin sears with the intensity of her touch. Her soft breath against my skin. She takes a deep breath. "Can I tell you something and you promise not to ever look at me differently?" Her finger continues circling along my chest.

My left hand caresses her soft, silky skin. "Cami, there is nothing that you can say that will make my feelings change for you."

Cami looks up at me, her eyes are gentle and contemplative. "After talking to Gayle the other day, I feel like a weight has been lifted. That I can finally talk about what I'm feeling, what I'm struggling with. I've never been one to be afraid of anything. I've never been one to keep anything from you, so I don't want to start now. I want to tell you what happened that night."

My fingers stroke her arm soothingly. "Cami, you don't have to tell me."

"No, it's time. I'm ready," she says firmly.

She lays her head back down on my chest. I don't say a word, I don't want to stop her from talking. "I fought back. The more I fought, the rougher he was with me. While he had the knife against my neck and was raping me, I wished he would have pressed it harder against my throat and killed me. I didn't want to live through it. I wanted to die, Jamie. For the first time in my life, I couldn't bear the thought of taking one more breath." There was a faint tremor in her voice.

"I prayed he'd press the blade harder, wishing he would pierce my throat. I would have rather have died than be coherent while he stripped me of everything I've known as a woman," she says in a choked voice.

Hearing that she wished she died, kills me. Curses fall from my mouth. I know what she looked like when we found her. Those images are burned into my mind. I don't think I will ever be able to erase them. As morbid as it sounds, I can understand her feeling in that moment that she just wanted to die . . . I'm eternally grateful that she's stronger than that.

I clasp Camryn's hands in mine, intertwining our fingers. She looks up at me with unshed tears in her eyes. "I'm tired of holding everything in, Jamie. I want what we have to be special. I won't let that bastard take that away from me. I won't give him that power."

"He doesn't have any power over you, baby."

Her tears run down my chest. I hold her tightly as she relives that murderous night. "How come I feel like all my fight has been stripped from me? I'm trying not to be weak, to allow him to have this kind of power over me. Am I wrong to feel this way?" She pulls away from me, wiping the tears from her face. She sits up crossing her legs over each other while she fidgets with her fingers in her lap before looking back up at me. I swallow hard, trying not to reveal how angry I am.

"Look at me," I take her chin and tilt it up to meet my eyes. "Do not let one night define you. That's not the Camryn I know. The Camryn I know would fight to get back what she feels she lost."

"I'm exhausted from fighting to be stronger than I feel. Some days I feel like I am a puzzle shattered into a million pieces, and I'm trying to find a way to put myself back together. I try to hide my emotions from everyone, but I'm failing miserably."

"You'll never know how strong you are until it's your only option." My arms tighten around her. "It's only been a month and I have seen how much you have changed. You're stronger every minute of every day you are fighting, we all see it. When you pass a mirror, I've noticed you can look at your reflection again. You can talk about the rape without breaking down."

I let her speak without interrupting her. As I look at her sitting before me, once again I realize that there isn't one particular thing that I can do to help her get past this. She needs to do this on her own, at her own pace. I can only be there to offer her my support and hold her hand along the way.

I lift our hands to my lips, placing small kisses on her fingers. "He did not rob you of your power. He just made you question it, but I'm here to make sure you get it back."

I gather Cami into my arms to hold her snug against me. She lays her head back on my chest. "I'm not going to surrender to this bastard. I want to be able to move on, to live my life like I was before this happened. I want to be able to leave the house without feeling like I could be walking down the same street as him."

"It'll take time, baby. Tell me what you want from me, what I can do for you. I never want to push you, I only want to be there for you every step of the way."

Cami leans in and places a soft kiss over my heart. "Knowing you are always here is the best remedy for this right now. Just promise me that you will be patient with me. There will be times that I will have my freak out moments."

I place my finger under her chin, lifting her face to look at mine. Once her eyes meet mine, I tell her without any hesitation, "I'm not going anywhere. No matter how hard you push, or how stubborn you will be, I will be there for you. Whether it is to hold you while you cry, or hold your hand while we walk down the street. There isn't anywhere else I plan to be than by your side for the rest of my life."

"I'm gonna ask you something now." Her hazel eyes were full of life, pain, and unquenchable warmth. "Can I kiss you?"

A smile spreads across her face, a genuine smile. "Yes, Mr. Banks, you may kiss me."

There's my girl.

I lean down and place a gentle kiss against her lips. The touch of her lips is a delicious sensation. I raise my mouth from hers and gaze into her eyes. She pushes up against me to meet my lips again. Cami showers kisses around my lips and along my jaw. The kisses are slow, sensual kisses that drive me wild. As much as I want Cami to be in the lead, I can't take the slow kisses any longer. My mouth swoops down to capture hers. She parts her lips granting me access to her tongue. My lips recapture hers, more demanding this time.

I pull away from her and gaze into her eyes. It was too easy to get lost in the way that she looks at me. I try to get a read on her thoughts. I don't want this to go any further than she is ready, plus her parents are down the hall, so I need to put the brakes on this. "Cami, we need—"

"No, I don't want to stop."

"Cami, we can't do this here. Not in your parents' house. Are you even ready for this? I don't want to push you if you're not ready for this."

My last words are lost as she smothers me with her lips. She climbs on top me, and straddles my waist. She draws my face to hers with a renewed embrace. My hands move slowly down the length of her back. The air around us electrifies. She leans down so her body is flush with mine. My heart hammers against my chest. Pressing her core against my groin, my cock becomes harder by the second. *Down, boy,* I repeat over and over in my head. I want Camryn. I want to make her mine. I have the unwavering desire to mark her. Make her scream my name. I've dreamt of this moment for years. But it isn't going to happen with her parents under the same roof.

My hands make their way to her face, cupping her cheeks. I'm able to break away from the breathless kiss. She bites her lip, and a groan passes through my lips. My chest heaves uncontrollably. My dick strains against my jeans. I will surely have an indented zipper mark on my cock. Besides the indent, I'm going to have a major case of blue balls when this is done with.

I reach out to stop her from grinding her hips against me. My resolve is seriously only as strong as the clothing that separates us at this point. I take a deep breath to gather my bearings.

"I can't do this with your parents down the hall. When we make love for the first time, it will be perfect. Just you and me. It needs to be that way. I've been waiting a very long time for you to be mine, and I will do everything in my power to make sure it's just right and, more importantly, that you're ready."

I use her parents being down the hall as an excuse. As much as I want Camryn, I need to make sure she is doing this for all the right reasons. I don't think she is ready. She may think she is, but if I am being honest with myself, I don't agree. I don't need the first time we finally make love to be the beginning of the first moment of regret she has. Right now, her decision is just as much about me as it is about her. Protecting her physically and emotionally. I will be her shield, no matter how long it takes, to fight off her inner demons.

Unshed tears fill her eyes. Camryn blinks quickly in an attempt to hold them back. I run my thumb across her face to catch the tear before it falls. I pull my thumb to my lip, kissing the tear.

"Don't cry, Camryn. I don't ever want you to cry because of me. Not unless they are happy tears. It will happen between us. Just not tonight, sweetheart."

Cami shifts herself off of me, snuggling close to my side. My arm wraps around her, pulling her close to me. Kissing her on her head, I say, "Come home with me tonight. Pack a bag for the weekend, stay with me." I pray she'll say yes. I need to be alone with Camryn, so I can have her all to myself.

Cami looks at me as her cheeks color under the heat of my gaze.

"Okay," she says quietly. She climbs off the bed, leaving me in her room. I hear her knock on her parents' door, then open it. She doesn't say anything, rather, I hear Mark say, "The keys are on the table by the door. You can use the car for the weekend. Just be safe."

I hear Cami, "Thank you, Daddy. Love you."

CHAPTER

Twenty-Six

Camryn

THE WEEKEND WAS PERFECT. I spent the last few days with Jamie in the City. We did a little Christmas shopping on Black Friday, saw *Wicked* on Saturday, and went to dinner at one of my favorite restaurants, Carmine's. Jaime has given me the mental space I need. I know he's allowing me to decide when I'm ready to be intimate with him and what I realized after leaving my parents' house is that I needed to be okay with leaving the safety net of their home and going back to Jamie's house before I have sex with him. Taking that successful step is allowing me to gain back some semblance of my life back . . . my new normal.

Jamie went to the studio this morning, leaving me in the apartment alone. I was a little apprehensive at first, but after giving myself a few pep talks, I forced myself to settle down. This is the first time I have been completely alone since I was raped. When Jamie left this morning, I felt a little uneasy, but I realize that I'm not always going to have someone with me twenty-four-seven. It's not practical and sure as hell not realistic.

My phone chirps from the coffee table. The screen reveals I have a text from Morgan. I haven't talked to her since the girls were over for lunch.

Morgan: Hey chickie. Linc said you're in the city. He said you stayed with Jamie this weekend. ☺ How did I not know about this??

Me: I needed a change in scenery and Jamie is exactly what the doctor ordered.

Morgan: Any plans for today? You with Jamie?

Me: Jamie went to the studio. I am at his place still ☺

Morgan: Do you want to meet up? Possibly go for coffee? If not, I can bring some to you.

Me: I think it would be good for me to get out. Regular spot. How about 10:30?

Morgan: Sure thing. There are a few things I need to talk to you about.

Me: Is everything okay?

Morgan: I'm hoping. I gotta jump in the shower. Cya in a little bit. Love ya

Me: Love ya too. Cya soon.

I call Jamie. He picks up on the first ring. "Is everything okay?" he asks, panicked.

I laugh. "Yes, babe, everything is fine. Morgan sent me a text asking if I want to meet up for coffee and I'm taking her up on her offer. We're gonna meet at Starbucks around ten-thirty. I just wanted to give you a heads up in case you came home and I wasn't here."

"That sounds like fun. You haven't spent much time with Morgan lately."

"She offered to bring the coffee here, but I think it will do me good to get out for a little while. I can't keep hiding from the world, if you know what I mean."

"Babe, you weren't hiding from the world. You were taking some time for yourself. Time to heal."

"I know, but I think it's time to get back out there. I need to spread my wings to fly again."

Jamie laughs, "You better not spread your wings too far. The only place I want you flying is right into my arms."

I walk into Jamie's bathroom and turn on the shower. "Did you just turn on my shower? Are you naked?" he whispers.

"Wouldn't you like to know?"

He growls at me through the phone. "Knowing you are naked there all alone is going to give me a severe case of blue balls."

A laugh escapes my throat. "Your balls are going to be like two prunes by the time you get some relief. You can't blame me for my lack of trying. The situation with your balls is all your doing."

Jamie knows I am right on this. I get why he wouldn't make love to me. He wants to make sure that I am one hundred percent ready for it. Whether it be physically or mentally. I am leaning more toward the mental part.

I have expressed my fears to Gayle. There is a part of me that is terrified to cross that imaginary line that we have with intimacy. When Jamie touches me, it is always calm and gentle. Never do I flinch when he caresses my body. He has yet to touch me where I need it the most, where my body aches for him to touch. I know Jamie would never push me, never force me to do something that I am not ready for. I'm the one who tried to push Jamie. But he knows me better than I know myself. I want to make love to Jamie, but somewhere in the back of my head, I have this horrible fear that once we get to the part where we would actually have sex, I panic. Fear of being intimate with Jamie is what keeps me awake at night.

"Cami. Cami. Are you still there?" Jamie asks in the phone.

"Yeah, I'm still here," I say, slightly above a whisper.

"Okay. Do me a favor. Go in the kitchen, open up the drawer next to the fridge. There's a new bottle of mace that I picked up. Take it with you," Jamie commands.

"And, one more thing. Please text me when you get there to let me know you made it okay." I can hear the concern in his voice.

"I can handle that." Smiling I add, "You do realize that eventually my life needs to get back to normal."

"Yes, I know. I just need to know you are safe, that's all. Have fun with Morgan. I'll see you when I get home after rehearsal around seven. We have a show this week, so Parker wants to go over some things."

"Sounds like a plan. I shall have dinner prepared and waiting."

I WALK THROUGH THE DOORS at Starbucks, and I spot Morgan at the table by the window. I make my way over, and nudge the table with my hip. "Excuse me. Is this seat taken?"

"Took you long enough. I've been waiting five minutes," she says with a fake pout.

"You said ten-thirty, it is ten-thirty. I am right on time, my friend."

She points to the two cups in front of her. "I got your usual. I hope it's still hot."

I pull the chair out taking the seat across from her. She looks like shit. Not that I'd tell her that, but her usual chipper self is not shining through. I relax against the back of my chair, really studying her face. Her eyes are puffy with black circles lining them. Morgan always has her A-game on. She never steps out of the house without looking flawless. She could rock a trash bag with a bedazzled belt and still put some people to shame. Something is off.

"Why are you looking at me like that? Spit it out, Cami." Her eyes narrowing.

Fidgeting in my seat, I'm not quite sure how to go about this. Do I just spit it out? Do I ask her what is going on? Ugh . . . she is my best friend. I should be able to say exactly what is on my mind. I know she wouldn't have a problem telling me. I decide to just rip the band-aid off. Since the attack, we haven't talked much. There's been some distance between us. Another thing that asshole took from me.

"You look like shit."

She scoffs at my statement. "Real nice, Cami. I ask you to come have coffee with me and you tell me I look like shit." She averts my gaze, then picks her latte up, taking a long sip then placing her cup back on the table. She raises her eyes to find me watching her.

Raising my brows at her. "Really. You are going to get defensive with me? Spit it out."

She lets out a loud exaggerated sigh. "I haven't been feeling well lately. I forget what it feels like to sleep, since it's evaded me for some time now."

Her hands are on the table. She avoids looking at me as she picks at the loose piece of skin on her thumb. "Morgan. What's going on? This isn't like you."

When she looks up at me, there are tears in her eyes. I immediately grab for her hands, clasping them with mine. "I need to tell you something. Something I should have told you a while ago, but I didn't know how to." Her voice breaks.

I stare at my friend sitting across from me. I have never seen her look so distraught. We have always been able to tell each other anything. We may not like what we have to say, but we respect each other's opinions. In all the years that we have been friends, I can't remember a time where we had a disagreement.

"Morgan, what is it?" Her silence scares me.

Tears stream down her face, like a dam has broken. She pulls her hands away from mine to quickly wipe them away. I hand her a napkin and she crumples the paper in her fist. "The night you were attacked, Camryn, it was my fault. I was the last person in the storage room. Lincoln checked the surveillance cameras. It was me."

I gasp and my eyes widen. Her words repeat silently in my head. A sharp jagged pain erupts in my chest. I want to make sure I heard her correctly. I want to be angry for the carelessness, but I can't. Seeing Morgan's tear-filled eyes, I have to accept it was a mistake. She's beating herself up more than I ever could. It was a mistake. It wasn't done on purpose. I reach across the table, taking her hand in mine. "Listen to me. It is not your fault."

She tries to slide her hand free, but I tighten my hold. "Yes, it is. The security footage showed me leaving the room, and the guy waiting in the hallway. When the door went to shut, he stuck his foot in the doorway to stop it. We saw him bend down and put something in the door to keep it open." She swallows hard. Tears glisten in her eyes.

"That's when we saw him taking you in the room."

My breath quickens from her revealing what she saw. This is not Morgan's fault. It's not my brother's fault. It's not Jamie's. And, it's not Lincoln's. But they all blame themselves. There's only one person to blame—the bastard who raped me.

"Listen to me. I do not blame you. You were not the one who brutally attacked me. This is not your fault, Morgan. Shit happens, it was an honest mistake that you didn't stop to check if the door clicked shut."

She wipes her face with her free hand. Her gaunt face and swollen eyes tells me this information has been eating her alive. The guilt is tearing her apart. "Cami, how can you say that? If I would have taken a second to make sure, this would have never happened."

"Look at me. I have replayed the events of that night over and over in my head. There are a million things that could have been done differently. Maybe in the end, it could have changed things. We will never know. But the one thing I do know is, this is not your fault. Not to mention the bastard would have found another place if not the storage room."

Morgan sobs across from me. I get up from my seat to sit in the chair next to her. I pull her into my arms. "I love you, Morgan. I know it took a lot of courage for you to tell me that you were the last person in the storage room. Look at me. I'm doing okay. He didn't ruin me. It might still haunt me, but I'm surviving and moving on. I can't imagine the guilt that you have been carrying." I rub my hand up and down her back, trying to comfort her.

Morgan throws her arms around me and hugs me tightly.

"Okay, on a lighter note, I have something to tell you."

Morgan draws back to look at my face. "Have you slept with Jamie?"

Chuckling at her assumption, "I assure you, I have not slept with Jamie. When I do, you will be the first to know."

She wipes tears from her face and takes a sip of her latte. "Shelby offered me a position here in the New York office. It is a promotion, actually."

Morgan claps her hands together. "Oh. My. God. You are coming home to stay?"

"I don't know yet. I haven't given her my decision yet. I have until the middle of January to tell her. I need to weigh the pros and cons."

Morgan and I talk about the details of my promotion. In the grand scheme of things, there really aren't any cons except my friends in LA. She asks what Jamie's thoughts are on this. When I inform her that I haven't told Jamie yet, she scowls at me.

"Why are you scowling at me?"

"How long have you known this little tidbit of info? Why haven't you told Jamie?"

"Slow down there, killer. You are the first person I told. I pretty much know the decision I am going to make. I needed to do what was best for me, what is best for my career. I know Jamie will support my decision no matter what it is, but I needed to be the one who made it. I didn't want any outside persuasion."

Morgan squirms in her seat with excitement. "You know you want to stay here for Jamie. I know you love your job, but you love that man fiercely. You always have," she says with a devilish grin on her face.

I can only sit here and laugh at her reaction to my news. "Yes, I do love him fiercely. I can no longer deny it. Now if I manage to tell him that before you do that would be a great start."

The two of us sit there for a while catching up on things that have happened over the past couple of weeks. Even though the two of us were texting while I hid away in my room, she had a lot of things to fill me in on. One being that Lincoln was tossing around the idea of selling Redemption. I make a mental note to have a sit down with him, as well. I won't allow him to sell his club because he feels guilty for what happened to me.

"Hello, ladies," a male voice says behind us. The hairs on the back of my neck immediately stand. A wave of apprehension sweeps through me. My stomach clenches. My pulse begins to beat erratically from the sound of his voice.

I don't need to turn to see who it is, it's Chad. He has an eerie grin on his face. Morgan kicks my foot under the table. I look over to her, her brows are raised almost to her hairline. I try to hold my raw emotions in check, but it's a damn struggle. I don't know what is wrong with me. One minute I was fine with Morgan, and now that Chad and his bandmate, Buffer, are standing by our table, I am a complete mess. Trying to reign in my emotions, I squeeze Morgan's hand for support. She gives me a look, asking if I am okay without actually asking. I shake my head back and forth, subtly, so only she can see.

Morgan speaks up taking the attention off of me. "Hi, Chad. What brings you and your friend to these neck of the woods?"

He nods his head at me, but focuses his attention on Morgan. "The band has a few more sessions set up with Christian. We need to fine tune a few things before the album is finished. Buffer and I were in the neighborhood, figured we'd stop for a cup of coffee."

Chad turns toward me. "Camryn, what's wrong? You can't say hello?" The sound of his voice makes me cringe. I am suddenly trying my damnedest to keep my coffee down before it comes back up my throat and makes an appearance here on the table. I raise my eyes and find Buffer watching me.

"Um . . . Um . . . Hi," I say quietly, trying to avoid eye contact with him. Something feels off. Very off.

Morgan gets up, her chair making a loud noise as it scrapes along the floor. She nudges my shoulder, "We were just leaving," she says.

I reach for my handbag from the chair across from us, then stand to my feet. Buffer steps to the side giving me room to move. Chad, on the other hand, is so close to me. I inch myself back from him. He is invading my personal space. "I've asked about you a few times. Hasn't your brother or that friend of yours told you?" he asks. When he said that friend of yours, his jaw clenched. As if speaking of Jamie infuriates him.

"Camryn, why don't you meet up with us to have drinks? You'll have a good time. I promise," Buffer says then winks at me.

I shake my head no without answering either one of them. Chad frowns, "I didn't think your friend would tell you, but I thought your brother would have."

Buffer doesn't say anything else. He simply stands there staring me up and down as if I was something he wanted to eat. Like I was his last meal on the way to the death chamber. It's as if he is eye fucking me in the middle of the coffee shop. A devilish smirk appears on his face as he raises his brows at me. For someone who doesn't usually have a whole lot to say, his unspoken words and actions, speak volumes.

Finding my voice I say, "That *friend* is my boyfriend. There was no need for him to tell me you said hi, since you seem to ask about me whenever you are in the studio with them. They probably figured we would run into each other at some point while you were there." Why is he so concerned about my relationship with Jamie? "As for meeting up for drinks, I'm sorry, that's out of the question." I eye Buffer letting him know that his invitation has been declined.

Chad eyes me suspiciously. A cold knot forms in my stomach. I feel like my chest is about to burst. "Then I guess me asking you out on a date is out of the question since you have a boyfriend?" he says with a devilish grin.

I look him straight in the eye. "Yes, I have a boyfriend. The only dates I will be going on are with him." Why is he pushing the issue about me going out with him? It's not gonna happen so back the hell off, dude.

Chad leans in to hug me but I step out of his way, moving closer to Morgan. Chad's jaw clenches, his eyes slightly narrow when I move away. I don't want him to touch me. My nerves tense immediately when it hits me. The scent of his cologne. Oh, my God. I'm gonna be sick.

Bile rises in my throat. I clamp my hand over my mouth and make a beeline to the restroom. I make it to the toilet just in time before I throw up the entire contents of my stomach. I throw up a few more time before there is a knock on the door.

"Cami, it's me. Are you alright?" Morgan asks from the other side of the door.

I reach for the toilet paper so I can wipe my mouth. When I open the door, the look on Morgan's face almost knocks me over. I walk over to the sink, so I can splash my face with cold water.

"What the hell was that about out there? You look like you saw a ghost?"

Looking at my reflection in the mirror, my face is pale, but I have red blotches on my chest and up my neck.

I turn to see Morgan's concern. "If I tell you something, you have to promise that you won't think I am crazy."

She nods her head. "Of course. I would never think that."

Clearing my throat, I try to make sense of what I am feeling. "When he walked up behind us, just hearing his voice gave me chills. I was barely hanging on by a thread. Then when he leaned in to hug me, I lost it. He smelled like the man who raped me, Morgan. That night. The man was wearing the same cologne that Jamie wears. That is why I thought it was Jamie behind me. Then when Chad leaned toward me, that was all I could smell."

Morgan doesn't say a word. She stares at me for a few moments. "I don't think you are crazy. Those guys give me the fucking creeps."

"I'm sure it's nothing. But the scent of his cologne was too much for me to handle."

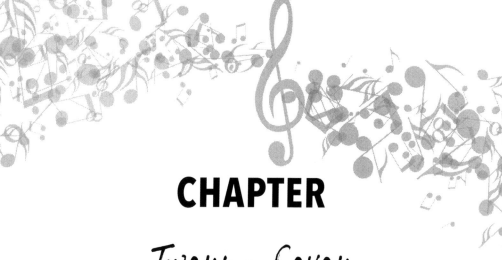

CHAPTER
Twenty-Seven

Jamie

A FEW DAYS HAVE PASSED since I last saw Cami. I miss her. Her lavender vanilla scent still lingers on my pillows, but my bed feels empty without her in it. Cami was only in my bed for a few days, but I'm like an addict and she is my drug of choice. I need my next fix of her, and I need it now. I've already grown accustom to her warm body wrapped in my arms at night, and her slow breaths lulling me to sleep.

She's supposed to come to Aces to watch Side Effects perform tonight. I offered to bring her with me, but she insisted that Morgan would pick her up. I would have preferred her to come with me since this is her first time out in a large crowd since the night at Club Redemption.

We have a few hours until show time, I am sitting at the bar, shooting the shit with Lincoln. I watch the guys up on stage getting their equipment set up for tonight's gig. Isaac, our drummer, is tapping out some beats, while the bassist, Alex, is fine-tuning his bass. Parker gives me a thumbs-up letting me know he is good to go.

A hand appears on my shoulder giving me a squeeze. The stool next to me slides out, then Christian signals to Lincoln. Lincoln slides a beer down to him, then he turns his attention on me.

"So, what's the deal with you and Cami?" he asks, his brows raised.

My mouth curves into an unconscious smile. I take a long pull on my beer before answering him. I'll let him stew for a bit. He knows my feelings for his sister. It's no secret—especially to him. I think every freaking person in a two-mile radius knows my feelings for Camryn.

"We're good. Things seem to be going smoothly."

Lincoln heads in our direction. "You guys up for shots or sticking with light drinks for now?"

"I'm good," I tell him as Christian nods his head.

"So, did this guy tell you he almost burned down his apartment while he was being a nosey prick?"

Lincoln lets out a hearty laugh, shaking his head.

Christian shoves my shoulder. I almost fall off the stool. "Look, dude, I already told you. I was making sure things were good with you and my sister."

I set my beer down after taking a drink. "Things were okay with Cami and me. You didn't need to be all Inspector Clouseau and shit with your ear up to the door."

Christian laughs. "I gave you my blessings with my sister, but I didn't say I was going to make it easy for you. You, my friend, need to step up to the plate. Lay it all out there. I want to see my sister happy again. Have you even told her how you feel about her?"

Lincoln stands there watching me—obviously stricken mute. He looks at Christian then back at me, like a damn volleyball match. He raises his brows to me, as if he's the judge and it's my turn now.

"Cami is special to me. You guys know how I feel about her. I'm in love with her. I have been for years."

Lincoln opens up a beer and takes a swig. "You know for such a smart guy, you are rather stupid. I have seen the way you have looked at Cami for years. You're gonna sit here and tell us that you haven't told Cami how you feel out of fear she might not feel the same way? Are you insane, man? I have sat back for years and watched the two of you go back and forth. The games the two of you play. Everyone sees it. We've been waiting for the two of you to see it. You've been wasting all this time over one little word."

Lincoln makes air quotes in the air, then says 'IF'. "If she feels the same way, if she wants you. If she is willing to see if things can work out between you two. You sure did give that little word a whole lot of power."

The look on Christian's face is priceless. He has a smug grin on his face, as if saying, duh, you dumbass. "Everyone knows how you feel about my sister, but Camryn."

After processing what Lincoln just said, I wonder if Camryn feels the same way, but was afraid that I didn't look at her that way. Have the two of us wasted years because we were both scared? I'm such a stupid ass. I can't believe I never had the balls to tell Camryn where I stand with her. If I could kick myself in the ass, I would.

"Dude, this guy knows his shit. It's like having a free session with Dr. Phil. Who would have thought Dr. Phil would show up in Aces tonight?" Christian says, pointing his beer bottle to Lincoln.

Christian turns his attention to me. "I gotta ask you something. Why did you and Tabitha break up? Don't bullshit me either. I want the God's honest truth," he asks.

I take a pull of my beer before I lay it all out there. I pick at the label. "The truth. I didn't love her. I couldn't see a future with her. I could never get those three little words to pass my lips." I finish my beer off and nudge the empty bottle toward Lincoln. He grabs another cold one from the case, and slides it in front of me. "I've never told a girl I love her. Those three unspoken words have ruined every relationship I've ever had."

Lincoln looks perplexed by this newfound information. "You mean to tell me that you never told Tabitha that you loved her and you dated her for over a year?" Lincoln asks.

Shaking my head, "Nope. I knew she wanted to hear them, they were just words that I never felt or could ever say. How do I tell someone I love them, when I didn't have my heart to give them? My heart was taken from me the moment Camryn stepped foot on the plane five years ago. Whether it was taken willingly or she stole it long before that, I'm not really sure." I shrug taking a long pull of my beer.

"When Camryn is by my side, I feel alive. I feel like I'm complete, the other half of my heart has found its way back to me. Yes, before you ask, I still have my balls." I stopped speaking and inhaled a deep breath. "You don't get it. I'm in love with your sister, dude." They just sit there staring at me when I finish talking.

"Lincoln, back me up here. You feel the same about Morgan?" Christian speaks up first.

"I get it, trust me, I get it. We know Camryn means the world to you. But don't tell *us* what she means to you, tell *her.* Show her how much you love her. You know how much she loves to see you perform, to hear you sing. Make tonight special when she comes. You need to go out on a limb, man. Camryn has been to hell and back. You have been there for her since we were kids, let her know that you plan on being there for her in the future. Tell her you love her. I bet money that she feels the same way.

I grab my beer and take a long swig. "You guys don't get it. We're seeing each other exclusively. I just haven't told her I'm in love with her. I got it covered. Stop with the advice."

"Don't get all defensive. I'm just trying to help. The two of you need to figure this shit out. And figure it out fast. She's only home till after the New Year, then she heads back to LA. Shit or get off the pot, dude. Make a move. Don't let her get back on that plane and take your sanity with her again." Christian shrugs matter-of-factly.

Lincoln looks at Christian like he has lost his mind. "What do you mean she's leaving in January? Morgan said she was offered a job here in the New York office, with a promotion. Morgan made it seem like it was a done deal that Camryn was taking it. It was a huge opportunity for her, one that she wasn't going to pass up."

When Lincoln notices the look of bewilderment on both mine and Christian's face, he holds his hands up in the air and backs away from the bar. "Look, I thought you two knew about this. My bad. Talk to Camryn. I'm sure there is a reason she didn't tell you yet."

A muscle flicks angrily in my jaw. Was she going to leave me again? Was she going to turn down this promotion? Was she even planning to tell me about it? I look to Christian and ground the words out between gritted teeth, "Did you know about this shit?"

He shakes his head. "This is news to me, man. I had no fucking clue. My parents haven't even mentioned it."

Lincoln speaks up. "Look, if it makes you feel better, she called me the other day when she heard I was contemplating selling Redemption. She didn't mention it to me either. It looks like she only told Morgan. Don't make a big deal out of this. Maybe she was waiting for the right opportunity to tell you."

"She has been with me since Thanksgiving. We've been inseparable for days. She slept next to me every night. Cami had every opportunity to tell me, yet she chose not to," I say through clenched teeth. My mind is a crazy mixture of hurt, deceit, and fear. I can't believe she kept this from me. How could she not tell me this little—hell, this big—tidbit of information?

Christian places his hand on my shoulder. "Calm down, man. I'm sure there's an explanation. Don't go all apeshit crazy and get pissed off. Give her the benefit of the doubt."

Taking a deep breath, I try and calm myself down. Talk myself off the ledge before I go balls to the wall on Camryn when I see her. "You're right. I'll wait it out. I'm sure she'll tell me."

IT'S ELEVEN O'CLOCK AND ACES is packed. Isaac announces five minutes to show time. We've gone over the playlist for tonight. The guys weren't happy that I've switched out a few songs, but they know the music, they can play the songs without any flaws. I look around the place—trying to see if Morgan and Camryn are here—when I spot them at the bar with Lincoln. I am proud my girl took a big step and came tonight. She's come a long way, and I love her more for fighting her fears.

For some reason tonight I am on edge. I'm not sure if my nerves are all over the place because of the bomb Linc dropped on me about Camryn's promotion or that this is the first time she has been out since the attack. Once Christian notices Camryn, he immediately heads in her direction. He throws his arm around her shoulder, pulling her body close against his side. Christian and I talked earlier today. He plans on staying close to her tonight to make sure she feels comfortable. It will definitely make me feel better, knowing she is with her brother.

Camryn spots me from across the bar. She grabs Morgan's hand pulling her with her through the crowd. When she reaches me, she stands on her tiptoes, touching my lips with hers. Her lips brush against mine gently. Raising her lips to mine again, she gazes into my eyes. My lips burn with fire from the contact. I want more. I need more.

"Hey, gorgeous. I missed you," she says in a silky voice. Damn, I want to take her right here and now.

Pulling her into my arms, I whisper, "I've missed you, too, babe. Are you staying for the whole set?" Biting her earlobe before pulling back to look at her face. She notices me watching her intently.

"Of course, I'm staying for the whole set." I want to ask her about this promotion, but now is not the time, so I push that thought out of my head for now

She leans in, kissing me again. Between each word, she plants a kiss on my neck, nibbles my ear, then my neck, and face before saying, "I don't plan on going anywhere except home with you at the end of the night."

When I hear those words pass her lips, "I wouldn't have it any other way, Tink."

Before she has a chance to respond, I hear my name being called, then Isaac is telling me to get my ass up on stage. Kissing Camryn lightly on her forehead, I help her get settled on the stool at the table near the stage. "Stay here, I'll be right over there." Pointing to the stage. "I'll be the one singing."

Camryn smacks my ass as I turn to head toward the stage. "I'll be right here. Make sure you put on a good show. I need a little entertainment tonight," she says jokingly.

I jump up on stage, grab my guitar from Parker, slinging it around my body. I have the jitters tonight knowing I am going to pour my heart out to Camryn through the words I wrote for her. I have always been good with words. These words came directly from my heart. Unspoken words that I have never said. I plan on telling Camryn I love her tonight. Not here in front of everyone at Aces, but definitely when we get home, when it's just the two of us. I can't contain the feelings I have for her. I don't see the point in wasting anymore time.

We start the set off with a song that I know Camryn will know is directed at her. Isaac taps out the beats, then I start to sing the words to *It Was Always You* by Maroon 5. My eyes lock with Camryn while I sing the lyrics. Every word that passes my lips meant for her. This song speaks volumes about how I feel for Cami. It's as if this song was written detailing our relationship. It's always been Camryn for me. It may have taken me some time to realize it, but I did. My entire life, the love of my life has been by my side. As the song says, we never crossed the line, but it's always been her. She has my heart, and it's about time I told her it's hers if she is willing to keep it.

Camryn doesn't look away from me the entire song. Her eyes tell me everything she is feeling. She discreetly wipes a tear from her face, not wanting Morgan and Christian to see her crying. She blinks several times, then focuses her gaze on me.

With each line I sing my heart out. Each word is filled with so much emotion. Emotions and feelings that I have been harboring for years.

Afterwards, we sing a few fan favorites to get the crowd into the music. The dance floor is packed with girls dancing and singing along with the lyrics. After a few songs, I slow things down with the song I wrote for Camryn called, *By Your Side*. With my guitar around my body, I feel my heart start to race. Isaac and Alex walk off the stage to grab a beer, while Parker stays with me. Only our guitars are needed for this song.

As my fingertips pluck the strings on my guitar, I can feel the music throughout my entire body. The rhythm of this song is steady, with a few smooth transitions to the chorus. The melody is soft. I grab the mic walking over to the corner of the stage close to where Camryn is sitting. I wink when our eyes lock and I blow her a kiss.

I'm nervous as shit tonight. I've put myself out there every time I perform. Nothing compares to the fear I have tonight. The words from this song come from my heart. I'm opening myself up for Camryn, for her to choose me, to love me.

The way we push, the way we pull.
I wouldn't change a thing

Through the years I've been fighting
Feelings I've been trying to hide

I capture Camryn's gaze with mine, analyzing her reaction to the unexpressed words that
have been living inside my heart for years. Her caramel colored eyes dart nervously back and forth. I search her face, trying to get a read on what she is thinking. I continue with the lyrics that I know will capture her attention.

You're the one who's got a hold on me
It's been you who has always had my heart.

You've held it in the palm of your hand,
Cradling it ever so gently.

I wonder what you dream about at night
It's only you I see when I close my eyes

Your smile that blinds me
Or your laugh that warms me

The entire song, I haven't taken my eyes off of her. Her eyes grow large and fill with tears. I can see there are so many thoughts running through her head. She has never been one who could hide her emotions from me. I watch the play of emotion on her face. Her lids slip down over her eyes as I sing to her. My eyes never leave her for an instant. This moment is about Camryn and me. I focus all my attention on her, as if it is just the two of us in this room. The sound of each pluck of the strings from Parker's guitar melt into the next as my vocals fill the room.

It took me some time to realize it,
But once I did, my heart only beats for you

For years I've watched us grow
Grow from friends to more

You know it in your heart
Even the times we've spent apart
You feel it too, I know you do

The huskiness lingers in my tone as I sing the last line.

Can we continue on this path from friends to lovers?

When the song ends, the entire room is silent. A few girls in the front of the stage wipe their eyes. I see Cami dab her face, then Morgan pulls her in for a hug. Morgan runs her hand up and down her back, then lifts her gleaming eyes to me. She gives me a thumbs up.

CHAPTER
Twenty-Eight

Camryn

JAMIE'S HAND IS CLASPED WITH mine as he pulls me into his apartment. Tonight was amazing. I was taken back a little by his performance tonight, but after seeing him on stage telling me how he feels, I realize my heart belongs to Jamie. It always has. As he stood on stage and performed those songs, it made it clear as day. I fall more in love with Jamieson Banks . . . my Jamie.

We've touched, we've kissed, but we have never actually made love yet. My body aches to be cherished by him . . . to have him inside of me. He never pushes me. Actually, I seem to be the only one pushing. He continues to put the brakes on our foreplay. I'm ready to take the next step. The thought of Jamie's hands on me doesn't terrify me, the way it would have weeks ago. My body craves his touch now, I need to rid myself of the visions and feelings that torment me and replace them with more pleasurable ones.

The poor man must have a severe case of blue balls my now. But at the end of the day, he has never once complained. I'm not sure if he stops because he thinks I need him to, or whether he stops for an entirely different reason. If I were to guess, I know it's because he wants our first time together to be special and doesn't want to feel like he is pushing me to do something I'm not ready for.

So tonight, I am taking control. Once the apartment door is shut, I free my hand from his then push his body against the door. His head draws back, his eyes are wide. I know I startled him with my movement. I have to say, I surprised myself. I have never been the aggressor in the relationship. The way Jamie focused his attention on me while performing sparked a raging inferno inside of me. One that only Jamie can put out.

His eyes move up and down my body, then lock on mine. He doesn't say a word while I slowly place my hands under his shirt caressing his ab muscles lightly with my fingertips. Jamie sucks in a breath, his muscles tighten under my touch. I trace the outline of his muscles, then gradually work my way over his chest. I focus my attention on his face trying to get a read on what is going through his mind as he continues to stare at me.

His jaw clenches, his eyes slightly narrow. Jamie is trying to control himself, fighting with the idea that I'm the one initiating this. He is the one who has always been in control of our make out sessions. Well, I have news for him, I plan on torturing him until the words "we need to stop" are no longer in his vocabulary.

My fingertips gently outline his nipples, causing him to suck in a quick breath. His nipples harden immediately from being teased. I gradually work my way back down his torso causing goosebumps to blanket his chest. I reach for the bottom of his shirt, pulling it up to reveal his beautiful body. His chest displays vibrant colorful designs inked on his skin. Jamie reaches behind the back of his neck, pulling the shirt quickly over his head, then tosses it on the floor.

Jamie's chest rises and falls fast and I can see that I'm having an effect on him. The fact he hasn't spoken a word since we entered the apartment says more than any verbal queues could tell me. The bulge that is straining against his jeans confirms it. I try to hide my smile knowing that I am capable of doing this to him.

My hand deliberately moves to cup his growing erection. Jamie leans his head back against the door, closing his eyes. Slowly, I massage him with my hand. My pulse quickens as his erection becomes harder from my touch. He is big . . . bigger than I remember.

A low growl escapes Jamie's throat. He lifts his head focusing his hazel eyes on me. His eyes shift from my eyes to my mouth, then to my chest, then back to my mouth. His tongue gently moistens his lips. His entire body tenses as I continue to massage his hardened erection. He wraps his arms around my waist pulling me flush against him, trapping my hand from moving.

With his one arm still wrapped around me, he takes his other hand placing a finger under my chin making me look at him. "Are you sure about this, Tink?" he asks with concern laced in his voice.

I nod.

"I need to hear you say it. I need you to tell me what you want."

Swallowing deeply, I tell him what he wants to hear. I tell him what I want him to do. What I need him to do. "I'm sure, Jamie." My voice shakes.

I stand on my tiptoes trying to get closer to his lips and whisper, "I want you to make love to me. I know you've been holding back, but I'm ready to take this next step." A little nervousness creeps up, but it's not because of what happened, it's because this moment is with Jamie. All about me and Jamie.

My lips brush against his, making my entire body tingle.

Jamie captures my lips with his. His tongue slides along to part them, causing me to open my mouth. Our tongues move slow at first, then our kiss grows heated. Jamie breaks the kiss, pulling away from me to cup my face with his hands. Immediately, I miss his lips on mine.

"I know you said you want this, baby, but if you change your mind at any time, we don't have to. I would never push you to do something you don't want to do," he says with trepidation in his voice.

I step back from him, and reach for his hand. I continue taking steps backwards toward his bedroom. "I've never been more sure of anything than I am of this right now. I know I'm safe with you. This is me telling you that I want you to make love to me, Jamie."

Unspoken words transpire between us as he watches me knowing I am giving him the silent okay that I am fine. My hands move toward my belt and Jamie stops me. "You are not going to undress yourself. That's my job."

He unfastens my belt, tossing it to the floor. Then his fingers unbutton my jeans. His hands touch my waistline causing goosebumps to cover my body now. The prolonged anticipation is almost unbearable.

He grips the hem of my shirt, slowly bringing it up my body and over my head revealing my black lace bra.

He scans my body slowly and seductively. His gaze slides downward taking in my body. My heart jolts and my pulse pounds. A look comes into his eyes, one that says he's so ready for this moment.

Taking a deep, unsteady breath, I step backward. An electrifying shudder reverberates through my body. Jamie reaches out, his strong hands grasp my hips, pulling my body flush against his chest.

Jamie places kisses on my chest, on the swells of my breasts and lightly bites my nipple over my bra. "No part is going to be untouched by me, baby."

My hands find the top of his jeans. I fumble with the button, then slide his zipper down.

"Let me help you out." His voice, deep and sensual, sending a ripple of awareness through me. Jamie quickly removes his pants and boxers, leaving him completely naked in front of me.

His tall figure moves closer toward me, leaving no space between us. He eases the lacy cup of my bra aside revealing my breast. He fondles one small globe, my rosy nipple is marble hard. His tongue caresses my swollen nipple as he continues his torturous attack on my breasts. My nipples are so sensitive, I could probably climax from just this.

Loving the reaction he is getting from me, he shows my other nipple the same attention, taking it into his mouth, sucking on my breast. A moan escapes me as his teeth bite down gently on my nipple. I need more than this, I need him inside me now.

I have dreamed of this moment. The moment that he would make me his. Mark me, claim me as his.

He unclasps my bra, and it falls to the ground, leaving my sensitive breasts exposed. He walks me backwards and the back of my thighs hit the mattress. Gently, he eases me down onto it. I scoot up the bed on my elbows, positioning myself against his pillows. He crawls up the bed, like a lion stalking its prey. Every hard inch of him presses against me as he leans down to kiss me. His tongue sends new spirals of ecstasy through my body. His lips are hard and searching.

He closes his lips against mine, "Are you sure about this, baby?" Jamie hesitates, measuring me for a moment.

Cupping his face in my hands, I speak with quiet, but desperate, firmness, "I need this, Jamie. Please . . . Don't make me beg you."

With a simple nod, he understands what I want, and most of all, what I need.

Jamie's lips hover before they claim mine. His kiss sends the pit of my stomach into a wild swirl. His tongue explores the recesses of my mouth. The kiss starts off gentle, then becomes demanding. He isn't just kissing me, he is claiming me.

His mouth works its way to my neck, nipping, sucking and biting with every kiss.

His hands move gently down the length of my body. He reaches my jeans and gradually lowers them down over my hips. I lift my butt off the bed, giving him the help he needs to move this along. Slowly, he glides down the bed, removing my jeans and panties at the same time.

His talented tongue makes a path down my ribs to my stomach. His teeth scraping as he goes. He murmurs his love for each part of my body. His movements are slow, gentle, and smooth. Every kiss, lick, or bite has a purpose and it is driving me crazy. I ache for him to be inside of me. Everywhere he kisses, my body ignites. My insides are melting from the pleasure of his touch. My hands rub the bare skin of his back and shoulders, digging my fingernails into his skin.

A delightful shiver of want runs through my body. My body trembles from his warmth. "Relax, baby. This is all about you tonight."

The more Jamie touches my body, the more my heart thumps erratically.

Every time my body rises from the bed he makes no attempt to hide the fact that he is watching me. He is enjoying working my body into a frenzy.

He spreads my legs further apart, leaving me completely exposed for his exploration. Slowly, he works his way to my core with light kisses on the inside of my thighs. His fingers slide through my folds as he plays with me like I'm his own guitar. His fingers are like magic. His tongue is his instrument.

My hips rise from the bed as I grip the sheets. Jamie's hand presses my body back down on the bed as he feasts on me. He licks, sucks, and nibbles on my clit. Bursts of fireworks are forming behind my closed eyelids. My back arches as I scream his name. My entire body is a raging inferno. He inserts one finger, then two stretching me a little. He moves his fingers methodically in and out of my body. Then a third. Oh.My. God.

His lips suck on my clit while his fingers are hard at work. I don't know which feels better, the pressure from his fingers, or the sensation of his mouth. Either way, I know I'm not going to last much longer. I grab his hair, holding his face against my core. My hips grind against his face as my body pulses with need. "Jamie . . . Oh, God . . . Don't stop . . . I'm coming . . ."

Once my body stops trembling, Jamie withdraws his fingers from me. He licks each finger slowly. My breath hitches. That was sexy as all hell.

"Did you like?" His voice husky from arousal.

I nod. A grin emerges on his face before his lips begin to sear a path up my stomach, taking my breast in his mouth. When he finally manages to work his way up, my lips recapture his. The taste of myself on him makes me want him more, if that's even possible. He did this to me. I've never felt this with anyone and I don't think I ever will again.

I reach over, opening the drawer to his nightstand. My hand reaches around until I find what I am looking for. I pull a condom out of the box, handing it to Jamie. "We need to use these . . . for now," I say in a broken whisper.

Unfazed, Jamie tears the wrapper open, sheathing his hard erection with the condom. He nudges my legs open wider as he slips the tip of himself into my opening. I push my heels into the mattress and dig my nails into his shoulders. I gasp in delight feeling his erection against my core.

Gradually, inch by inch, Jamie presses himself inside of me. I inhale sharply as my body adjusts to him.

"Ah, baby, you're so tight. You feel so good." His cheek brushes along mine.

Slowly he pulls out of me, then enters me again. With each thrust of his hips, he gets deeper inside of me. My hands work their way to his ass, wanting to feel all of him. He withdraws again, and I wonder if he wants to prolong this. But I don't think I'm capable.

"Jamie, don't stop. I need you."

"You're mine, Cami, you always have been."

"Oh . . . Jamie . . . harder . . . please."

He thrusts his hips harder, filling me. "You are so beautiful. God, Cami. I can't get enough of you," he says in between each thrust.

My body is on fire, my core is tingling with desire. As my climax ricochets through my body, a moan of ecstasy slips through my lips. My whole body floods with desire. "Jamie, don't stop. Just like that. Keep doing that." I bury my face into his throat as my body begins to tremble from my orgasm.

He whispers in my hair, "I love you. I've only ever loved you. I've never loved anyone else before, Camryn. You own my heart. You always have."

A soft gasp escapes me. His declaration, makes my heart beat rapidly. He thrusts his hips a few more times, reaching his climax. I can feel the pulse of his erection as he empties into my body. I wish there didn't have to be something between us, no barriers, but a condom is a must.

Tears began to pool in my eyes. Cupping his face, "I love you too."

WE MAKE LOVE SEVERAL MORE times throughout the night. I'm not sure what time it is, but the sunlight is sneaking through the blinds. With my head on Jamie's chest, I can hear the beat of his heart. A heart that beats for me . . . and only me, as Jamie told me over and over last night.

I slowly trail my fingertips along the design on his chest outlining his tattoo. I admire his body art. I could stare at the tattoos that cover his arms, shoulder, and chest for hours. Jamie's hand begins to trace little circles on my left arm as he holds me against his chest.

This is where I want to spend the rest of my life. Wrapped in the arms of the man I love. The man I want to wake up every day next to and spend every day with. Jamie represents everything from my past and I hope he represents everything in my future.

After those three little words left my mouth, I felt as though a wave of euphoria washed over me. I have never told a guy I love him because I knew all along my heart belonged to Jamie. Hearing Jamie tell me how much he loves me only reconfirmed what I already knew. This man is everything to me. He is my world. He always has been and always will be.

Was I a little shocked when Jamie told me I am the only one he has ever said those words to? Absolutely. He wrapped me in a silken cocoon of his love. I would have thought he'd told Tabitha he loved her. I guess that's what I get for assuming.

Jamie's voice breaks me from my string of thoughts. "Can I ask you something?" he asks quietly. I almost didn't hear him.

"Sure."

"No secrets, right?" He speaks in an odd, yet gentle tone.

"Of course, no secrets. We didn't do secrets before, so we aren't going to start now." I say a little more harshly than how I wanted to. Why he is accusing me of keeping something from him? We've been down this road before and I refuse to go down it again.

"Were you going to tell me about the job offer?" His soothing voice says matter-of-factly.

I pull away from him and sit up, wrapping the sheet around my body, then cross my legs over each other.

"How do you even know about that?" I study his face unhurriedly, feature by feature trying to get a read on what he is thinking.

His eyes are now studying me with a curious intensity. He's upset with me. Did he actually think I wouldn't tell him about this? He is one of the reasons why I'm going to take the job. To stay in New York—with him. I want to see where this relationship is going. I knew the moment

Shelby offered me the job I'd take it. Granted, the salary increase and the promotion are amazing, but the opportunity to stay here with Jamie outweighs any financial incentive.

He picks at a piece of lint on the blanket avoiding eye contact. "Lincoln told me. He dropped the bomb on me right before you got there. I didn't have a chance to talk to you about it before our set started. Why wouldn't you tell me?"

I reach for his hand, clasping it with mine. "Look at me." He needs to look at me when I tell him my answer. I want him to see how much love I have for him. His dark eyes bore into me while I begin to speak.

"I had every intention of telling you. There wasn't a doubt in my mind that I wanted this when Shelby offered me the job. Yeah, the raise is amazing. Yeah, having more people work with me on my column is great. But those aren't the reasons why I'm taking the job. You are the main reason I am taking this position. I want to live my life waking up next to you, and loving you."

His eyes are wide as if I shocked him with my response. "I wanted to surprise you with the news. I had plans for the two of us going to dinner to celebrate, then afterwards I was hoping we would head to my parents' house to fill them in on the details. I wasn't trying to keep anything from you. No secrets."

He cups my face between his hands. "I'm sorry I thought the worst. I didn't know if you wanted to go back to LA to get away from here. To get away from the bad memories. I was dreading taking you to the airport. It would have been like *deja vu* for me. The day you got on the plane to head to Stanford, that's the day my life changed. In that moment, I knew I was in love with you. You took a piece of my heart with you to California."

A soft gasp escapes me. I hesitate, blinking with bafflement. "Wait. Did you just say you've loved me since I left for college? Why didn't you ever tell me?" I can't believe he's felt this way for years and never told me.

His gaze lowers, as does his voice. "I didn't want to chance telling you in case you didn't feel the same way. I wasn't willing to risk our friendship. For years people always assumed something was going on between us. We were always together, always joking around, always flirting. It was how we were. But the moment you weren't going to be there next to me, everything changed. I felt like a part of me was missing when you boarded that plane. I know it sounds absurd, but I struggled for months when you first left. Yeah, we talked all the time, pretty much every week, but it wasn't the same. I was used to looking at your beautiful face every day."

Licking my lips nervously, I say, "Since we're being honest here. I think you are the reason my relationships never worked out. Not that there were many of them. I always seemed to compare them to you. They weren't funny like you, they didn't make me laugh, treat me like you did. In the end, they just weren't you. I confessed to Morgan a while back that I thought my feelings for you were more than friendship. She kept pushing me to tell you, but, like you, I was afraid that you wouldn't feel the same way. She told me that I would never know unless I told you. So when I found out that I would be home for three months, she told me this was my opportunity to put myself out there. To be honest with you about my feelings. I had intentions of telling you, but I wanted to put some feelers out there to see if the feelings were reciprocated."

Jamie reaches out with his powerful hands, and he yanks me up toward him. His arms encircle me, one hand on the small of my back, while burying his other hand in my thick hair. His expression grows serious. "Well, my love, the feelings are definitely reciprocated. I am head over heels in love with you and I wouldn't have it any other way. I'm just thankful, that you feel the same way. I'm glad you took a chance on us and opened your heart to me."

Gently he eases me down onto the bed. I moan softly as he lies on top of me. My hands caress the planes of his back. I am loving the feel of his body pressed against me. I could definitely get used to waking up like this every day. The weight of him is my protection against the world in this moment.

I quickly sneak a kiss in. "I'm in love with you too."

THE PAST FEW DAYS HAVE been a blur. Most of my time has been spent wrapped in Jamie's arms in bed. We have christened every piece of furniture in his apartment. I can't get enough of him. The more time we spend together, the more I want. He surprised me with breakfast in bed this morning before he left for the studio, so I figure I'll return the favor and bring him and my brother lunch.

When I enter the studio, Christian turns to see who is coming in. He gives me a quick smile then nods his head toward the table, and continues working the gadgets on the sound board. Jamie is rocking his head to the beat of whatever is being played through the headphones.

I place the bags of food on the table near the door and walk over to stand behind Jamie. He doesn't realize that I am here yet. I place my hands on his shoulders, giving him a firm squeeze, and place a kiss on the side of his neck. His head tilts to the side, giving me more access. I give him a series of slow, shivery kisses as I make my way to his cheek. He slides his earphones off. He crooks his finger at me. I lean in and kiss him on the lips. The kiss deepens as he slips his tongue against mine. A few more kisses on the lips, then he swats my ass as I turn to walk back towards the table.

A chill courses through my body, causing my skin to crawl. I turn to look into the studio and I see Chad.

"Why is Troubled Pasts here? I thought they finished up last time they were in town."

"Chad said he wanted to make a few changes to a song. Christian had them come back in. I can't wait to get the douche out of here and back on a plane to LA."

Christian says into the mic, "That's a wrap. We got what we need." Buffer's eyes fixate on mine through the glass as he says, "Now that's how it's done, sweetie."

My entire body starts to shake. My drink slips from my hand, smashing on the hardwood floor. My shaky hand covers my mouth as my eyes widen in horror. I stare at Buffer through the glass as the blood drains from my face. His eyes are trained on me as he laughs with the guys in his band. The look on his face causes goosebumps to blanket my body.

Buffer's eyes are locked on mine. Jamie jumps up from his chair, quickly pulling me into his embrace. "What's wrong, Camryn?" I don't answer. "Baby." He shakes my arms. "You're scaring me."

Even as Jamie holds me, my body won't stop shaking. I manage to get out. "That's what . . . the guy said . . . to me when he . . . finished raping me," I say in between shaky breaths. "It's him."

Buffer exits the recording booth and I pull away from Jamie's hold. I lunge at Buffer striking him in the face. I hit him repeatedly, before Christian grabs me, wrapping both of his arms around my body holding me tightly against his chest.

Jamie lunges for Buffer once Christian has me. They fall to the floor. Jamie throws punch after punch, making contact with Buffer's face.

Christian whispers in my ear. "Please, calm down. Listen to me, Cami. We will take care of this. You are safe now."

Chad and another band members pull Jamie off Buffer.

Jamie breaks from their hold and makes his way to me. I have no intention of allowing myself to be his prey again. I will fight back with everything I have. He can't hurt me. Jamie and Christian are here. I thrust against his hold, trying to break free. But the more I fight, the tighter Christian's hold becomes.

"I'm gonna fucking kill him. I swear, I'll kill him with my bare hands," Christian mutters. Christian reaches for the phone, calling 911. He tells the operator that an officer is needed to arrest a rape suspect and provides his name, my name, and the address to the studio. When Christian hangs up the phone, all hell breaks loose again.

"You're crazy. I didn't touch you," Buffer screams.

Jamie lunges at Buffer again knocking him to the ground. Jamie lands several punches on his face. The members of Troubled Pasts just stand there watching Jamie and Buffer wrestle on the floor. I'm surprised they are just standing there. His friends are watching him get the shit kicked out of him. Jamie lands another few punches, as he yells, "Come on. Hit me. You get off on beating and raping innocent women. Come on, you pussy. Hit me."

Buffer tries to slide out from under Jamie, but his knees are holding down his arms. My brother lets me go, placing me in a chair. "Sit there and don't move!" he yells.

Christian scrambles to pull Jamie off of Buffer.

Jamie is immediately by my side. He places his hands on the side of my face. "Are you okay?" I nod my head. Jamie pulls me into a hug. I can feel his heart pounding in his chest.

Chad pulls Buffer up from the ground and throws him against the wall. "What the fuck did you do, man? Did you rape Camryn?" he yells.

Buffer pushes Chad away from him, then says, "I didn't touch that bitch, she's crazy."

That comment scores him a punch to the face from my brother. My brother grabs the sleeves of his shirt, pulling him up. Faint scars appear on his forearm from where I scratched him.

"Really, dude? She's crazy? How'd you get those marks on your arm?" Christian replies sharply.

Buffer doesn't answer my brother's question. He turns his attention to me and his lips turn up into an evil smile. My brother slams him into the wall. Chad quickly wraps his arms around Christian's body pulling him back.

"Dude, as much as you want to kill him, you can't. Leave it for the authorities," Chad says to Jamie and my brother.

The police arrive within minutes and Buffer is removed from the studio in handcuffs. I'm advised that I should come down to the station to meet with the detectives.

Jamie comes over and squats down in front of me taking my hands in his. "I'm here, Cami, he will never hurt you again. Do you hear me? He will never touch you again."

I lean in and kiss him, then wrap my arms around his neck burying my face in his shoulder. Feeling Jamie's protective arms wrap around me, I lose it. I cry because this nightmare may finally be over. I let out all of the pent up emotions that I have been concealing deep within me.

CHAPTER
Twenty-Nine

Camryn

I LIE ON MY BED reading the latest release from one of my favorite authors until a soft knock taps at my bedroom door. Shifting my gaze from the Kindle to the door I instruct whoever it is, "the door is open."

My mom peeks her head in. "Are you busy, sweetheart?" she asks. I close up my tablet, placing it on the nightstand next to my bed. "Nope, I have nothing but time on my hands, come in."

My mom makes her way over and sits at the foot of my bed. A thoughtful smile curves her mouth.

I have yet to tell her everything that happened that night. I have been working on how to express my feelings and fears with my family. My visits with Gayle have helped me tremendously. The way she has me open up to her astounds me. I was never one to feel comfortable talking with strangers, especially about something so personal, but Gayle has a way of making me want to talk about it. It's as if the floodgates open and I can't control the emotions that I express during my sessions.

Knowing that the monster who raped me is no longer walking the same streets has given me a newfound strength to move forward. A little part of me has healed knowing he's behind bars. The detectives obtained a court order for Buffer's DNA. It was a match to the samples in my rape kit. I no longer feel the need to constantly look over my shoulder, thinking it could happen again.

Every day my feelings for Jamie grow. I'm irrevocably in love with the boy who has always been by my side. From my first baseball glove, to my first scraped knee, my first black eye, to all of my birthdays. Even when Jamie and I were apart, there wasn't a week that went by that we didn't speak. I may have been on the other side of the country, but he always made me feel as if he was right there with me.

There are days that I can't believe I am a rape victim. Days that I can't believe I am now a statistic. Every day I face the ghosts of that night. But I don't have to do it alone. My family and friends are an amazing support system.

My mom clears her throat pulling me from my thoughts. "How are things with you and Jamie?"

My cheeks flush just thinking of Jamie. "I'm in love with him, but I think you've known that for quite some time, haven't you?"

"The two of you have been inseparable since you were young. I think Michelle and I knew that the two of you had something special a long time ago. The way the two of you could finish each other's sentences, the way you always had each other's back. The two of you were always protective of each other. Yes, there was always Christian and Morgan in the mix, but you two always managed to venture off on your own. Whether it was to practice on your catching or pitching. Sometimes the two of you would leave the group just to go sit in the tree house out back by yourselves. He has always been there for you, Camryn. I think he's held your heart for a very long time. Do you remember the time you fell out back by the pool? He wouldn't leave your side then either. The two of you were the only ones who didn't see it. Everyone else around you knew the two of you would end up together. It just took you two a little longer to realize that you have been by each other's side the entire time."

How did I forget about that day when I fell and split my chin? I remember Jamie telling me that everything was going to be okay. That he would stay with me until my mom got there. Hearing my mom bring that up has that day fresh in my mind.

It was a hot summer day. We were probably around six or seven, at most. My mom had just gone in the house to get us something to eat for lunch. We were told to stay out of the pool until she came back outside. Jamie was at the other end of the pool drying off with his towel. Christian snatched my towel off of the chair. "Hey, put my towel down!" I yelled.

Christian ignored me as he continued to dry himself off.

"Christian, put my Tinkerbell towel down now. You're not allowed to use it, it's mine."

Christian dried his head off with my towel, "You're such a baby, Camryn."

I went over to where he was standing and tugged on my towel. "I'm not a baby. Give me it, it's not yours." I yelled at him and tried to pry it from him.

Christian pulled back the towel, pulling it from my hands. "Fine, if you want it so bad, go get it." He said then tossed it in the pool.

Shocked that he did that to my Tinkerbell towel, I screamed "I hate you!" then kicked him in his shin. He leaned down to grab his shin and I pushed him, making him lose his balance and fall on the ground.

He screamed, "I'll get you, Camryn, and when I do I'm gonna punch you really hard." I started to run to the house to tell my mom what he did.

He jumped up off the ground and began to chase me. I heard Jamie yelling, "Leave her alone, Christian. You started it . . ." I tried to run as fast as I could. He was going to hit me back. I wanted to reach the house before he could catch me. I turned to see how close he was behind me when I stubbed my toe on the ground making me lose my balance and fall. My face smacked the ground and there was blood everywhere. I screamed from the pain and from seeing the blood. Jamie was by my side handing me his towel. I didn't know what I was supposed to do with the towel, so I just held it to my chin.

"Go get your mom," Jamie told my brother.

"No, you go get her. I'm staying with her."

"Go get your mom. You're the reason she fell!" Jamie yelled at him.

Christian had tears in his eyes. "Fine, you stay with her," he said before running off toward the house.

Jamie held the towel under my chin where my hand was. "It's gonna be okay. I'll stay with you until your mom comes. She'll fix it for you," he said calmly.

My mom ran out of the house with a dishtowel and a bag of ice. When she reached me, I was crying really bad. She kneeled down next to me. "Here, let me see."

She pulled the towel away from my face. I knew it was bad by the look on her face. "Put this ice on your chin. Hold it there, okay."

She scooped me into her arms, carrying me into the house. The boys followed close behind. My mom reached for the phone. "Mark, Camryn fell in the yard. I'm taking her to the emergency room. I think she needs stitches. I'm gonna call Michelle to see if she can keep the boys."

I started to sob on the kitchen stool. "No, please don't take me to the hospital. I hate needles. Can't you put a band-aid on it? Please, don't take me there."

Jamie rushed to my side. "It's gonna be okay, Cami. The doctors will make it all better."

The memory warms my heart. Jamie's been by my side all of my life. I can't believe I forgot about that. I run my fingertip along the faint scar that is still there. I look at my mom, "I've had feelings for Jamie for a while now. I used school and softball as an excuse as to why I never had time for a boyfriend. I think Jamie was the true reason why I was never interested in anyone else."

"Honey, when you compare everyone else to the one guy you want them to be like, then you know that *he* is the guy you *should* be with. Follow your heart, Camryn, it will lead you down the path that is truly meant for you." My mom says with a knowing smile.

"Have you talked with Gayle about your relationship with Jamie?"

Fidgeting with my fingers on my lap, I peer up at her. "We've talked about it. I've voiced some of my concerns. Things between us are going really well. There are days that I feel like my old self again, but then there are days that I feel like it's a struggle to get out of bed. When I'm with Jamie, things are great. I laugh, I catch myself smiling uncontrollably. But then when I'm by myself, my mind wanders and I am taken back to that dark place that I don't want to be anymore."

"Come here, sweetheart," my mom says as she rises from my bed gesturing me to follow her to stand by the full-length mirror in the corner of my room. "Come stand here with me for a minute." She spins me around so that I am looking at my reflection in the mirror, never taking her firm grip from my shoulders.

"You know what I see, Camryn? I see a strong-willed woman standing in front of me. One who has never backed down from anything." She squeezes my shoulders.

"I mean anything. You have to start with the girl in the mirror, sweetheart. That's where the change needs to start. It's up to you on what your future holds. Only you. The past is the past, and that is where you need to leave it. What happened to you that night was horrifically tragic, but it does not define you. Only what you do can define you. We will be by your side every step of the way. Your healing is our number one priority."

THE SOUND OF CHRISTMAS MUSIC being played in the house awakens me. I lean over to grab my cellphone from the nightstand. Jamie already sent me a text wishing me a Merry Christmas. He told me to let him know when I was up and dressed and he would come over since he spent the night next door at his parents'. Well, I wouldn't say spent the night, I don't think he left here until well after two in the morning.

We laid on the couch last night and watched *National Lampoon's Christmas Vacation*. No matter how many times we see the movie, we laugh our butts off each and every time. Watching this movie is sort of a tradition for the three of us. Jamie, Christian and I used to watch it every year then head to bed and hope to hear Santa arrive.

I jump in the shower and dress quickly, tossing an oversized sweater on over a pair of black leggings.

When I make it to the kitchen, Jamie's parents are at the island talking to my parents as they prepare breakfast. "Merry Christmas, sis," Christian says behind me. I turn and give him a hug and wish him the same.

The doorbell rings, then the door immediately opens, revealing Jamie standing there in a pair of dark denim jeans, and my favorite light blue Henley shirt. A smile immediately forms on my face. Jamie's arms are filled with gifts. He teased me last night and said he didn't trust me to leave his presents here cause I would probably open them then re-wrap them, hoping he wouldn't notice. Okay, sue me. I did it once. I was young, probably eleven. What did he expect? That is like taking a kid in a candy store and telling them they can't have a single piece.

Not. Going. To. Happen.

So now he doesn't trust me.

Jamie sets the presents on the floor by the coat rack in the foyer and pulls my body flush against his, holding me tight. His mouth is on mine before I can protest. Not that I would. He can kiss me whenever he wants to.

I stand motionless in the doorway, as Jamie's hand squeezes my ass. I hear someone clear their throat behind us. "Are you going to let him in the house, honey? Or are you going to keep making out in the foyer?" My mom jokes.

Taking a deep, unsteady breath, I step back and put a little space between the two of us.

He walks over to my mom, giving her a kiss on the cheek, "Merry Christmas, Gwen."

My mom tiptoes to kiss Jamie on his cheek, "Merry Christmas to you, too. Here let me help you with those." Jamie leans down and picks up the gifts. My mom takes a few gifts from Jamie's arms then heads toward the family room where my dad and Christian are already sitting.

Jamie and I follow my mom and I am taken aback by all the presents surrounding the tree. "It feels like old times when you kids were little," my father says. "You would think Santa was here. You would never know you kids are twenty-four years old. I think you two are a little spoiled, if I say so myself."

My mom walks over, placing her hand on my dad's shoulder. "Honey, our kids will always be spoiled by us even when they are grown with a family of their own. If we are capable of spoiling them, we will."

My dad pats my mom's hand. "I know we will. I was just teasing."

Jamie and I sit on the sofa. Christian walks over to the tree and starts handing out presents to all of us. Each time he calls my name, he shakes the box and tries to guess what may be inside.

We each take turns opening presents. It seems like we were opening presents for hours. Wrapping paper is all over the floor.

Jamie hands me a small box with a red bow on it. "Here, this is yours too." His voice is low and smooth.

I know it's not a ring, the box is too big for that. Not that I'm expecting a ring or anything. Awkwardly, I clear my throat. My fingers tense in my lap.

Slowly I remove the bow, sticking it on Jamie's shirt over his heart. Once the paper is removed, I slowly lift the lid from the box. A gasp leaves my throat and my hand covers my mouth.

A platinum bracelet with a heart-shaped charm is nestled in the box. I remove the bracelet. "Turn the charm over," Jamie says.

There is an inscription on the back, just like he did with my locket. I read the inscription. "You have my whole heart." When I look up at him, his eyes are full of promises. He smiles at me, and says, "It's all yours."

I throw my arms around Jamie's neck, pulling him in for a kiss. My lips brush against his "I wouldn't want it any other way."

CHAPTER
Thirty

Camryn

SIDE EFFECTS IS PERFORMING AT Redemption tonight to ring in the New Year. Knowing that tonight will be the first time I've been to the club, I am definitely on edge today. I just got back from a long run in Central Park with Morgan. I needed to feel the thump of my steps on the concrete.

When we approach our halfway mark for our run, I told Morgan that I was apprehensive about going to Redemption tonight. I was in need of support to know that I could get through this.

Jamie has asked repeatedly if I want to go or not. He has been telling me for days that he would completely understand if I didn't go to their show tonight, but I need to go. I need to go for Jamie to show my support, but more importantly, I need to go for me. To walk through those doors again will be a huge step in my recovery.

Buffer's bail was revoked. It seems that I wasn't the only girl he raped. The detectives came by the other day to advise me that he's been linked to two other rapes in Los Angeles. His DNA retrieved from my rape kit was able to link him to those. So not only do I have closure to this nightmare, but two other girls do as well.

I know walking through the doors at Redemption will take all the strength that I have, but I will do it. I know that Buffer can no longer hurt me, that I can go tonight and not have to look over my shoulder the entire time, thinking someone is watching me. I know I will always be guarded, always be observant of my surroundings. After my sessions with Gayle, I now know that it wasn't my fault what happened that night. My outfit didn't provoke him, I didn't make any sort of inviting eye contact with him while I was dancing like he told me I had.

What happened to me at Redemption, could have happened to me walking home from getting a cup of coffee, or while on a run in Central Park. There are sick people out there, I was a victim of circumstance.

The other day, I received a thank you card from the local rape crisis center thanking me for my generous donation. When I opened the card and saw who made the donation, I cried. Lincoln made the monetary donation on my behalf. He never ceases to amaze me. He truly is a one of a kind guy. Morgan sure is lucky to have him.

Jamie isn't home from work yet. I told him I would get ready at his place, rather than back at my parents'. After the set tonight, we are going to dinner at one of my favorite restaurants in the Upper Westside.

I emerge from the bathroom in my robe, and hear Jamie calling out my name. "In here, babe," I yell.

He walks into the bedroom, then stops immediately when he sees I am only in my robe. His eyes rake up and down my body, taking my appearance in.

I hold up my hand. "Don't get any ideas, Mr. Banks. My hair and makeup are already done, and you have twenty minutes to get ready. We have to be at Redemption by eight o'clock. It's an early set tonight."

He walks slowly toward me. When he reaches me, he pulls me against him, grinding his growing erection against me. "I think we're gonna be late tonight. The band can't start without me."

Looking up at his face, I can see he has one thing in mind. ME.

I need to put this fire out now before it even begins to ignite. I place my hands on his chest, "Babe, we will have plenty of time to play when we get home. I am here for the weekend. Save your stamina for after the show."

I wiggle out of his hold, smacking his ass as I walk over to the closet to retrieve the dress I am wearing tonight.

He grunts as he removes his shirt, and tosses it in the hamper. "Are you sure you don't want some of this before we leave?" he asks waving his hand in front of his bare chest, like Vanna White does as she reveals the letters on *Wheel of Fortune.*

A laugh escapes me. "You are too much. I definitely want some of that, just not right now. You have a show to perform and we have to be out of here in twenty minutes. You never finish what you start in twenty minutes."

I step into my dress, then sit on the bed to put on my strappy fuck me heels, as Jamie refers to them.

"Let me get in the shower. If I continue to stand here and stare at you, I'm going to have no alternative but to be late for my show." He glares at me then retreats to the bathroom.

That man has problems. He just got some this morning. He has no room to complain. The man sure does have a sexual appetite, not that I'm complaining. I seem to be benefiting from it as well. I don't think I have had as much sex in my life, as I have had this week alone.

WHEN THE DOOR TO REDEMPTION opens, the loud thumping bass of the music reverberates through my entire body. The club is dark and the strobe lights are going along with the beat of the music, highlighting the people dancing. My eyes immediately scan the club. I begin to shake as the fearful images build in my mind. Pausing at the door, Jamie mouths, "You okay?"

I quickly force those images away. I nod, then give his hand a reassuring squeeze. He smiles back at me and we continue to make our way through the sea of people.

By the time we get to the stage, the band already has their equipment set up and they are at a nearby table drinking their beer.

As we approach the table, my brother stands and pulls me into a hug. He whispers in my ear, "You okay?"

I nod and smile knowing that everyone is worried about me. "If I need to leave, I'll let you or Jamie know. But I think I can handle being here."

My brother nods, acknowledging what I said.

Jamie puts his arm around my shoulder, pulling me against his side. "I just ordered you a beer. I'm gonna head up on stage in a few minutes. If at any time you feel the need to leave, you let me or your brother know, got it?"

Leaning up on my toes, I place a soft kiss on his lips. "Thank you for looking out for me. I'll be okay. My brother is here, all the girls are coming as well. I'll be fine while you are on stage. I promise."

Side Effects opens the night with a few fan favorites of their original material. There's a bachelorette party going on tonight and they seem to have quite a crowd with them. The girls are all wearing white t-shirts with sayings embossed on their shirts in neon coloring. Some say 'Suck It', 'Bite It', 'Lick It', 'Kiss It', and 'Nip It'. Those are just some of the few that are PG-rated. Some of the other girls have more explicit sayings on their shirt sleeves in the same neon coloring. With the black lights at the club tonight, they seem to be standing out in the crowd.

I know for sure, that is not what I would want for my bachelorette party. I would much prefer a weekend in Miami Beach, or even Las Vegas with my friends, possibly even a joint celebration with the guys, that is, unless, Jamie has other ideas.

The guys sound amazing tonight. The crowd is going crazy when the first few beats of the song tap out from the drums. Jamie is bouncing up and down on his feet, with his hands in the air. When Jamie starts with the lyrics, *Shut Up and Dance* by Walk the Moon, the crowd erupts. The noise is deafening. I absolutely love this song. I am up on my feet dancing along to the music. My body begins to sway to the beat. This song's tempo is infectious. It makes your body move. There's a tap on my shoulder. It startles me, making me jump. When I turn, Lincoln is standing next to me with his hand extended. "Come dance with me, baby girl."

Before I can even answer his question, he captures my hand and leads me to the dance floor. Jamie sees me with Lincoln and nods his head. Lincoln grabs my hips, pulling me close to him. I throw my head back and laugh. This is the side of Lincoln that I don't get to see often. The happy-go-lucky, carefree side. Usually when he is here at the bar or at the club, he is in business mode, always making sure everything runs smoothly.

I throw my arms around Lincoln's neck as my hips move to the beat. We take turns singing the lyrics to each other. The facial expressions that Lincoln is making are cracking me up. With each line he sings, he raises his eyebrows at me signaling for me to sing the next. He is really into this song. I throw my hands above my head, moving them to the tempo of the song.

Jamie is working the crowd in front of the stage. The thump of Isaac's drum is all you can hear as it echoes throughout the entire club. When Jamie reaches the chorus, he holds the mic stand over the crowd and they all begin to sing. Parker is behind Jamie clapping his hands above his head. The crowd follows him. I look around the dance floor and everyone has their hands above their heads clapping and singing along.

This is definitely a crowd favorite. I think almost everyone in the club is up on their feet dancing.

I make eye contact with Jamie, he smiles and winks at me. I'm sure he was nervous about me coming here tonight. Seeing me having a great time with our friends probably helps ease his fear as well, which I am glad. I didn't want him to worry about me when he was on stage.

I see Morgan working her way through the crowd. When she reaches us, she pulls me into her and starts dancing with me.

Lincoln leans down, placing a kiss on my cheek, "I got some shit to take care of. Thanks for letting loose for just a few minutes with me."

I pull him in for a hug. "I needed a good night out, thanks for making me laugh my ass off at you. I loved your rendition of the song."

"Anytime, baby girl, you know I love to see you smile." Before he turns to walk away, I notice the look that passes between him and Morgan. Huh, what was that look about? I'll have to make a mental note to ask her what's going on between the two of them.

I spot Lindsey and Karsen half way through the first set. After dancing several songs, we head over to the table to grab a drink.

The lights in the club dim, with one light focusing on Jamie. He lifts the hem of his shirt, wiping the sweat from his face. I see his perfect abs glistening from his exertion. The girls in the front hoot and holler when he lifts his shirt. He laughs at them, shaking his head in amusement.

"I want to wish my beautiful girlfriend a Happy New Year's. This year will be better than the last. I promise. His voice, deep and sensual, sends a ripple of awareness through me. His gaze roams and lazily appraises me. The heat in his eyes makes me squirm in my seat.

I blow a kiss to Jamie, which he pretends to catch, then touches his lips with his fingers.

Jamie starts performing *One Life* by Boyce Avenue. He knows this is my favorite band, so I give him my undivided attention, my eyes focusing solely on him while he performs.

The lights on the stage go black for a brief moment. A spotlight appears on Jamie, and a second spotlight appears off toward the side of the stage.

Oh, my God . . . the lead singer of Boyce Avenue, Alejandro Manzano, steps out on stage. I cannot believe what my eyes are seeing. The lead singer of Boyce Avenue is walking across the stage with a mic in his hand singing along with my boyfriend. No way.

The two begin rotating verses. Jamie walks over toward the side of the stage where I'm now on my feet, lifting his brows at me as if saying, do you see this?

When the song ends, the rest of the Boyce Avenue band members come out on stage. The members of Side Effects leave the stage. Jamie introduces the rest of Boyce Avenue to the crowd and cheers erupt around me.

I am stunned when he tells us that Boyce Avenue is taking over the rest of the set and he has a hot date to get to. Jamie jumps down from the stage, making his way over to me. Before he even makes it to me, I launch myself at him, wrapping my arms around his neck. Jamie hoists my legs around his waist. I kiss my man with everything I have.

Jamie squeezes my ass, making me remember that we are in the middle of the club, surrounded by thousands of people, even our friends.

"Hey, get a room," I hear my brother yell at us.

"Zip it, dude, she's mine. You better get used to seeing me with your sister," Jamie says to Christian.

"Yeah, yeah, don't remind me. Just remember, she's still my sister. I will still kick your ass if you hurt her," Christian says.

I place my hands on Jamie's cheeks bringing his attention back to me and ask, "How did you pull this off?"

"Your brother and I have been in the studio with them this week. I asked for a favor and they were more than happy to comply when I told them that they were your favorite band, well besides, Side Effects," he says the last part jokingly.

"You are my favorite, babe. But they do come in a close second."

Jamie places me on the stool, then stands behind me. "Sit back and enjoy the show, babe. After their set, I have a surprise for you."

I tilt my body, so I can see Jamie over my shoulder. "You know how much I love surprises."

"Yes, I do. Sit and enjoy the show. It's not every day your man has Boyce Avenue come to perform just for you."

For the next hour, I sit on the stool with Jamie's arms wrapped around my shoulders. Boyce Avenue closes out their set with *Keep Holding On*. Jamie leans down and I feel his breath on my neck as he sings the words of the song in my ear.

As I lean back against his chest, I know there isn't one thing he wouldn't do for me. His love is unconditional. I am where I belong. Right here with Jamie . . . my Jamie.

ONCE BOYCE AVENUE WRAPPED THINGS up on stage, Jamie leads me outside to a cab that's waiting for us. The temperature has dropped since we arrived at Redemption. Our breaths leave white puffs of air hanging in front of us. I wouldn't be surprised if it snows tonight.

Jamie opens the door, gesturing for me to hop in. "My dear, your chariot awaits you."

I get into the cab, sliding across the seat. I rub my hands together trying to get warm. Once Jamie is in, he places his arm across my shoulder, pulling me into his side. I snuggle up against him, placing my cheek on his chest.

Jamie moves his hand up and down my arm while we travel to the unknown destination. I am trying to figure out where we are going by keeping an eye on my surroundings. The cab stops on the East Side of Central Park on 62nd Street.

Jamie pulls out some money to pay the driver and gets out first, holding the door for me. He leans into the cab and tells the driver something, but I can't hear him.

"I thought we were going to dinner?" I ask.

"Change in plans," Jamie takes my hand, entwining our fingers together. We enter Central Park and I am taken aback. All of the trees are lit with white lights, making it look like a winter wonderland. Jamie and I walk hand in hand until we reach a bench by the rink.

With its romantic backdrop, Wollman Rink puts us beneath the magical New York City skyline and its twinkling lights of the night.

There are two sets of ice skates sitting there. When I look at Jamie he has a mischievous grin on his face. "What?" he asks.

"We're gonna ice skate, in the middle of the night, on New Year's Eve at Central Park?"

"Skating on Wollman Rink is a winter tradition for us. We did it every year growing up. Come on, I'll help you lace them up."

I sit on the bench and take my heels off. I am not dressed to go ice skating. Thank God my coat is long enough in case I fall. I slip my foot in the skate and Jamie laces it up tight for me. He repeats the process with my other foot. Once I am laced and ready to go, I stand on my blades with wobbly knees. I haven't skated here in years . . . maybe since high school, if I remember correctly.

Jamie gets suited up with his own skates, and he takes my hand, leading us to the rink. He is a natural on the ice, whereas I seem to have shaky legs tonight. I grip the side of the rink, helping hold myself up.

We start slow. Once I feel steady on my feet, I let go of Jamie's hand. He spins and begins to skate backwards, keeping his eyes on me. Jamie has always been a good ice skater, even when we were little. I find a rhythm on the ice finally and pick up some speed.

There are tiny snowflakes falling from the sky. I skate over towards the wall. Once I reach it, I tilt my head back and I stick out my tongue to taste the snowflakes.

Jamie skates over to me, wrapping his strong arms around my waist. I turn around and wrap my arms around his neck. He hoists my body up and I wrap my legs around his waist. Jamie starts to skate with me attached to him. I tighten my grip around his neck so I don't fall. "Don't worry, babe, I'll never let you fall," he whispers in his husky voice.

Snow falls lightly from the sky, blanketing the grass and ground around us. It's a picture perfect wonderland. We skate around the rink a few times, until he gently lets me down. We make our way back over to the bench.

Jamie squats down in front of me, on one knee to remove my foot from the skate. A touch of snow falls on Jamie's hair and water droplets glisten on his face. The snow covers everything around us. It's like our own personal snow globe, like when you tilt it upside down and everything turns white. I turn to grab my shoe and when I look back, he has a ring box in his hand. His handsome face is kindled with a sort of passionate beauty.

My hand immediately covers my mouth. Jamie has a huge smile on his face. He removes my hand from my mouth, bringing them together and covering both of them with his own.

"When I look at you, I see my future staring back at me. You are the love of my life . . . you are my life. No one compares to you, Camryn. Your fingerprints are all over my heart because you have touched me in so many ways. Love is just a word without meaning till the right person comes along and changes everything. You are my everything. I love you more than I can ever describe. I want to spend the rest of my life with you by my side. Not just as my best friend or my love, but as my wife. Will you take this journey with me? Will you marry me, Camryn Elizabeth Townsend?" The warmth of his smile echoes in his voice.

Tears stream down my face. I attempt to wipe them, but they continue to fall quicker than I can wipe them away.

"Yes . . . I've always been yours."

He takes my left hand, placing the three-stone, princess-cut diamond engagement ring on my finger. The band has additional princess-cut diamonds lining the shank.

My ring is absolutely gorgeous. I drop to my knees, throwing myself against his chest. The force of my actions makes Jamie lose his balance falling backwards into the light coating of snow that layers the ground.

I cup his face with my hands, "I would love nothing better than to me Mrs. Camryn Elizabeth Banks."

When I pull back to look at Jamie's face. I see the boy who I have spent my entire life chasing. The boy who has been by my side for every milestone in my life. He was my date for the homecoming dance, we went to our junior and senior proms together. He held my hand before I boarded the plane to head off to California by myself for college. There isn't a moment in my life that Jamie wasn't there for me . . . not a moment he wasn't with me. As I look at the man before me, I know I was meant to spend my life with him. He's the boy I had my first kiss with, and he will be the man who takes my last.

CHAPTER
Thirty-One

Jamie

I OPEN MY APARTMENT DOOR, then kick it shut with my boot. I pick Camryn up by her waist, and she wraps her legs tightly around me. I carry her to my bedroom that is illuminated with candles placed all around. Rose petals are sprinkled in a path from my door to my bed. There are vases of stargazer lilies and Gerbera daisies, Camryn's two favorite flowers, on my dresser and on the nightstand.

I spoke to Morgan earlier in the week to fill her in on my plans after I asked Camryn's parents for permission to marry her. Morgan was a huge help tonight. I gave her my apartment key before we left Redemption so she could get things set up for our arrival.

Camryn breaks the kiss when we enter my room, seeing the room lit by candlelight. Her eyes begin to fill with tears. She looks at me with wonder and awe. There is no doubt by looking at her, she truly loves and adores me.

"Oh, my goodness, Jamie," she says, her hand covering her mouth. "How did you do this?"

I turn Camryn around, pulling her back against my chest so she can take in the ambience of the room. I wanted to make tonight special. My girl deserves special.

"I wanted to make tonight a night that you will never forget." I whisper against her ear, kissing her favorite spot, just below her ear. I suck her earlobe into my mouth, then nibble on it before I release it.

A soft moan escapes her. Cami's body shivers. I turn her in my arms, guiding her backwards towards the bed until the back of her thighs hit the mattress.

I find the zipper on the back of her dress, pulling it down ever so slowly. My hands push the dress off her shoulders, revealing her soft skin as the dress falls and pools at her feet. She stands before me in black lacy underwear with a matching bra. I gaze at her realizing I need to touch her more than I need to stare at her right now. I unclasp her bra, sliding the straps off her shoulders, then toss it on the chair.

She goes to kick off her shoes. "Leave the heels. Those fuck me heels are exactly what I intend to do."

I tug her panties down her legs and spread her thighs apart where I can see how aroused she is. I slip my finger in.

Camryn tries to close her legs. "Relax, baby. It's just me and you," I say. I hear her take a deep breath and let it out.

I move my finger inside her, hitting the spot within her that she loves. The spot that causes her to grip onto me so tight like there's no place else she'd rather be and no one else she'd rather be doing this with.

Her hands caress the length of my back.

The warmth of her soft skin is intoxicating. I withdraw my finger slowly. I'm not letting her come yet.

I cup her face with one hand and the other goes to her hip, "Tink, I love you."

She leans up on her tiptoes, touching my lips with hers. "I love you too."

"Lie down, baby."

Gently I ease her down on the bed. She shimmies herself back towards my pillow and leans up on her elbows, watching me undress. I pull my shirt over my head, tossing it on the chair, then unbutton my jeans, pulling them and my boxers off quickly. "I could have helped you undress," she says seductively, biting her lower lip.

"I'm going to worship you tonight. I intend to lick every inch of my fiancé's body. I want the neighbors to know you're mine as you are screaming my name."

Her wetness coats my finger immediately when I slide it through her silky folds. Slowly, I move my finger over her clit, making her hips jerk up from the bed. I spread her folds with my fingers, putting her on display for me.

My dick is hard as steel and is aching to be inside her. But I want to make her come before I make love to her. I want to make sure she is ready for me. So, I slowly add another finger and begin to move them in a scissor motion, stretching her out.

Camryn moans my name, "Jamie . . ." Her hands grab my hair, pulling on it roughly. She is tugging it harder with every whimper escaping her lips. My dick hardens the more she doesn't hold back and shows me what she wants.

The need to taste her is overwhelming.

Camryn cries out when I suck on her nub, lightly nibbling on it. Her hips grind against my face in a slow motion. She arches her back from the bed when I stick my tongue in her opening after I remove my finger. She pulls against my head, pulling me closer to where she wants me. I continue my assault on her, licking, and sucking.

I look up and see Camryn's head thrown back against the pillow. The sheets are fisted in her hands. "Do you like what I'm doing?" I ask.

She simply nods her head. "Yes . . . Yes, I love what you are doing. Please, don't stop. You're gonna make me come." She pants out between breaths.

"Tell me what you want, Cami. Do you want me to keep eating your pussy until you come, or do you want me inside of you?"

"Make me come, then I want you inside me. Don't stop . . . Keep doing what you're doing." My girl is greedy, she wants it all.

A moan of ecstasy slips through her lips as I do what she begs for. Every muscle in her body tenses. Her thighs grip my head like a vice as she pulls my hair roughly. She screams my name out as her orgasm hits.

I gently lick her sensitive clit as her body still trembles from her orgasm. When Camryn's breathing evens out, I slowly make my way up her body. Kissing a path from her navel to her breasts. Gently, I capture her nipple between my teeth, tugging on it. Sucking it into my mouth.

Her body tingles from my touch as goosebumps form on her skin.

My tongue circles the rose-colored nipple that is swollen from arousal. Camryn grabs my face, pulling me toward her. She crushes her mouth against mine, her tongue sending shivers of desire racing through me. I grind my dick against her core.

"I can taste myself on your lips." Her lips brush against mine as she speaks.

"I love the way you taste. You're so sweet, I could lick you all day." My last words were smothered by her lips. Her tongue traces my lips, making me growl.

"I need you inside me, Jamie. I want you to make love to me . . . now."

"Your wish is my command. I'll never deny you anything, baby." I rub the head of my dick against her entrance, teasing her. She is so wet. So ready for me.

"Don't tease me. Give me what I want." She says as her hand grabs my rock-hard dick. She pushes my hand away and begins stroking me. It starts off slowly, then she begins to stroke me faster. I can't let her keep doing this, or I'll come in her hand like a teenager.

I laugh. "I'll give you what you want." I place my hand over hers, slowing the pace. "If you keep doing that, I'll come in your hand and this night will be over before it even begins."

I pull my hips back, grinding against her core. Her hands are caressing my back. She moans softly with an erotic pleasure as I enter her inch by inch, as she welcomes me into her body.

Once I feel her body adjusting to me, I push all the way in. My balls hitting her ass. She clenches me tightly. "Jamie . . ." she moans as I move slowly inside of her. I pull all the way out, then enter her body again with more force than I did the first time.

I am so hard, I don't know how much longer I'm going to last. She feels so good, so tight. I can feel the pulsing of her pussy on my dick. Shit . . . Shit . . . I forgot to put a condom on. My body stills.

Camryn notices. "What's wrong?"

"Baby, I forgot to put a condom on."

Her eyes widen at my confession. "All my tests came back negative. I'm on the pill. We should be okay."

"Do you want me to put one on? I can, if you want."

"I love the feeling of you inside me without one."

I push back into her, then slowly begin to find a rhythm.

"If you're okay without them, then I am. I don't want anything between us. I want to feel you clench my dick when you come. I want to feel your come on me."

She nods her head accepting my response.

Our bodies are in exquisite harmony with one another. Our pace is slow at first.

My tongue explores the recess of her mouth. Our kiss is anything but gentle. She bites my lip, then sucks it into her mouth soothing the pain that she just caused. I growl from the pleasure she elicits.

She wraps her trembling legs around my waist. I thrust again, deeper, harder, faster. A tingling sensation forms in my spine. I'm not gonna last much longer. She claws at my back. I lift her leg above my left shoulder, so I can get a better angle. Hit that perfect spot she loves.

Her hands grip my ass, squeezing it tightly with her fingernails.

"I want you to come again," I say as I push into her. I know she is close, I can feel her pussy pulsing in time with my thrusts.

"You're killing me, Jamie," she whispers, her breath hot against my ear. Her body slowly tenses beneath mine and then I feel her release. Her muscles clamp down around me, pulsing. My dick is going to explode.

Her hazel eyes close as she finds her climax. "Look at me, baby. Don't close your eyes. I want to see you come. I want to see what I do to you."

She opens her eyes, her whole body flooding with desire. Her hands grip my waist, pulling me into her more. When she does that, the tip of my dick hits her G-spot, causing me to come with such force like I never have before.

Once I catch my breath, and can feel my legs again, I pull out of Camryn. I roll to the side of the bed, bringing Camryn alongside me.

She lies there panting, her chest heaving.

"I love you, Camryn . . . soon to be . . . Mrs. Camryn Banks."

She laughs, "I love you too . . . my soon-to-be husband . . . Mr. Banks."

Epilogue

Five Months Later ~ May

Camryn

I CAN'T BELIEVE THE IMAGE staring back at me as I take in my appearance in the full-length mirror that stands before me. How much I've changed in a year. My life is filled with joy. My reflection shows a woman who is truly happy where she is in life. My eyes are bright and shine like the stars in the sky on a dark night. The smile I have on my face today radiates with excitement.

I no longer feel like I was stripped of my spirit, dignity and hope. There were moments that I thought I no longer wanted to live. That I wished Buffer would have killed me when he had the chance. There were moments that I didn't think I had the strength to get through this. I was wrong. That night had the power to destroy me. I made the choice not to allow it to dictate my destiny.

For a period of time, I thought it was only my burden to bear. But with the love of my friends, family, and Jamie, I knew I didn't need to go through it alone. I have the best support system a girl could ask for. My parents stood by me, supported my decisions, showed me that there was a light at the end of the tunnel. My brother has always been an amazing listener. Many nights he sat by my side, allowing me to cry, holding me while I broke down in his arms. Not once did he ever push me to talk, rather he simply listened. Christian encouraged me to talk to Jamie, which I knew I had to. I just needed to do it at my own pace.

Scars take time to heal and in time mine did. I no longer view myself as a victim, but rather a survivor. I am now helping others who have endured the same as I did. I volunteer at a rape crisis center twice a month. Some months it is more difficult than others with my schedule for work, but somehow I make it work. I continue to see Gayle when I feel overwhelmed with my emotions.

I rub my palms on my dress to ensure there are no wrinkles. The tiara that rests on my head with my veil attached makes me look like a real life princess.

Since I was a little girl, I have always imagined what my wedding would be like. I never thought the man of my dreams would have been by my side my entire life. He was there to wipe my tears when I skinned my knee. He was there to help me learn how to catch a ball. He was there for all of my firsts. My heart belongs to him . . . it always has.

Today I will walk down that aisle to marry the love of my life. And I couldn't wish for anyone else to be waiting for me at the end of that aisle.

All of my girls are here in the room with me. Each of them promising not to make me cry. There is a soft knock at the door. Lindsey opens the door to find my brother standing there in his black tuxedo, looking handsome as ever.

"Hot damn, you look fine," Lindsey says with a whistle.

I hear my brother's hearty laugh. "Thanks, you look beautiful as well."

Morgan quickly walks to the door, trying to block his view of me in the room.

"You know the rules, no seeing the bride until she walks down the aisle with your dad," Morgan says firmly.

"Relax, Maidzilla. I'm not trying to sneak a peek. I came bearing a gift from the groom." Lindsey takes the box from Christian, while

Morgan shuts the door in his face.

"Men. . . ." Morgan mutters hastily.

Morgan's phone starts to ring, I can tell it is Lincoln by the assigned ringtone, *Fall Into Me* by Brantley Gilbert. She looks at her phone, then tosses it onto the chair with a huff. Morgan seems a little off today.

"Is everything okay?" I ask while I watch her in the mirror. She makes eye contact with me and quickly averts her gaze.

She bites down hard on her lower lip. "Everything's fine. Today is your day. You don't need to be worrying about me."

"I know you're lying. I know you better than this. I'll let it go for now, but this isn't over. We'll talk about this tomorrow. Deal?"

"Camryn, don't worry about me. Today is your wedding day. It's your special day."

"You are my best friend. When something bothers you, it bothers me. Promise we'll talk tomorrow before I leave for the airport."

"Okay, if you insist," she says as she walks over to the couch to gather her belongings.

I know my best friend is lying, but I'm not gonna push the issue. Not today, I won't. If I had to guess, I think she's a little disappointed that she's not the one walking down the aisle. Things between her and Lincoln have been strained the past few months. A couple weeks ago I asked what was going on with her and Lincoln, she simply said, "I need more than unspoken promises from Lincoln."

Breaking the moment, there is another soft knock at the door. My mom makes her way over to open it. My dad stands there in a black tux, looking just as I'd always envisioned he'd look like on my wedding day.

He makes his way toward me. He takes my hands in his, leaning in placing a kiss on my cheek. "You look absolutely beautiful, sweetheart," he says with unshed tears in his eyes. I am sure this is tough on him. But I will always be his little girl. No matter how old I am. This man has taught me what to accept from a man by showing me his unwavering love for my mother.

"Thank you."

"Are you ready to become Mrs. Banks?"

"You better believe it."

My dad extends his arm to me. I lace my hand through his elbow and we walk out of my

bridal suite silently.

We make our way down the hallway to the double wooden doors leading to the Wedding

Pavilion. Jamie and I opted for an outdoor ceremony. The location is enchanting. Handsomely landscaped, it features a beautiful pergola covered with flowering wisteria and a winding brick walkway leading to a charming, open-air gazebo.

Music is playing from the violinist. As we line up, I see Christian escort my mom down the brick walkway, then each of my bridesmaids make their way to the front of the garden to stand near the gazebo.

When Morgan reaches the front, I inhale a deep breath before my father and I begin our

walk down the winding brick walkway. My eyes immediately lock with Jamie as he stands at the gazebo waiting for me, as always.

THE END

Make sure to check out UNSPOKEN PROMISES, Lincoln and Morgan's novel coming Fall 2016

Playlist

Hanging On by Ellie Goulding (Divergent)

Toyfriend by David Guetta

Desnudate by Christina Aguilera

Not Myself Tonight by Christina Aguilera

Love Somebody by Maroon 5

Crazy Bitch by Buckcherry

I Won't Let You Down by Static Cycle

Down on Me by Jeremih & 50 Cent

Every Breath by Boyce Avenue

On My Way by Boyce Avenue

You Got Me by Gavin DeGraw

Shut Up and Dance by Walk the Moon

One Life by Boyce Avenue

Keep Holding On by Boyce Avenue

Fall Into Me by Brantley Gilbert

Acknowledgements

FIRST AND FOREMOST, I WANT to thank my husband for his un-wavering love and patience with me. There have been plenty of nights that my face has been buried in my laptop and I have ignored you. Don't ever forget how much I *want* you in my life. You are my heart, my soul, my whole world. I love you.

To mother, father and brother, you have supported me through all of my hiccups in life. There have been times where I fell on my face and you have always been there to help pick me up. You taught me to reach for the stars and never to settle for less.

Michelle Kemper Brownlow, THANK YOU . . . These small words just don't seem enough to show you how grateful I am for our friendship and for the amazing support you have given me. You have been there since these characters began speaking to me. You have held my hand since last year when I wrote my first word. You allowed me to bounce ideas off of you every day. You are the reason why these characters made it to paper. You pushed me to have the confidence to write this story.

Michelle Lynn, thank you for the countless hours you put in with helping me. You have a way to know what I want to say without unspoken words on my part. I can never thank you enough.

Megan Smith, you are my girl. Words cannot explain how much I value our friendship. I know I can always count on you to be honest with me no matter what the subject is. Who would have thought our friendship would have formed from simply our love of books.

Michelle, Megan, and Michelle, you ladies rock. You have been there from the very beginning. You answered countless questions and the three of you have held my hand throughout this entire process. I will forever be indebted to you.

To my betas, Heather, Chrissy, and Jennelyn you girls rock. Thank you will never be enough. I appreciate your feedback and how you love Jamie and Camryn as much as I do.

Elaine, girl, you nailed my cover. You were able to take my vision and make it real. Your editing skills are amazing. You were able to work your magic on my manuscript and have it say exactly what I wanted it to.

Christine at Perfectly Publishable, you nailed my vision. I am beyond thrilled with the final copy. Christine, you are AMAZING!

And of course, YOU, the readers. Thank you for supporting me and buying my debut novel, *Unspoken Words*.

Thank you to the bloggers who have shared my posts, read *Unspoken Words* and provided a review. All of your hard work does not go unnoticed. I myself am also a blogger, so I know the time and dedication it takes to run a successful blog. Word of mouth is the best way for me to get *Unspoken Words* in the hands of readers. So once again, I thank you from the bottom of my heart.

About the Author

H.P. DAVENPORT GREW UP IN Philadelphia, graduated from Temple University, and is currently living in southern New Jersey. She is a litigation paralegal by day and romance genius by night! When she's not tending to her furry children and her handsome husband, H.P Davenport is seamlessly carving beautiful stories from her mind in her comfy PJs.

Follow H.P. Davenport and follow her writing journey, on the following social media platforms.

Facebook
www.facebook.com/hpdavenportauthor

Website:
www.authorhpdavenport.blogspot.com/

Instagram:
www.instagram.com/h.p.davenport/

Pinterest:
www.pinterest.com/HpdavenportAuth/

Twitter:
www.twitter.com/hpdavenportauth

Goodreads:
www.goodreads.com/author/show/14927304.H_P_Davenport

Want to receive up to date news relating to H.P. Davenport, sign up to receive her newsletter. You will receive bonus scenes, release information, exclusive giveaways and many more exciting things.

Newsletter: *http://goo.gl/forms/B1qgOnYucW*

31628503R00152

Made in the USA
Middletown, DE
05 May 2016